Shoot!

* * *

George Bowering

*for Sarah,
The lucky driver*

George Bowering

KEY PORTER·BOOKS

Canadian Cataloguing in Publication Data

Bowering, George, 1935-
Shoot!

ISBN 1-55013-606-2

1. McLean Family – Fiction.   I. Title.

PS8503.0875S56   1994   C813'.54   C94-932084-6
PR9199.3.B68S56   1994

The Publisher gratefully acknowledges the assistance of the Canada
Council and the Government of Ontario.

Key Porter Books Limited
70 The Esplanade
Toronto, Ontario
M5E 1R2

Printed and bound in Canada

94 95 96 97 98 5 4 3 2 1

A passage from chapter 4 was published in Books in Canada.
A passage from chapter 8 was published in Quarry.

This story is dedicated to Aimee August,
Bill Arnouse, and Adeline Willard

I

THERE WERE THREE brothers walking around the dry country, doing their best to change things. The sun was beating on their heads, but they had a job to do. The sky was wide and blue, just as it is today. Red willows grew beside the river. There was not much in the way of green, except high on the hill where the pine trees stood apart from one another. In a few months there would be a lot of white on practically everything.

The three brothers were changing things so that the new people could live there.

The country was full of people-killers, so Thlee-sa and his brothers had to be sharp. If the new people were going to make a go of it, they could not always be looking over their shoulders for people-killers.

Ike Willard said that in those days Rabbit was a people-killer. Ground Hog was a people killer. Thlee-sa and his brothers fixed things so that when the new people came they could kill rabbits to make tobacco pouches for themselves and meat for their dogs. They fixed things so that their dogs would chase ground hogs into their holes.

Ike Willard knew what he was talking about.

Thlee-sa and his two brothers spent the last part of their lives putting things in order for the new people. When they werent working they were camped at Kamloops, because tobacco grew there. They would sit and smoke their pipes and cook fish because that is where they kept their fire.

They were always working, changing things for the new people who would not be animals at all.

Archie McLean was fifteen years old, he figured, and he was sitting in a jail cell, waiting to get hanged. He wasnt old enough to be anything but tough. It took a lot of guns to get him here, a lot of guns and a government. The government was made of rich men with names something like his. He was famous.

But he was shut up in the Provincial Gaol in New Westminster. Allan had a plan. Allan was able to see things, he said, and who wouldnt believe him? Right now, Allan, what does the river look like? What colour are the aspens? Who are you talking to?

Allan McLean was sitting in his own cell with his jacket buttoned, and there was a young woman sitting on a kitchen chair outside his cell, reading the paper to him. The paper is all about how outraged the citizens are that those outlaws are getting a new trial. She's the same age as Allan, about, but she's married to her husband, so her name is Mary Anne Moresby. Moresby is the warden of the Provincial Jail in New Westminster.

Mary Anne Moresby is the first woman who ever sang songs for Archie McLean.

"If you're finished reading that there noose-paper, ma'am, would you sing a song for us?" This was Archie. He was the youngest, but he was tough enough to be funny.

And she sang.

She was twenty-three years old, and had a collar that came up to just under her ears, and hair piled up in light brown curls that she must have done herself because they were better in front than behind. She stood up and put her hands together behind her back and rotated her body a little as she sang.

Thou dear companion of my early years,
Partner of all my boyish hopes and fears,
To whom I oft addressed the youthful strain,
And sought no other praise than thine to gain —

There was very little light in that place, but Archie saw Mrs. Moresby's eyes as she sang. They were not there, not anywhere in there, a little like Allan's eyes when he was talking about the things he could see.

Archie was going to die without ever doing whatever you do with a girl. Allan had a wife at Douglas Lake, and a son, and now he was going to have another boy, he said. His son would be born the year Allan died. Archie was born the year his father died. The McLeans were like that.

Their mother was always telling them what the McLeans were like. She always told them to fight back against anyone who wanted to take what was theirs, put them in jail, insult the family.

"Your father died fighting," said Sophie. "I expect you not to give in to them."

But their father died fighting Indians. They were now fighting white men who kept coming from Scotland and taking the best country along the rivers.

"You're McLeans," said Sophie.

They looked at each other's faces, and saw McLeans. There were McLeans, they knew that, in Scotland, but they would never see them. The McLeans in Scotland would have white faces like their father's face.

Archie did not remember his father's face.

"Are we white men?" he asked his mother.

His mother was pulling the warm stuff out of a chicken with no feathers. She was wearing a dark dress that came up to her chin, and an apron over the dress. Her hair was done the way the white women in town did their hair.

"You are McLeans," she said. That was supposed to be enough.

"Are you a McLean?" asked Archie.

He was a troublesome teenager. But he had been riding horses since he was three years old, and he had been working on other people's ranches since he was nine. He wore boots that had once belonged to a man twice his age.

"My name is Sophie McLean," said his mother. "Your name is Archie McLean. You can write your name," she said.

They taught him how to write his name at the school in Cache Creek, the town named after something his father did.

"Our father died fighting Indians," said Archie. "We fight Indians sometimes, but one at a time. Most of the time we have our troubles with white men."

Sophie separated the parts of the chicken stuff she wanted to save and handed the bucket with the rest in it to her son.

As usual there was a dog at the door, lifting its muzzle, hoping.

"Donald McLean had his troubles with white men," said Sophie. She had a large knife in her hand.

The geese flew north, every day and into the early darkness. Large bodies in the air, like people, heavy in the air, a sky full of them day after day. They made a whistling sound, a whisper that anyone who was quiet could hear.

Two Wasco men listened to the large birds in the darkening sky. Nothing was more important; how could it be?

There was no story they knew about the soft whistling that filled the air for a while and fell to the earth so they talked about it.

"That sound comes from their wings," said one man.

"No, it is a sound that comes from their beaks," said the other. "If we were men flying heavy through the air we would grunt with the effort. We would gasp."

"We would labour to move our wings, our arms," said the first man.

"Such labour would make us breathe heavily."

They listened as another flock of geese whispered by, barely visible in the low shadowed air.

"I hear their big wings flapping, the air whispering as they move, like paddles in the river," said the first man.

"You are as stupid as the hard ground," said the other.

"Wings."

"Dumb as dirt."

Donald McLean had trouble with everyone, with Indians, with white businessmen, with his own families, with the Hudson's Bay Company. He was a pillar of the community but he was a nasty man, cruel and self-important.

He was born, conveniently in 1800, at Tobermory on the Island of Mull. It was a very old place that was just getting started. Like most people, he left to go somewhere where he would no longer be a hopeless case. He wanted to become powerful.

Donald McLean worked hard and never smiled and got to be in the room when it was handy to be there, and fought his way up the ladder inside the Hudson's Bay Company.

The Hudson's Bay Company built trading posts called forts and asked the Indians to come in with furs. In exchange for the furs the Indians were given items of European manufacture that were in Europe deemed far less interesting than furs. Rich fat men in London wore beaver hats, and thin Shuswap men in Kamloops carried rifles that would not shoot straight.

Years later Donald McLean's sons had quite a few rifles. Local people were surprised to see how well they could hunt with rifles that white men would not tolerate.

Donald McLean worked hard and in front of the right people, till he became Chief Trader at Fort Kamloops, in the district called New Caledonia. He seemed to hate everyone. He shared a nineteenth-century European notion that the world he had come to was a vast disorder that could be organized with the application of strength and will. He went and got himself a second wife. He never learned a word of her language.

The geese continued to fly overhead. North they went, whispering through the sky. And the argument continued. It was accompanied by angry facial expressions and unkind words. The man who said wings got together with his immediate family and some friends and explained his point of view. Soon there were quite a few people who argued for wings.

There were also quite a few people who argued for beaks. Sometimes the argument was made of reason. Sometimes it consisted largely of scornful laughter, and in the case of the middle-sized children, of shoving and tripping and name-calling. If there had only been an old story about the whispering of the geese, there wouldnt have been any of this trouble.

But among these people there was a traditional desire to stay away from big trouble, so a few of the more level-headed people on each side of the dispute took the problem to their Chief. He listened and retired to his sweat house beside the creek that emptied into the big river.

"Wings," he could have heard people saying outside the sweat house.

"Beaks," too.

Early in the morning, while the first light was showing how high the clouds were going to be that day, he stepped out and stood in front of the sweat house. Geese were going by, unseen yet, but whistling by the hundreds.

Later that morning he put on his medium-important clothes and called together the first two disputants and their brothers and his own immediate family.

"Beaks," he said.

"Hooray," some of the people shouted. A brother of the original beak theorist whistled through his teeth.

His opponent was moved by the disappointment and anger of his faction, and demanded a Council. Such were the traditions of these people that a Council was called, to deal with the issue fairly.

"What will we do," said the wing man's wife, "if the Council decides for them rather than us."

Her husband looked around the settlement, at the slow green river gathering itself. In the north it had plunged white between stone walls. He saw the bright sun removing the last of the morning clouds. Tiny in the sky an arrow of geese flew northward, too high to be heard.

"The Council cannot decide against wings," he said. He sounded confident, as he was brought up to be. He was a man of the river people. But she saw that this morning he had been counting his arrows, checking each for its workmanship.

That evening, with the proper fire, and after more than the usual number of fresh fish inside them, the Council met and listened to every word of the arguments. Every person who desired to speak was listened to. Then the people whose job it was to decide matters spoke, not among themselves, but to everyone there.

Beaks, they announced.

If Donald McLean had heard this story he would have sneered. Geese are geese, put on this earth for use of God's people if they happened to want them. Not as good eating as grouse or pheasant.

If Donald McLean had heard the story about the geese he would have said, "Isnt that just like an Indian, to argue about such a thing?"

His wives would have kept quiet.

All right, said the defeated wing supporters, we know what we are listening to when we hear the geese going north, and we cannot stay and be surrounded by tyranny and error. We are leaving.

They followed the great river until they found a place far enough away and good enough to live in. The following spring they travelled some more. So every year they travelled, looking for a really good place. They met other people on their way, and traded stories and food. Occasionally someone would decide to marry someone and learn a new language. At other times someone would fall in love and join their group, bringing a little extra language and new stories.

So they went from year to year, up the side of the river, until they came to a beautiful place where another river entered, and they stayed for the winter. In the spring they went north along the side of this smaller river. They were in a valley of brown grass with walls of striped rock on either side. They ate the fish from the river as they went. In another year they found another river meeting this one, and they followed the new river, north.

This was a very beautiful river, shallow, with fast water over round stones. The fish in this river were smaller and better tasting.

"I am really glad I was on the wing side," said one young man.

"Me too," said his young wife. She was as beautiful as the river.

"But you werent even there," said her young man. "I met you one river away from home."

"Home? What is home?"

"No, I mean you were never at the argument. When we met I could hardly understand what you were saying."

"You quickly found a way to overcome your linguistic difficulties," said his wife, pretending to blush.

"So how could you be glad to be on the wing side of the argument?"

"No. You said that you were glad to be a wing enthusiast," she said, looking down to see what he was doing with part of her body. "I was agreeing. I am glad that you left that place."

"Home," he said.

"That place."

If you were looking at a map of the wing people's sojourn, you would say that so far they have travelled up the Columbia River to the mouth of the Okanogan River, and up the Okanogan to the mouth of the Similkameen River. They went up the Similkameen for a year or two, till they found a place we call Keremeos. At Keremeos there is a conical mountain on the side of which is a huge letter K made by ancient shale slides.

The place they found was at a turn of the sparkling shallow river, under a mountain the local people called Chopaka. These were some Okanagan people who called the newcomers En-koh-tu-me-whoh, and treated them very well.

So for some years the two peoples lived together, married each other, and told each other's stories.

The great Okanagan writer Mourning Dove says that the southern strangers' women were fair and pretty.

She says that the Keremeos Indians taught the strangers their language, and the strangers taught their hosts how to make pit houses for the winter.

This is the way the Shuswap people responded to newcomers.

They would be that way when the white fur traders came too.

Some years later the people from the south left again, without an argument. They left with their two languages and their new children, and travelled north again, up the glistening Similka-meen until they found smaller waters. They went as far north as they ever would, and over time they became the Nicola people. They began to forget their grandmothers' words, but they remembered some of the stories.

They remembered the story of the geese's wings.

Those Wasco people weren't the only strangers to come into the country, as we all know. Not much later the Yankees came up from the south too, up through the dry Okanagan valley and down the other river they called the Thompson. When they got there the Kamloops people showed them how to find animals and such.

"Is there anything else you need?" an Elder asked the white men.

"Well, where can we find some – "

"What? Some what?"

"Well, you know – "

"Tell us," said the Elder, baffled by the unusual reticence in the newcomers. "You know that we like nothing better than to help people far from home."

The white men looked at the ground. One of them drew semicircles in the earth with his toe. There was a snicker from someone in the back of the group, or the first half of a snicker.

"Well," said one of the white men. "We have been away from Fort Astoria for many months."

"White man mighty traveller," said one of the Kamloops people noted for his humorous attitude.

"So, uh, naturally we havent had an opportunity to meet any women, you know what I mean, for social purposes."

Now their hosts got it.

They stepped away from the fur traders and formed a group of their own. Once in a while the white men would see one or two of them look over toward them, but they could not hear what the Indians were saying.

One of the Indians was saying, "You should remember what happened when the Chilcotins came over here pretending they wanted to play a sports tournament. These white men – maybe they only pretend that they want animal skins. Maybe the reason they came here was to get our women all along."

"Oh, now really – " began another.

"No, I mean it." And now this man's voice became really animated. "And think about this: if they can somehow manage to take our women, or some of them, even, maybe they will get the idea that they can take away our land."

The others all laughed.

Here is why the McLean brothers and Alex Hare were in jail in New Westminster, where they listened to the warden's wife singing songs made out of poetry.

One cold winter morning in 1879 they were camped among the trees overlooking the Nicola Valley, one young man and three boys full for the past few days of whisky and rum manufactured by the Hudson's Bay Company.

Recently they had acquired a dandy horse that a rancher named Palmer thought was his. They had also acquired a lot of whisky and rum.

———— SHOOT! ————

When Johnny Ussher, special constable, Government agent, tax collector, jailor, assessor, Clerk of the County Court, Registrar of the Supreme Court, and mining reporter, rode into their camp, the McLean brothers and Alex Hare were liquored up against the cold and particularly interested in their own story.

Johnny Ussher thought they were just boys on a tear. He was a special constable without a gun.

By noon he was a corpse in the snow.

Ike Willard the story teller told us what happened to Thlee-sa and his two brothers.

They walked south along the river till they came to the place where it took a little bend and joined the other river. They crossed the river and found themselves in a place called T-kam-loal-pa. It was Things Getting Ripe month, and they picked as much tobacco as they needed, and sat around smoking for a while.

Salmon went by them, eastward. The sun beat down hard. They smoked their pipes.

Then they walked east with the salmon. They camped at a place called Hu-su-loat.

Early in the morning Thlee-sa got up before the others and went for a walk, checking the condition of the berries, looking to see that there were plenty of the plants required when people get sick. He was a few years older than his brothers, so he did a little more thinking than they did. He could see things that they had not learned to see yet.

He saw a young woman in a small clearing. She was dancing

in the morning light. He watched her dancing for a while. Once he thought he saw her eyes fall on him for a moment, but then she continued to dance.

Thlee-sa went back and found his brothers just waking up.

"Come and see something," he said.

"Something to which we have to give order?" asked one brother.

"Something to see," said Thlee-sa.

So the brothers walked up the slope toward the small clearing and hid themselves behind a chokecherry bush. They watched the young woman dancing in the morning sunlight. She was wearing buckskin, and all over her buckskin were hanging tassels made of hair, in all the known colours.

Her eyes fell on them from time to time, as she danced. Their eyes fell shut, opened a little, fell shut, opened hardly at all, fell shut, and stayed shut. They slept in the morning sunlight.

The young woman danced around their sleeping bodies, and soon they were not people any more. They were three pointed mountains, side by side. They would last forever while the new people came into the valleys.

Just a little south and west of Monte Creek, you will be able to see them, Thlee-sa and his two brothers, covered with trees. You have to lift your eyes a little to see them.

2

WHEN DONALD MCLEAN arrived in Kamloops to be the chief trader, he had a family. His wife was a Spanish Indian woman, she said, from Kalispell. She had gone with him from his job on the Snake River, to the Chilcotin, and then to the confluence of the Thompson and the North Thompson. They had six children. He abandoned her and took up with Sophie Grant.

There is not enough information about Sophie Grant, and there are more than enough stories about her.

Why did Donald McLean get another wife when he had already brought one with him? And how did she get the name Grant?

Some people say that Sophie Grant was from Kamloops. Some even claim that she was a daughter of Chief Louis. That would be a nice allegory of life in the old west, but then why did Chief Louis have a daughter named Grant?

You begin to wonder whether it was a mystery to Donald McLean, or if anything was. He certainly was not. He hated Indians, and treated them with monstrous cruelty, but he lived with at least two Indian women and created a lot of children with them.

With his first wife, whom he may have married and may not have, and whose name we did not bother to remember, he had six children who managed to grow up and become what local folks called at the time "fine citizens." They were named as if they were Scottish, and not Salish: Duncan, John, Hector, Alex, Donald, and Christina.

In 1854 Donald McLean took up with Sophie McLean, and made five more children: Allan, Charlie, Annie, Sophia, and Archie.

Donald McLean liked to shoot Indians and create halfbreeds.

There was a time when the word "halfbreed" was used as an unpleasant epithet. Knowing what we know, that seems to be a stupid notion.

When Charlie McLean bit the end off an Indian boy's nose he may have ruined any chance of winning Indian sympathy for the McLeans later on.

This happened when Charlie was fifteen. The boys spent a lot of time on the reserve. Most of their friends were Indians or halfbreeds like themselves. White people were generally their employers or the sons and daughters of their employers.

Charlie was fifteen and more than half drunk. It was not hard to get a hold on a bottle of whisky in those days. You either bought if off a grown man or you stole it out of someone's kitchen. Charlie was a quiet boy, and he grew even more quiet when he was drunk. When he started talking it meant that he was getting ready to start fighting.

It was a beautiful spring day and Charlie had been drinking since late morning. He had been fired from the Palmer ranch the day before, for a good reason. Now he was using up the little bit of severance pay he had been handed, some greasy notes from a Victoria bank.

His Indian friend was fifteen too, but he was not drunk. He was a Christian.

They were standing at the bank of the river, skipping stones in the spring-quickened water. Some of the stones were old arrowheads. They skipped nicely because they had been chipped flat.

"There, eight. I got an eight," shouted Charlie. "Beat you all to shit, you dumb Indian."

"Five," said his companion.

"Fucking liar," said Charlie, still skipping stones. "I got an eight."

His friend smiled his famous Shuswap smile and gave Charlie a little friendly shove on the shoulder.

But Charlie was fifteen and drunk, and newly unemployed.

"Hey, watch it, you fucking Indian," he said. "Fucking loser," he added.

His friend decided that companionship was more important than competition. In that way he was enacting the normal spirit of his people.

"Okay, you got an eight. Beat me by four. I feel pretty good, getting half of what my best friend got."

Charlie had very dark and thick eyebrows.

"What's that? Some of your Jesus shit? You doing Christian shit at me?" He was making himself sound as mean as he could in the spring sunshine.

"Naw," said the other boy. "It's an honour to get beaten by just four by the great Charlie McLean."

Now Charlie didnt know whether he was being laughed at or not. He scrambled up from the loose gravel slope, falling to his knee once, enraged by this awkwardness, and threw himself at the Indian boy. They rolled in the spring dust, and the enraged Charlie, his anger fuelled by whisky, found his hands and feet occupied in holding on. His teeth were available and he used them to bite the end off the boy's nose.

Then he got up and kicked the boy, who was lying in a circle with his hands to his face.

He strolled to his horse and rode it at a walk off the reserve.

SCHEDULE OF WAGES

WILL BE PAID BY

The Contractor

TO

WHITE LABORERS

ENGAGED TO WORK ON THE

C A N A D I A N

PACIFIC

R A I L W A Y

IN BRITISH COLUMBIA

On The Line Between

Emory's Bar

and Savona Ferry.

Allan McLean was a handsome man with a black beard and black eyebrows. He liked being a handsome figure, the oldest son in the second family. He had a black clawhammer coat and a black hat. He had black boots with no laces, which he kept clean even in the dirtiest bunkhouses or camps. He had a shirt and collar and necktie, which he wore on Sunday, even when he had no particular place to go. He thought of himself as an Indian McLean, or sometimes a McLean Indian.

He liked the idea of being historical. He would be a leader, not just of his boy gang, but of a new society. He had heard these words from a man in Mara's hotel. The man was reading a newspaper from Victoria. "The sons of Britain are forging in the new colony of British Columbia a new society," the man said aloud. Then he guffawed and looked around the lobby in Mara's hotel. Allan did not laugh.

He could lift a rifle and shoot a crow out of a ponderosa pine that most men would have trouble seeing. He heard a voice he feared and liked. He was a man of vision, some newspaper writer from Victoria might say, and he was ready to meet such a writer if he ever showed up.

The voice told him important things. When you were eight years old, it said, your father was killed by a smart Indian man. Your father killed many Indians, and he hated the ones he had no reason to kill. Now you are the oldest McLean in your family. You can bring all those Indians back to life.

"I am not an Indian," he said. "I am Allan McLean."

You have a black beard and black boots, said the voice. But you are not a white man. You do not own a ranch. You will not own any land while the white men live in our river valleys. You are not a trader at the fort. Your wife lives with her people.

Your baby child can already see farther across the land than any grown white man.

"The Indians give too much away to the white men," said Allan. "When the first white men came here from the south, the Indians started to give away everything."

Keep talking, said the voice.

"They gave away the land, they gave away the stories, they gave away the fish and the skins. They gave away the women."

Allan McLean spit on the ground, right in front of his shiny boots.

The white men brought their famous law with them, said the voice. It was a real voice; there should be no mistake about that. They brought their famous law and their judges and jails and priests to discolour the earth. The voice spoke in the language that Allan McLean's father had never learned.

"Their law will not enclose me," said Allan. "Their law will not take away my wife. She is a Nicola woman. Her children will take the land and the fish and the stories back from the white people. They will be called McLean but they will not be sons of Britain."

You are nearly ready for the vision, said the voice.

"I am ready," said Allan.

He spent many hours at campfires with the people at Douglas Lake. There they spoke the real name of the lake, and some of them said that the white people had taken the land away and the other things. But they needed Allan McLean with the black beard to tell them about the future.

Special Constable Ussher managed to arrest Charlie the day after he had bitten off the end of the other boy's nose. In the

Government building the Justice of the Peace, John Tait, took care of the bother.

This is how you got to be a Justice of the Peace in Kamloops in the 1870s: you worked as a factor for the Hudson's Bay Company, and you went into business or farming or both. John Tait had worked his way up in the Company, but he was a bad businessman and no great shakes as a rancher. Mr. Mara and Mr. Wilson were the best businessmen in town, and eventually they squeezed Mr. Tait out. In the spring of 1877, Tait was a Justice of the Peace.

He listened to the case for the prosecution. He looked under the bandage on the boy's face.

He did not bring up the topic of evidence for the accused.

The accused was one of Donald McLean's bad boys.

He sentenced Charlie to three months in the Kamloops hoosegow.

This place was a subject of some local political dissatisfaction. Just about every time they would put a McLean inside, someone would help him get back outside. The little back yard was surrounded by a high fence made of lodgepole pines. The doors were fitted with hasps that were not as tight as they could have been. The bars in the window, as Charlie remarked on his way inside, looked as if a man on a horse could yank them out on the end of a worn-out rope.

Constable Ussher had written four letters to Victoria, suggesting that for a hundred dollars he could fix up the Kamloops jail so that a McLean would have considerably more trouble getting out of the place. The Government of the Colony of British Columbia informed Ussher that these were tough times. The gold rush had been over for fifteen years.

Johnnie Ussher spent a few of his own dollars at Mara's store and put new screws in the door hinges.

In the hoosegow Charlie shot the breeze with the only other prisoner. This was a quiet little fellow with a foreign accent, called Everyday Luigi. He had not bitten off anyone's nose. He had got in the way of a Hudson's Bay man who had been threatening violence to an Indian woman outside the Dominion House. It turned out that the Indian woman was the man's wife, so Everyday Luigi also lost the day in the Government office before Justice of the Peace Tait.

"Why did you bother sticking your big nose in, anyway?" asked Charlie.

"Oh, I come from a romantic family," said Everyday Luigi.

"Your romantic family is going to get you killed one of these days," said Charlie.

But he liked the little foreign man in the flat-heeled boots. He took him with him when he went over the fence.

Now Allan had a plan for getting out of the Provincial Jail in New Westminster, but this was not the Kamloops lockup. The brothers and Alex Hare spent a lot of their time shackled to their walls. The jailers had empty cells between each prisoner. The cells were inside a cell block inside a wall. They were on a hill overlooking the wide Fraser, but they could never see the river.

You would need an amazing plan to get out of this place. You would have to have help from an army of Shuswaps and Okanagans and Chilcotins intent on recovering their land, but they were not coming. You would have to receive power from the spirit people who made the land ready for the new people before the new people were pushed into corners by the white men. You would have to be Thlee-sa and his brothers.

Were they Indians in jail, Allan, Charlie, Archie?

Or were they McLeans? Or were they paying with their short lives and long death for the evil nature of black-eyed Donald McLean?

Donald McLean's hatred appeared every day, as his sons shouted and threw things, raising as much of a commotion as they could. They would not submit.

Except to the stories and songs of Mary Anne Moresby, the warden's wife. She had her little son Willie with her again, and Willie really wanted to get closer but he had been told he could come only if he remembered to keep away. Farther away a very big man in a uniform with a round cap was standing where the lamp light was even weaker. Mary Anne Moresby was sitting in a chair outside Allan's cell, reading from the Victoria *English Colonist*.

She read the paper, including the advertisement for white workers on the new railroad. She conveyed all the gossip. She sang songs she had procured from some odd place seldom visited by colonial wives, much less roustabouts:

> 'Tis true, that in this climate rude,
>   The mind resolv'd may happy be;
> And may, with toil and solitude,
>   Live independent and be free.
> So the lone hermit yields to slow decay:
> Unfriended lives — unheeded glides away.

Archie listened to her thin British voice and let his ear lie down on it. But he did not hear the words. He imagined the voice slipping around on his body. He saw little Willie's wide round eyes looking at him out of the yellow light.

By 1833 Donald McLean was an apprentice clerk for the Hudson's Bay Company, a long way west of Hudson Bay. He traded objects for furs with the dark-skinned people at Fort Hall, Fort Boise, Fort Colville, Fort Chilcotin, where there were many languages he could not understand, and one that he spoke. He spoke it with impatience and contempt. By 1853 he was the Chief Trader at Fort Alexandria.

He made McLeans and killed Indians. His successes were detested by the other hard Scottish men in the Hudson's Bay Company.

When his son died he composed a poem about love and heaven. The next afternoon he deafened a middle-aged Indian man by hitting him repeatedly on the side of the head with a stick of wood. When his daughter Elizabeth died he composed another poem, about the Creator's will.

In early 1849 Donald McLean was holding the fort at Alexandria, surrounded by people who hated him.

One of these people was a halfbreed named Alexis Belanger, who had been beating his wife for ten years because she had slept with a white trader. Another was a Quesnel Indian named Tlhelh, whose wife had recently died. Tlhelh believed that if the white men were not in the country his wife would still be alive.

Tlhelh vowed to avenge his wife with the death of a white

man. In the gunsight of Tlhelh's musket Alexis Belanger was a white man.

Tlhelh painted himself dark and waited on the cliff over-looking the confluence of the Quesnel and Fraser rivers. When Belanger's boat came within range Tlhelh began his revenge. His first musket ball plinked the edge of the boat and fell into the water. Belanger turned to scan the line of the cliff. A second musket ball buried itself in his chest. He fell backward, into the arms of three Hudson's Bay Company Indians.

They didnt like Alexis Belanger much at the Hudson's Bay Company, but he was a Company man, and he had been killed by a member of the community that had been here before the Company people had come in. So they had to make a posse and go after Tlhelh. The Company gathered a dozen people, and gave the head job to Donald McLean.

It was not so much that McLean loved this kind of work, not exactly. It was just that while he was doing it he felt useful to destiny. He saw issues clearly and sharply: an Indian mur-derer had to be brought to justice. McLean would be justice.

McLean and the posse rode to the Quesnel village where Tlhelh lived. But the fugitive was gone, and so were nearly all the other men and women. The posse rode their horses very carefully around the nearly deserted village. They looked as far as they could into the dry countryside next to the village.

McLean sat upright and still in his saddle. His chest seemed to stick out, as if to offer a target.

They looked across the creek and saw a figure in a doorway. McLean rode his horse right to the open doorway of the hut. Then he walked right into the hut without knocking at the loose open door.

Inside they found an old man and a young woman who was holding a baby to her chest.

"That's the bastard's uncle," said a man with a Scottish accent.

Donald McLean slapped the old man across the ear. He spoke while his interpreter listened, and listened while his interpreter spoke. While he listened his black eyes were emptied of light.

"Where is Tlhelh?"

"Tlhelh is in another place."

He struck the old man's ear with his open hand.

The old man did not cringe. He stood as straight as he could. He was short but he stood straight and his eyes looked as well as they could through the clouds in them, at McLean.

"I am only a man," he said, and the interpreter translated as well as he could, having changed from Carrier to French and then from French to English. "How am I to know where they have gone?"

"They?"

"Tlhelh."

McLean was furious. His chest seemed to stick out even further. Now there was a pistol in either hand.

"You are an unfortunate old savage, then," he said. "For today you shall be Tlhelh."

He fired both pistols at the old man, and missed his mark with both. The woman ran from the room. McLean was infuriated. Several men had seen him miss the old man at close range. He stepped outside to his horse, pulled his musket from its scabbard, and went back inside the hut. There he took close deliberate aim and shot the old man in the chest.

A young man came running out of the other hut, his hands empty. The entire posse turned their weapons on him and killed him again and again.

McLean had reloaded his musket. Now he walked with even steps to where the woman was kneeling in the horseshoe-marked dirt. She held her baby before her, speaking Carrier and weeping. McLean lifted his musket and blasted the baby's head away. The posse rode back across the creek. The woman lay among the horseshoe marks, bleeding from a wound in her shoulder and neck, holding a crooked package of blood.

One day Donald McLean had Tlhelh's other uncle brought to the fort. He handed the man a gun and some ammunition. The old man did not want to take them.

"I will give you one hundred skins," McLean said.

Finally the old man said some words in Carrier, very quietly.

"What must I give you?" the interpreter repeated.

"One skin," said McLean, and now he smiled, a smile that would never be answered by any man, Scottish or indigenous. "The scalp of Tlhelh."

"No," said Tlhelh's uncle. "We do not do such things."

McLean explained his terms.

"If you do not bring me Tlhelh's murderous scalp, I will first kill all your family, and then all your associates, all the old men. You have heard that babies can be killed too, have you not?"

The old man said that he would do this white thing.

"I wish," said McLean, in the company of his fellow businessmen, "that the sensitive people in Victoria would spend some time up here. Then they would see that educated men in the middle of this accursed country can never expect these savages to understand and obey the imperatives of a Christian service."

There was a round of throat clearing, which he took as agreement.

Netzel knew where his nephew was keeping himself. He went to his camp.

His nephew had no paint on him.

Netzel raised his gun and shot Tlhelh in the chest.

Then he put down the gun and the rest of the ammunition, and sat beside the body of his nephew. He thought about his family and the old men and the babies.

He used Tlhelh's own knife to remove his scalp. It was a more difficult job than any skinning he had ever done.

Then he burnt his nephew's body.

Then he stayed all night. In the morning he raised the gun and looked down the long barrel into the dark.

But Tlhelh appeared in the morning light off the water and told him to go back to Alexandria.

The old man gave the gun and ammunition to a young Carrier man who had just received his name. Then he went to the fort.

McLean stood in front of his furniture and waited until his interpreter arrived.

"What have you brought me?" he asked.

Netzel took his nephew's scalp from his bag, where the dried blood was sifted with medicine. He held the end of the black hair and whipped Donald McLean's face with what was left of the skin.

3

* * *

THE SHUSWAP PEOPLE were by nature a little wary of half-and-half-breeds. As with most things, the origins of this wariness could be found in one of their old stories.

Some people say that the Elders told two kinds of stories, the ones that were about real things that happened to real people and explained the way things were now, and the ones that were invented, about things that really could not have happened in a million years. Some of the Elders said that there was no difference, that all the stories were true. Some of the younger folks said that they were not sure they should believe anything the Elders said when they got into story-telling.

But no one ever scoffed at an Elder.

So the famous halfbreed story, or legend, or history, whatever it was.

In those days the people waited to be told what to believe. In addition they had been led too far away from home, too far away from the thick forests full of deer and rivers in which the fish were still silver and firm. Now they waited for someone to come and tell them why they were there or where they were going to go next. So when a walking person with ghost-white skin and red hair arrived from the rising sun they said this must be the one they had been waiting for.

Some people called him, for a reason no one could remember, K'etzalcoat'l. An old man with particular knowledge tried to get the red-haired man to wear feathers, but to no avail. The red-haired man carried a black leather thing and told about a great ghost who would arrive later.

Meanwhile he took someone else's woman and lived apart with her. This was, though the people did not know it at the time, the beginning of a pattern. Eventually the red-haired man was touched with the people's fingers, and touched with the children's arrows, and finally given the gift of death. The woman died too, and that was the end of that. The people were disappointed, and made a little wary.

But then the yellow-headed boy with no shadow appeared one afternoon on the woman's grave. The people were still hungry enough and sentimental enough to desire a great strange being among them. They called this one K'umkleseem, and told him that he had been created to fulfill their needs. The boy grew up like one of the people, but this time the people watched very carefully, to make certain that this one did not take one of their women.

He was not white like a ghost. His skin was dark, but his hair looked a little like the sun flowing down the side of a rock cliff. This one, they were certain, would lead them to a place where the animals stepped into traps and the silver fish swam into nets.

And so he did.

The people loved him, and made for him a place to live, and spoke to him with proper distance and respect. They understood when he left them for a month or more. Once he left for all of Deer Travel Month, and when he came back he was wearing a strange red shirt, and said that his name was now Yellow Hair.

He stayed with the people for a month, and then he left again. Some of the people said that he was gone on their behalf, searching for animals to bring to their place. Others said that he was abandoning them, speaking words they could not understand.

Still, all the while he was gone, the people laboured to make a splendid new house for him. They swept the path and cleaned the skins. They said that he would return. When they heard a sound among the trees or beside the river, they thought he was nearby.

All winter long, said an Elder, smoke rose from the new house the people had made for Yellow Hair. Every night an owl perched in the nearest tree and hooted from the darkness there.

Constable Johnny Ussher sincerely wished that he did not have this problem with the McLean boys. The problems were getting worse and worse.

They got drunk. They bragged about themselves. They got into scuffles in the street in front of bars and on the reserve and at the ranches where they still managed for a while to be employed.

Every time a storehouse was broken into, or a cow was killed for steaks, the angry ranchers claimed it was the work of the McLeans.

He liked them, and he was sad. He was afraid of where this was all leading them – and him.

He was afraid there was a pivot coming, and that he and the McLean boys would be at that pivot. He did not want, as some of the local businessmen and politicians wanted, to be a stopping place in history.

This time he had brought them in, Allan, Charlie, and Archie, on a charge of horse stealing and roadside robbery. Maybe they had thought that the people they had robbed would not recognize them on someone else's horses. Maybe they just did not care. Johnny Ussher tried to talk to them.

"There's plenty of good working jobs around these parts," said Ussher, compromising inside his head. "Boys like you can make an honest living."

"Boys like us?" asked Allan.

"Your brother Alex has a good steady job at Palmer's."

"Our brother Alex, he's a white man, aint he?"

That was Charlie. Charlie had the hottest head in the whole McLean family. When he was eating a peach the circling wasps would send him into a fury. He did not wrap his knuckles in cloth when he smashed windows.

"Now you know he aint a white man," said Ussher. "But what does that matter in the end? Does the church keep you out because you're not a white man, exactly?"

"Does the god damned jail keep us in because we're only half white?" asked Allan.

"This sorry cow's arsehole of a jail dont keep us in much at all," said Charlie.

Johnny Ussher liked these sons of Donald McLean.

"I'm just concerned that it is getting late for you boys," he said. "Getting into fights or breaking a few locks is one thing, but – "

"That's two things," said Charlie.

" – stealing horses is just about the worst thing you can do in this country. Stealing horses and robbing people on the highway is about as bad as you can get, next to murder."

Allan McLean fixed Johnny Ussher with his black eyes.

"What about stealing women?" he asked. "What about taking young girls and filling their heads with white man's lies and filling their stomachs with Hudson's Bay whisky and making a white man's whore out of them?"

Is he talking about his mother, the constable thought.

"I'm talking about my sister," said Allan McLean. "I'm talking about your famous King Mara, the big white lord of everything in this town, including you, Johnny Udder."

The constable stayed inside his head a little longer. The story about Mara and Annie McLean was in there somewhere. He decided to talk to these dark angry boys another time.

Alex Hare was in love with Annie McLean. This made it complicated to be in Allan's gang. He could be around Annie with a good enough reason if her brothers were too. He could say decent things to her and that would be all right because it showed respect for your friends' sister, a good idea any time. But it was complicated. Naturally Allan and his brothers wanted Annie to do well in life. Even if they thought more of themselves than anyone else in the Valley, they did not want Annie to live the kind of life they were living. They would not be very happy if she made an arrangement with someone like Alex Hare. Alex Hare was an outlaw. He sat in a saddle for a week at a time without ever taking his clothes off. He smelled as bad as they did.

Once Alex Hare had taken a deep breath and told Charlie, his best McLean friend, that he thought a great deal of Annie.

"That's good, Alex," said his friend, who was skinning a calf at the time. Alex saw fat on the edge of a Bowie knife.

"I would be honoured as all creation to step out with her," said Alex, keeping his eyes now on the cork he was trying to get out of a bottle.

"Annie dont go to town with low lifes," said Charlie, and he smiled while he pulled on the hide.

Charlie did not often smile, and when he did, people around him were careful.

"This fuckin' horse has threw a shoe again. I gotta take him over to Palmer's and get another one," said Alex Hare.

John Andrew Mara was what people such as he liked to call a respected citizen.

John Andrew Mara owned just about everything that the Hudson's Bay Company did not own in Kamloops in 1879.

He owned the general store and then he fixed it so that the new stage line ran from Nicola to Savona and stopped right at his front door. Then Mara built steamships that ran the length of the lake and up the river. Traders and travellers paid high rates on those ships, but what could they do? The days were gone when a man in animal hides could carry everything out of the mountains on his back.

Mara had businesses in the Kootenays and the Big Bend

country. He had people to see in Victoria. He had places to live all over the new Province. In Kamloops he built a mansion on First Avenue. The stage from Savona brought him the right wines to drink with Grade A Kamloops beef.

John Mara was a big salmon in a regular-sized river. Naturally he became a Justice of the Peace. He became a Member of the Provincial Parliament.

He could give you a job. He could put warm clothes on your grandmother.

He gave Annie McLean a good job washing things.

When Annie was fifteen years old she had a pale baby. She stayed with her mother Sophie and her sister Sophia, and her brothers brought her things she needed, fresh meat, candles, cotton.

"I will be sixteen next year," she said. "I am a woman."

"I'll never make it to sixteen," said her brother Archie.

It got to be well known around the Thompson and Nicola valleys that the McLeans wanted revenge on John Mara. They sent messages to the store. They were going to kill him and skin him. They were going to sell his skin at the Hudson's Bay store.

People were getting tired of the Wild McLeans.

They called them murdering thieves.

But so far the McLeans and Alex Hare hadnt killed anything but some people's cows. They were famous as good shots. They won the shooting contests and they won the horse races. Allan McLean shot crows out of trees. They knew firearms as well as anyone on the plateau. But they had never killed anyone.

Not like their father.

But some people say that when John Andrew Mara seduced a fifteen-year-old girl and got her pregnant he set the stage for a new act in their career.

To him it meant nothing. He was just another white Overlander taking hold of an available girl. It was traditional. There was land to be had and women to be had. Land was going to be valuable.

The three horse thieves were in the Kamloops jail for four days this time. The lads yelled and sang white men's songs, they hollered jokes at Constable Ussher whenever they saw him. People walking by in the street could hear the uproar inside.

Annie came to visit them. She was wearing a new wool jacket with a Stuart plaid pattern. She gave bannock and honey to her brothers, and spoke to them in two languages Johnny Ussher did not know.

Johnny Ussher looked at her sadly. She was a beautiful girl with black eyes and no smile. He knew about Mara and the pale baby. He wished he could do something good for her. He wished he could keep her brothers away from trouble.

When he said hello to her, she lowered her eyes and walked past. She spoke to her brothers in Shuswap. She listened to their loud voices without smiling. She managed a youngster's contemptuous expression while Ussher investigated her basket for weapons, and then gave her brothers the food from home. She gestured toward Ussher with her head, and spoke Chinook with her brothers.

Johnny Ussher wished things were different. He had a pile of warrants for her brothers. If they would go away and never come back he would not chase them. He might follow them a few miles up the river and then turn around.

After Annie had gone the boys raised their noise again. They ate some of the bannock and threw the rest at each other.

The horse thieves were supposed to be locked up in the Kamloops hoosegow until the circuit judge made his next visit. Johnny Ussher would be glad when he got here and the trial could begin. The noise was making him less and less sympathetic to Allan and the kids. He was glad that he had to be away from the jail on his other business.

The rules said that if the constable had to be away from the jail on other business, the prisoners were not to be left in the yard. They were to be contained in their cells. Anyone who lives and works hundreds of miles from Victoria knows how to apply the rules. If Victoria will not send you a hundred dollars to make repairs to your jail you might as well let the boys spend their time in the fresh air of the yard. A quarter of an hour after you left the office they would be out there anyway.

Twenty minutes after Johnny Ussher left to investigate a small fire at the back of the Cosmopolitan Hotel, the boys were out in the yard, talking loudly, smoking Bull Durham and throwing stones at birds. A rope came over the wall and missed Charlie by inches.

One by one the McLeans held onto the rope and walked up the wall. On the other side were Alex Hare and their half-brother Hector McLean. Hector knew the inside of the Kamloops jail pretty well. He knew where to throw the rope. Alex Hare knew where to catch the boys' horses. Away they went.

For the next few days Johnny Ussher took two out-of-work wranglers and rode around the country, asking questions and looking at hoofprints. Then he called it a week. He figured he would have another chance at the McLeans, sooner than he would like.

Alex Hare was a short skinny boy with a bad attitude. Some people said he was a French halfbreed, what they called back east a *Métis*. But his father was a Cherry Creek rancher named Nick Hare, a sullen angry man who never spoke to his neighbours unless he was selling or buying something. He was a bad rancher, and every year he had fewer cows. Every time a cow disappeared he would bang one of his dark children over the head with something made of leather and metal.

They said Alex Hare's mother was a Siwash. Some people said that was a kind of Indian from the coast. Other people just used the word to mean the kind of Indians that didnt come up to scratch.

When Alex was in school at Cache Creek they called him Rabbit. That's why he learned to ride and shoot so well. He pretty well kept up with the McLeans.

He developed his sense of humour. After the boys were captured at Douglas Lake he spotted an old friend in the posse, a roustabout from Scotland. This roustabout was missing an eye. "You be there at the hanging, Scotty," he shouted amid all the noise of the capture. "You can help yourself to an eye before they throw us in the hole." Everyone laughed except Charlie.

The young man Allan with his black beard, and the three boys with smooth cheeks, never read any books. There were quite a few books in cow country but there were a lot of boys who could not read. For a year or two Charlie McLean could read because he had been in school at Cache Creek, a town that was named after his father's hidden gold. Alex Hare had learned to read too, and he could still read. But he didnt read anything except the odd wanted poster. He could write a little too, so sometimes he wrote a little extra on the wanted posters. He always added his name if the posters just mentioned the McLean brothers. He wrote his name bigger than theirs.

They liked these posters. They always said there werent enough of them, and they were disappointed that they didnt mention a five-thousand-dollar reward living or dead.

Whenever they could, they would boast about their exploits and future victories and spreading fame. If there was someone else to boast to they would boast to him. If there was not, they would boast to each other.

"Took that cow right out from under the eye of Palmer."

"Took the horse right out from under his ass."

"Shot the heels right off his boots."

"Remember the time you shot his hat full of holes and ventilated his chaps?"

"Nothin' compared to the time we rode an hour in front of a posse of a hundred armed men. Rode straight up a hoodoo and down the other side."

"Two hundred Pinkertons had us trapped in that box canyon and we rode right up the cliff, driving ten of Palmer's shorthorns in front of us."

"We're some rightful bad boys, all right. All's I can figure is them Scotchmen better hightail it back to where they come from."

"And leave our women behind them."

"Aint a ranch this side of Monte Creek going to have a cow standing on it, just a flock of blackbirds swoopin' down on the shit."

They laughed in the darkness, four country boys sitting around a campfire they didnt bother to hide from the law. The law was too scant and too busy to be out in the jackpines looking for chicken thieves.

The people in neckties reading newspapers in Victoria never saw that campfire. As far as they were concerned these were the four horsemen of the Nicola Valley apocalypse.

Charlie McLean was trying to grow a mustache. That was the only thing his white father had given him, the promise of a mustache. Allan had a black beard and a dark look to his eyes. He would look good on a wanted poster, but the McLeans had never had their photographs taken. They were clear faces in people's memories. Charlie was seventeen years old. He had been wrangling cows for eight years.

Charlie was born in 1862, the year the Indians were dying of smallpox. The gold seekers brought smallpox with them. Victoria vaccinated the white people. The Indian people fell dead in the forest. When Charlie was born his mother waited to see whether he would escape the graveyard. But Charlie was a tough baby.

Now he was trying to grow a mustache. An outlaw without a mustache would not go far on the plateau. Charlie liked to make jokes with his brothers around a campfire, but when there were other people around he was tough. He liked to drink whisky out of the bottle, and run the back of his right hand over his mouth. He thought he could feel whiskers on his hand.

He carried a beauty of a gun. It was an SA .44, a long-barrelled revolver. When he had enough shells he practised with this heavy pistol. He held the open whisky bottle in his left hand and the .44 in his right. He could hit a crow three times before it finished falling. When he was drinking and counting.

Once he put three .44 bullets in the hump of a camel. He said he wanted to see whether water would come out.

One of the few things Charlie would not shoot was a coyote. The white ranchers hated coyotes. They claimed the coyote killed chickens and calves, and could not be trusted around children. There was an Englishman over at Ashcroft Manor who claimed to be a senator. He would get his friends dressed up in high black boots, and hold a fox hunt, packs of howling dogs chasing across the sage after coyotes, trumpets in the morning, Englishmen in high black boots galloping over the plateau.

Usually the coyotes got away. The white ranchers tried to kill them with poisoned meat. The white ranchers thought the coyotes were a nuisance on their range land, like Indians by the river.

The Indians never killed coyotes. What Englishman would wear a coyote skin?

Sometimes Charlie would point his .44 at a coyote. The coyote would sit panting, tongue halfway to the ground. "Bang," Charlie would say. The coyote would jump and turn at the same time, hustling off, rear end low.

4

The Wild McLean Boys.

That phrase was in my head when I was a boy in school in the Okanagan Valley. The Wild McLeans. They were not gun-toting cowboys, exactly, not USAmericans. The fear that had once run like grassfire through the whole Province had drifted away like smoke as people died, especially the McLeans. It was succeeded by a kind of avarice for legend. If people in Victoria exaggerated the misdeeds of the McLeans in 1879, so did their descendants around the Interior in the next century.

We didnt play McLeans and Lawmen. We played USA cowboys and Indians.

In elementary school, I was in a class with Kenny McLean. Years later, when I was going to college, Kenny McLean was the world's champion bronc rider. There used to be a sign about that on the highway coming into Okanagan Falls.

When Kenny McLean was seventeen years old he could handle a horse with a saddle on it like nobody's business. Four years later he was better than anyone in the world. I dont know how he was with a gun.

The white people had their stories to tell. They told them in newspapers. Newspapers were very important to the "frontier." Settlers needed newspapers to make what they were doing real. If they had newspaper stories they felt as if they belonged to the place, they were the first chapters in the place.

If the proprietor of the Continental Hotel had a piano carted in from Victoria it would stay there. It was not a guitar that could be carried to the next gold field. Some woman in a brocade dress could play Franz Liszt. It might get reported in the newspaper.

First the newspaper was published in Victoria and horses brought it to the plateau. Then the newspaper was published a hundred miles up the Fraser River at Yale.

Those who were in this Province in 1864 have good reason to remember the excitement of the Bute Inlet massacre of whites by Indians in July of that year; others who have read or heard of the dreadful affair may feel curious to learn particulars.

Last Spring, while we were in New Westminster, we learned that one of the survivors of the massacre was then an inmate of the Royal Columbian Hospital, where he had been for nearly a year suffering from rheumatism. Accordingly, in the interest of an eastern newspaper, we called to interview him, and, from a few notes still in our possession, submit to our readers the following account as told to us, prefacing the narrative by stating that the information we received was from a French Canadian by birth, who had been brought by his parents, while a child, to the country now Oregon, where he had grown up and lived until a young man, when he came to British Columbia and worked in the lumber district, on surveys, etc. He appeared medium size, dark complexion, and gave his name as George Catman, aged thirty-seven years. Mr. C. looked somewhat thin, but seemed wiry-looking and capable of enduring hardship, and appeared to bear his present ailment in a rational manner.

Finally the newspaper was moved to Kamloops and the Wild McLean boys were dead. The local hotel men and mill owners had a place to advertise. The more money they managed to gather together, the more the stories came to favour them. The surviving McLeans stayed out of the newspapers.

The Shuswap Elders are still telling their Indian stories. Sometimes white people from Victoria come and get them on spools of tape. In recent years they have taken to paying for them, and giving copies of the tapes to the people. It just goes to show.

There have always been Elders around. You never know, looking at a yard full of Indian kids, which ones are going to be Elders. The ones that learn the most stories are the ones who get the oldest.

The Elders never seem to look as old as they say they are. Take Bill Arnouse, for instance. Last time I saw him he was eighty-four. Hard to believe. If they put him in a movie they'd have to put white stuff in his hair. Some time you ought to get me to tell you, the best I can remember, the one he told us about the guy visiting bear country.

I dont know whether it was supposed to be slu-hai-yum or s-chip-tak-wi-la. True story, that is, or legend, as we would say. If you're an Elder, and you have been telling stories long enough, really, what's the difference?

Thlee-sa and his brothers are now three little mountain peaks southwest of Monte Creek.

All around the Thompson country there are creeks and mountains and lakes with people's names on them. Ussher Lake, for a good example. All the businessmen and most of the white ranchers got their names on the map.

That's what happens when people become history and paint themselves for a while on geography.

Before the white people came the land was unsettled. It was always moving around, nervous. It could not sit still. Those rolling hills were rolling. You could not count on anything. Rock slides slid. Snow melted and rivers overflowed. Fish came home every four years and then they took off again, gone to see the water around Japan. You could not count on the weather.

And the Indian people. They could not seem to settle the land. Spent serious time playing a game with sticks.

When the McLean boys were the scourge of the Nicola Valley and the whole damn Province, the newspaper readers in Victoria and New Westminster were afraid of an Indian uprising. Some of the Nicola Valley ranchers were also afraid of an Indian uprising, and they saw Indians every day.

They thought the Indians had settled down. At bottom they thought they had settled for what they had now. But this Allan McLean was talking about some vision he had, talking about organizing the Indians. An uprising. The ranchers did not think that was a funny word.

Donald McLean wanted to be a legend. He went around killing Indians all his adult life, and that was part of what he came to the new world to do. He was a successful fur trader. He started the first cattle ranch on the plateau. He could not make any white man like him. He did not want the Indian people to like him. He killed Indians. He wanted them to make him a story.

So he went to a blacksmith and had an iron breastplate made. It did not fit perfectly. It did not hold his pectoral muscles like a hard woman. But it could be tied to his body underneath his jacket so it didnt show. Donald McLean was conquistador on the Thompson River. Indians could not kill him.

From time to time they fired shots at him and they saw some hit him. The bullets tore his jacket and knocked him out of the saddle, but he got back on his horse and chased Indians. Every time he killed an Indian there was a brother who wanted to ambush him.

Donald McLean had three Elders brought to his office.

"I am Donald Iron Chest," he told them. "I cannot be killed by Indian bullets. I am the scourge of the range land. I hang Indians who laugh at the law. I am protected by a magic you have never seen. Indian bullets bounce off me. Go tell your people."

The Elders adjusted their blankets and turned to go.

"Powerful magic," said Donald McLean, in his Tobermory accent.

In 1864 the Chilcotin people still had rings in their noses, and they wore wolf capes turned inside out. There were no French priests among the Chilcotins.

In Victoria a Forty-Niner died of smallpox, so they

vaccinated the white people and told the Indians to get out of town. The Indians got out of town, taking bacilli with them.

Indians died faster and faster. Their families became too weak to bury their children. Bodies were left where they fell. Indians arrived at the forts and asked for food. They were told to get out of town.

At Bella Coola some smart businessmen took blankets out of houses filled with dead people and sold them to other people a little farther inland. At Bella Coola there was one living person for every two dead people.

In Yale and Fort Douglas and Kamloops doctors and nurses vaccinated the white people. In some villages the population went to zero. Archaeology began.

Some white men were building a little bridge in the middle of the forest. They had lots of tools and horses and Indian women who had escaped the bacilli. They had lots of food and no whisky. They were not USAmericans. In front of them were a hundred steep mountains covered with night-darkened needle trees.

One day a dozen Chilcotin men arrived, walking out of the forest. They had wolves on their shoulders. They did not have pock marks on their skin. They looked at the camp and walked up close without smiles on their faces.

White men sat on stumps and held axes in their hands. The people they called their squaws were bent over steaming pots.

"You boys are a long way from home," said John Brewster, the chief of these surveyors.

"We are without food," said a Chilcotin man with a ring in his nose.

"I always heard you boys could live off the land," said Brewster.

"Will you give us a little food?" asked the Chilcotin man.

There were eighteen other white men there, heroes with no time for inconvenience. The Indian women attended to their fire.

"I'm sorry, boys, this here food is property of the Company. It's for the progress of the highway to the Fraser. Sorry as them there cooks are, they are cooking for citizens. You will have to stay with your savage ways. Wish we could help you."

The Chilcotin man looked at Brewster as if his eyes were a precious metal no white man should ever reach for. Then the Indians walked back into the forest. They were followed by guffaws from the surveyors.

The surveyors retired to their tents with their temporary women and did not hear the feet approaching over old needles in the cedar darkness.

That night seventeen bodies were dropped into the stream and carried toward civilization. George Catman and another white man with blood on his face spent a week walking between the trees until they saw smoke.

"Murdering thieves," he told an enquiry in Victoria.

Eight years later some Government men came upon the site. They found tools leaning on trees, boots and hats on the ground, remnants of tents wrapped around undergrowth. They were lucky archaeologists.

In 1864 the Chilcotins decided they had had enough, and began an uprising. That's what the white people called it. The Chilcotins did not know they had ever been down.

When the ranchers and fur traders talked to the government they said the Chilcotins were on a rampage. They didnt mention the women. For a while there were incidents at places lived in by white men who had felt the need to take Chilcotin women.

It is not easy to start an uprising when smallpox has been in your people for two years. The people were not getting enough to eat. The white people had all the land along the rivers. When your people are dying every day it is not easy to reach the anger on the other side of sadness. Not when your bodies are skinny on horses.

But the white people saw an uprising.

Red-headed Donald McLean volunteered to lead a force against the Chilcotin uprising. He wanted to be in the story. He thought he might go into politics now that his fur-trading career was over and he was a rancher. He wanted to destroy Indians. He wanted to ride into camp with Chief Klatssassin on a rope.

He gathered twenty-four men, fifty rifles and fifty revolvers, and joined up with another posse of forty men riding from the west. He took his son Duncan McLean to teach him colour. McLeans are not Indians, they shoot Indians.

He left his three older sons in Kamloops. He left the children, Allan and Charlie and Annie in Hat Creek. He left Sophie with a bairn in her abdomen.

He told his posse he was Captain McLean. Under his tunic he wore a heavy iron plate.

There were not many Indians left, so the posse thought they knew who they were looking for. The Indians knew who Captain McLean was. He walked into a person's house and shot uncles and babies.

In the morning the grey light came off Tatla Lake as if it were rising from beneath, grey light surrounded by black trees.

Captain McLean was already on his horse, and with him was an Indian the white people called Jack. McLean's dark beard was carefully combed. His long red hair was smooth.

"I have decided I want to kill a couple Indians before breakfast," he said, to no one but history.

So with Jack as company he rode his beautiful horse along the water's edge, and coming upon a promising defile he dismounted, saw that Jack did the same, and proceeded by foot up the slope on the west side, weapons all over his body. Up the hill they went, without more than ordinary care, Jack a few paces behind. Red McLean eyed every tree, every bush, every pile of long-ago fallen rock.

Then he saw a slightly unnatural pile of fir boughs beneath a tree just behind the edge of the forest. McLean smiled and cocked his rifle. He would pretend that he had not seen the blind, get a little further into range, and before the enemy could act, blast the unbeliever to whatever afterlife might be waiting for him. He did not signal to Jack because he did not want to give any hint of his increased alertness.

The pile of fir boughs had been built by a man named Anukatlh just the afternoon before. As McLean raised his firearm, so Anukatlh, who was not in the blind, but behind McLean, raised his own, and immediately after the sudden morning noise McLean lay dead on the sloping ground, his breast plate beneath him. Anukatlh prepared and fired again, over Jack's head. Jack ran down the hill, and Anukatlh walked uphill into the sunlight, into the darkness of the forest.

They turned Donald McLean over onto his back and opened his tunic. It was the first time anyone but a blacksmith had seen the iron chest. But Captain McLean was dead now and his magic would not reappear until his grandson George captured a lot of white men at Vimy Ridge.

Now Duncan McLean raised his borrowed pistol. Tears were running through dust on his face. He put the pistol to his head. But another young man grabbed his arm and took the gun away from him.

They dug a hole just above the lake and buried the Donald from Tobermory. The pursuit of the thin massacre warriors would continue without pure-white McLeans.

Jack did not feel as if the white men trusted him. When they woke up the next morning he was gone.

The killing of Donald McLean was an execution. His executioner was never punished by the British Government.

Anukatlh died in 1901. He was an Elder who told excellent stories, but he never told the one about the man with the metal chest.

In 1880, when Judge Henry Pering Pellew Crease pronounced sentence on Allan and Charlie and Archie McLean, he said, "You have disgraced British Columbia, and you have disgraced the name you bear, instead of honouring it."

One hundred and twelve years later two new histories of British Columbia were published to considerable acclaim. Neither mentioned the McLeans. The McLeans are not in history.

When Donald McLean rode to Tatla Lake and never came back to the ranch, Allan was eight years old. Charlie was two. Archie was moving his hands and feet in Sophie's womb.

Annie was one year old. She played with the younger dogs outside the log house her father had built at Hat Creek. She looked up and saw a mother almost six feet tall. When she was stepping inside the house, her hair missed the lintel by inches.

When she was old enough to walk Annie followed her brother Charlie around the ranch. When she was two she stood for half an hour looking at a rattlesnake that was coiled and holding its head still. When the baby Archie was born she brought him insects and leaves.

She was a beautiful girl, and her mother dressed her in white on Sundays. She had light brown skin and dark red hair and white clothes. Her brothers paid little attention to her, especially lonely Allan, who was often away from them all, standing in the middle of a field and listening to something. He would not let her come to the middle of the field.

When she was four some white men came to the ranch and took everything out of the house. They loaded everything onto two wagons, and the children too, and for five days they rode in the wagons, toward the sun.

When Donald McLean did not come back from the Chilcotin, his property became of interest to a large number of people. He left behind the first ranch on the plateau, the stage depot at Hat Creek, a lot of horses and some cows and equipment. He left a treasure buried somewhere near the confluence of Hat Creek and the Bonaparte River.

Nine of his eleven children and at least one of his wives were still living. In London, England, his sister Anne received the news of his death and hired a lawyer. In Kamloops J. A. Mara began to think about Hat Creek and the coach road that ran north past McLean's door.

The Hudson's Bay Company argued for half a year, and then gave Sophie Grant McLean eight pounds a month for five years. She was an Indian, they reasoned. Indians have their own economy.

When Annie was fourteen years old she was not as tall as her mother but she was a tall girl and as poor as any halfbreed in Kamloops. White women thought she was a red-haired Indian girl. Indian women thought she was a caprice of nature. They respected nature.

J. A. Mara did not have to respect nature. He offered Annie McLean a job.

Annie never told her brothers what Mara had done to her, but they knew. Charlie and Alex used to board at the school in Cache Creek, and the school was on the property of C. A. Semlin, and C. A. Semlin told them. Mara was the father of their nephew.

Archie and his brothers told everyone that they were going to burn Kamloops to the ground and kill J. A. Mara. Alex Hare was in love with their sister. He did not tell them that he was going to beat them to J. A. Mara. He was going to ride away from Kamloops wearing Mara's suit.

5

SINCE MORNING THE hard pieces of snow had been hissing through the air at an angle. The four young men were sitting as close to their fire as possible. Each time the whisky was passed, the recipient would remove his deerskin glove to hold the bottle and tip it up to his mouth, then pass it on before replacing his glove. There was an outline of dry snow on the horses, which had got as close as possible to the small pine trees. The four young men sat with their shoulders as close as possible to their ears. They had scarves under their hats. From time to time they put their boots next to the fire.

Allan was looking straight at the moving flames. He had not said anything for hours. The younger ones joked and jostled each other despite the cold, and passed the whisky around. Allan was not drinking whisky. He was somewhere else. They were used to his travelling.

Archie passed the bottle to Charlie.

"I was talking to an American guy in Savona. He called me a nigger boy."

"I saw a nigger in Kamloops," said Alex.

"What did you say to the American?" asked Charlie.

"I put him on the floor, and then I showed him my knife."

The three of them laughed. They looked at Allan. He was staring into the far place in the fire.

The wind had died down, and now the snow was at least coming straight down. Even this close to a big campfire fed with greasewood the snow piled up on their hats. Almost everyone living on the great Interior plateau was indoors, safe behind hand-axed logs, warm as an iron stove could make them. Sometimes the winter wind came down one valley, sometimes another. It slipped between logs in a low wall and someone stuffed old cloth in the aperture. Not many people were outdoors. Most cows were in the barn or in the yard. The hilltops were abandoned to the dark snow. To be outdoors you had to be an idiot or a fugitive. You had to be unlucky.

"I seen some niggers that were so black it scared you, and others that are called niggers but look as if they'd just walked a little slow through one of their villages," said Charlie.

"They dont have villages," said Allan. He took off a glove and reached for the whisky bottle, just in time to polish it off. He threw the empty into the fire.

"We're talking here mainly about the States, where the Darkies come from," he said. "Down there they got Darkies just about everywhere you look. Matter of fact some parts of the States there's more of them than there is of us."

"What d'ya mean, us?" asked Charlie.

"I mean there's more of them than there is white people."

"Oh, us *white* people," said Charlie.

Alex and Archie laughed. Allan nearly smiled.

"Anyway," said Allan, "down there in the States you're either a white man or a nigger. If you're half nigger you're a nigger. If you're a quarter nigger you're a nigger. I heard about people was niggers in the States and when they came up here they was all of a sudden white men."

"Aint life strange?" enquired Alex Hare.

Mrs. Ana Richards never saw a bear at the Inlet and up here in the higher country she would never see a bear.

She had left a little grave on a high piece of land overlooking salt water. Now she lived alone again, in another shack, this time overlooking ice. A woman of a certain age. She made no friends easily.

Here she was again, older, her shoes in imperfect repair, a woman eyed by the rancher fathers and the women behind lace curtains. They might nod to her on the street because she was the schoolteacher, and they might whisper once she had passed because she had no history.

And when she first saw Allan McLean with his collar turned up and crystals of ice in his black beard, she had no grammar.

You will find Johnny Ussher's grave in a little square park in the middle of Kamloops, beside the joined Thompson rivers. "In Memory of John T. Ussher – 1844-1879 – Killed by the McLean Bros." He is a pioneer with a lake named after him, and even the Shuswap people call it Ussher Lake.

He was once a thin young man who didnt look young at all. Now he was forty years old, and skinnier than ever. Some people called him frail. Older women with big bums wanted to bring strawberry pies to his office.

He had his own woman at his own ranch; they had been married a year. She made wonderful strawberry pie, but the ranch hand ate most of it. One time two of the McLean boys came round looking for work and she gave them an apple cobbler almost worth dying for.

"I havent got time to eat," Johnny Ussher often said, swinging his leg over the pommel. "Save me a piece for tonight."

As he rode toward town, the dogs running after his horse, Mrs. Ussher stood on the mean porch of their unpainted house, one hand shading her eyes from the blasting sun, the other holding a well-worn broom. She watched him ride out of sight around distant rocks. She looked at the apron over her flat belly. If she could get a little boy she would cram his mouth with pastry.

Johnny Ussher's father was an Anglican minister in Montreal. He had always expected a lot from his son. Now Johnny Ussher did not think about this, but he expected a lot from himself. He did not have time to eat pie.

A lot of the gold rush boys came from California when they heard there was gold up north. When that petered out, they were gone again, to Alaska, to Mexico, wherever they could hammer in little posts and spend their dust in a tent full of familiar women. Johnny Ussher made a tidy stake in the Cariboo gold fields, and while most of the gold boys were dancing back to Victoria to get on a boat, he bought land outside of Kamloops and started feeding cows.

But there were getting to be a lot of ranchers in the Thompson country. When the railroad came through there would be a lot of railroad workers who would want to eat beef. When the track was finished the trains would carry cows to the coast. A man who wanted to have rich grandchildren would get a ranch with good bottom land as soon as possible.

But there were a lot of ranchers now. Johnny Ussher wanted

to be something more. His wife would have liked a few more picnics near the creek.

"Give me a few more years and you'll have your picnic on a street in Paris," he said.

She stood on the porch and shaded her eyes.

The Provincial Government was going through some hard financial times, so John Ussher was the only regular constable in the district. There were still a lot of Americans around, so guns went off from time to time. In the old days the Hudson's Bay Company whipped Indians and threatened their families. The Americans shot them. Now the Provincial Judges came around on their circuits and hanged them, and sometimes hanged white men who got liquored up and shot people. From time to time John Ussher had to hire deputies and write letters to Victoria, pleading for expenses. Victoria usually chiselled him down. A lot of the time he didnt chase outlaws unless the ranchers and businessmen came thumping on his door.

Johnny Ussher was overworked. He got skinnier.

He was also the Government agent, the tax collector, jailor, property assessor, the Clerk of the County Court, Registrar of the Supreme Court, and the mining reporter. He was a part-time policeman on a salary that was decent but not grand. He did not spend a lot of time drinking tea at the Dominion Hotel.

He looked at the land around him and became a businessman. He was a partner with J. A. Mara in the Shuswap Milling Company. It was the most promising sawmill in the Interior.

There was smoke in the air over Kamloops.

The James brothers and the Younger brothers robbed their first bank in 1866, when Jesse was nineteen years old and just recovered from the last Civil War bullets.

Billy Bonney started shooting people around 1873, when he was fourteen years old.

In 1881 Billy Bonney was found guilty of murder, but he killed two guards and got away. Pat Garrett knew where to get him, and told Billy who he was in the dark by plugging him.

In 1882 Jesse James got shot in the back of the head by a gun in the hand of a Mr. Ford.

Alex Hare and the McLean brothers died six months before Billy did, and a year and a half before Jesse did.

Canadian history is mainly written by schoolteachers who know a lot about the Government. If an individual with a gun shows up, he had better be an American or else.

In the Kamloops museum there's a display including pistols about Bill Miner the train robber. He was an American who snuck into Canadian history with a gun in his hand.

People dont want to know about the McLeans. They werent Americans. They werent white people and they werent Indians.

They might as well have been dead all along.

Allan McLean was having a talk with his wife on a brown grassy slope that ended in a line of willows and rocks at the edge of Douglas Lake. When they had a talk they did not talk much.

They were offering emotional information to each other.

They were talking about the baby and his name.

Allan was an outlaw leader and he had something like visions when he made himself alone, but this was the daughter of an

Okanagan Chief. If she assented, she agreed. But she was no white man's wife.

"It is normal," he said in Okanagan, "to have a white name."

She nodded a little, watching the baby at her breast.

"I favour the name George," said her husband, whose eyes never stopped searching the edges of hillsides in the beginning of the dusk.

She assented.

Her baby had an Okanagan name. Next year he would have a new one.

"I would like," she said.

"Yes?"

"I want to purchase his name from the brother of the house chief," she said.

"I know his name," said Allan in Okanagan.

There were not many whistling swans that year, but in the silence that followed Allan's words, the three people above the lake heard a whistling swan.

The gold rush had ended and the railroad was not here yet. From 1870 to 1879 the depression worsened in the Nicola Valley and along the Thompson rivers. If you were not doing well in 1870 you were almost gone in 1879. Then the winter of 1879-80 came as a dark stone of cold. It was the worst winter anyone had ever seen. Hard thin snow caught in the bent hair of cattle caught outdoors, and cows froze standing on level ground. Men gathered their small families and walked away from their frozen soil. The large owners acquired the small lost ranches. They diversified, building sawmills and hotels, forming meat cartels, in possession of riverside tracts the Canadian Pacific would need. They sent away to Europe for pianos and mirrors.

The CPR surveyors did all their business at the store and mill owned by Mr. Wilson and his senior partner Mr. Mara, the local Member of the Provincial Parliament. Every worker for the line bought his boots from Mara because he knew that Mara had to approve every man's job for the survey. Mr. Mara's other partner was John Ussher, the only constable in the region.

Mr. Mara did not feel the cold of 1879-80. He ordered more Hudson's Bay blankets. He sold whisky to the Indians across the river. He waited for the McLean ranch to become available. He leaned his whiskers on Annie McLean's light brown chest.

The rifle felt like ice on Charlie McLean's cheek. He held a glove in his teeth and his right hand was naked. He was learning how to fire quickly, one shot after another. Then he would put his hand in his left armpit for a minute, and shoot again. There was lots of ammunition – it had come from the back of the bastard's store, through a window whose boards had cracked loudly in the windy night. He grinned and his teeth felt as if they would freeze.

They were shooting targets on the slope above Hector McLean's cabin, where they had been sleeping these mornings. Allan was the best shot, but he seldom practised. Archie was the best rider. He won the wranglers' games when he was too young to enter. But Charlie wanted to be best. He used a lot of Mara's ammunition.

"Are you going to eat that crow you just shot?" Allan asked. He sounded stern, the big brother, the outlaw leader. But they knew Allan. He was in a light mood despite the cold.

"I will shoot ten more and make you a stew," said Charlie.

Below them the wide river was frozen solid. Wagon tracks crossed the snowy ice everywhere. Along the south side of the river thin smoke rose straight up from every chimney.

An unfortunate crow allowed himself to fall from a tall red pine, speaking first, then swooping downward before he bent his wings and began to rise. At that moment Charlie and Archie raised their barrels together and fired. The crow disintegrated, black pieces scattering on the white ground.

"I think I will call that fellow Mara," said Allan. He was leaning back on a boulder, his rifle leaning beside him.

"You sure as hell aint going to eat that one," said Charlie.

"Why dont we just go right down there and shoot Mara right now?" asked Archie. He was the youngest person in the gang. He felt that it was his function to be the hothead.

"Mara will be the climax," said Allan. As usual, his eyes were scanning the hills and the edges of the treeline.

"What the hell does that mean?"

"This is a lot more than just us and Mara."

"Yeah," said Charlie. "It's us and Tait and us and Trapp and us and Palmer and us and McLeod."

"It's more'n that," said Allan.

"Allan, you're irregular. Pardon me, but you're some irregular Indian or something. You got a problem with seeing stuff us regular folks cant see," said young Archie.

"It's them white store owners and politicians and ranchers got a problem," said Allan. He took up his rifle and shot a sparrow hawk out of a tall tree. The others had not noticed it. The Chilcotins had no fish and no bannock. They could not light fires. Some of them had the marks of smallpox under their paint. They were thin and slow in the mountains.

The white people had an invisible spirit weapon that left people lying on the ground without a wound. The white people took their women after the children died.

Now Klatssassin and his men were nearly ghosts in the mountains. They were ready for diplomacy instead of musket fire.

So a white man named W. G. Cox sent them a message. Cox was a Gold Commissioner, and he had a posse of volunteers from the Cariboo who did not want to ride too far into the mountains.

Come down to the enclosure. Make your camp nearby. We will give you food and tobacco. The war is over. We will arrange a meeting between you and the Big Chief. If you do not come down, we will send in an enormous army, and kill all the Chilcotin people that are still alive. We will kill all the women and all the children.

Klatssassin and his people came down. A deputy showed him a picture of the Big Chief. This was Governor Seymour. Klatssassin and his thin warriors smoked tobacco.

"We understand your situation," said Commissioner Cox.

"We are not murderers. We are killers," said Klatssassin.

"You are savage murderers," said Commissioner Cox, "and you are under arrest."

Klatssassin stood up, his old weak body as straight as possible. He had no paint on his face.

"We want to speak with your Big Chief," he said.

"You will see the Big Chief," Commissioner Cox said. "Matthew Begbie."

The Hanging Judge.

It bothered Judge Begbie that they were now sentencing these thin men to whom they had offered an amnesty. It seemed that there might be some moral hesitation, and even something legally imperfect.

Oh, what the hell! He heard the jury decide for guilty without leaving the box, and sentenced five of them to hang.

It would save lives, in the long run, and the Colony required settlers. It must not be left to the hordes of drunken gunmen from the States.

Still, Begbie did not feel right.

But he sentenced them to hang at Quesnelmouth on October 24, 1864.

Tah Pit, Pierre, Tellout, Chessis and Klatssassin.

Side by side. Chilcotin men with their arms bound to their sides.

Deputies went around to all the villages and pointed rifles at the people. They had to walk to Quesnelmouth. Old women leaned on short sticks. Those children who could walk walked. A wisp of smallpox air hovered over their path.

Two hundred Indian people surrounded the shining lumber of the gallows. They were well-managed, said the report to Victoria. No one was to make a speech.

Five more Indian men were hanging from ropes.

Only the people who had been compelled to come and watch knew who these men were. They knew what their powers had been. They knew who was an uncle, and they knew who understood salmon.

"Whatever happens to us, they're going to hear about the

McLeans," said Archie. He could feel terror inside his body, rising like dark water in a cistern.

He had never gone to the mountains alone to look for something.

His brother Allan had a bullet in his body. He had to lie down on his side. He was with them but somewhere else too.

"They have already heard about us," said Allan, pain in his mouth.

"I mean a hundred years from now. They are going to say the McLeans, and they'll be scared," said Archie.

There had not been a shot fired for an hour or more.

6

✹ ✹ ✹

"ONE OF THESE DAYS we ought to be rich," said Alex Hare. "You see this here pistol? One of these days it's going to make me rich."

It was a beautiful pistol. It had letters etched onto it along the side. Professional letters. AWH. Alex waved it in the cold sunlight, and then stuck it back into his waistband.

They were riding slowly downhill toward one of the skinny lakes in the Nicola Valley.

"We will never be rich," said Allan, who was willing to speak today. "We will ride around this country all our lives till they hang us, or till we take it back offa them."

"Who is this we?" asked Charlie.

Allan turned in the saddle, using his hands on the pommel to lever his rear end up for a moment's rest. He fixed a fierce brotherly stare on Charlie. There was frost in his black beard.

"This here was Sophie Grant's land before them damn Scotchmen and politicians and railroaders came in," said Allan. "I have been pondering on getting it back for her."

"Listen, Allan, big brother, deep thinker," said Charlie, trying to keep it light. "For one thing, a name like Sophie Grant aint any more Indian than a name like Sophie McLean."

Archie giggled. He had a mouthful of whisky.

"I dont know about you, but my mother's important to me," said Allan.

"Hey, us too," said Alex.

"She aint your mother," said Archie, and giggled.

Charlie thought about how they were always on an edge like this with Allan. They could make a few jokes, but they didnt want to make him angry.

Once they were sitting around a fire after a day of branding for the Palmer ranch. Everyone was worn out from the twelve hours of hot dirty work. They were half-sitting, half-lying against their saddles on the ground.

It took less than a second for this to happen. Allan reached the shiny Bowie knife out of the sheath on Alex Hare's hip, held it by the tip beside his ear, and threw it across the yard, where it entered a white chicken's chest and sent the body of the bird fifteen feet along the dust in a whirl of feathers.

No one asked him why he did that.

Charlie hummed a song his mother had taught him.

"We could of been rich," said Charlie.

They were riding slowly downhill through the shallow snow. Clouds of steam came from their mouths and from the noses of their horses.

"We could of owned the Hat Creek Ranch. We should of. Government would of made us rich."

"J. A. Mara's the Government," said Allan.

Charlie rode up beside Allan. Didnt look at him. Just talked loud enough so he could hear and so could the others.

"Big brother, if the white men are so bad, how come our

mother stayed with our father so strong? Stayed with him all those years, and years later."

"It aint our job to know what there was between Donald and Sophie McLean."

"We're their breed kids!"

"It aint our job to know what there was between them. That aint the story of what's happening in this country," said Allan.

On the sloping ground beside them was a white pile. On top was a layer of snow. Under the snow was a frozen calf.

"Must of broke off the glacier," mumbled someone.

"What?"

"Never mind. Tell us how we could of been rich."

Some white people were priests with another language and another religion. In black gowns they were making their rounds, and a lot of the stories they were telling sounded familiar to the people.

They said they ought to forget about Coyote. He was just an animal with parasites on his body.

They said no more Shuswap language. Got enough to do with these other languages, French and Latin and English. And no more Shuswap dances – they might have been choreographed by the Dark One.

And another important thing. No more polygamy.

There was not much future in the river country for abandoned wives.

Little statues of a young wife in a blue garment began to appear around the country.

The McLean gang lived it up. They drank a lot of stolen whisky and boasted about their rampage. They knew there werent any buildings in that country that a person with a rifle butt could not break into. They ate people's food and wore people's clothes and carried people's guns. If they didnt like a gun after a while, or they couldnt find the right ammunition, they would throw the gun into a creek.

Sometimes they would kill a chicken just for fun. Or piss on a floor. They even robbed an Indian house from time to time. They had a lot of revenge needed getting.

Sometimes they would get Alex Hare to leave a note.

They sat around the fire and drank a little, but they were all looking at Allan. Allan was a hundred feet away, sitting on a big flat rock at the edge of the cliff. He was sitting with his back straight and a blanket over his shoulders. It wasnt snowing, so he had his hat on the rock beside him. His hair was a little long and he had it pushed straight back. If it was any longer he could have tied it together in back.

Old Allan. He was twenty-four and they were all under eighteen. Between them lay three McLean babies who had died while their eyes were still blue.

After a while their old brother came back to the fire. He had his hat on. He kept the blanket around his shoulders. When he sat down he waved his hand at the offered bottle, no.

"Allan, what were you doing over there?" This was Archie the Kid.

Allan waited a while, as some men do, before he answered.

"Listening," he said at last.

"For what? Timber wolves?"

"I didnt hear nothing for a long time," said Allan. He poked at the fire and a lot of sparks flew up. "Then I heard a voice talking to me. It was talking, and then it was talking to me."

"What did it say to ya?"

Allan waited for a while. He was getting to be like certain men who wait a while before they answer your question.

"Said I am in a dangerous business. Said I might get shot, maybe more than once."

"Wouldnt be surprising," said Charlie.

"I might get shot, he said, this voice said. Might get shot, more than once. But no bullet will ever kill me. That's all he told me," said Allan. "Except then he started saying something in another language. Old language. I couldnt understand what he was saying. Sounded like he might of been singing."

"Have a drink," said Archie.

The McLeans had just about the best weapons in the country. When they were holed up in the Douglas Lake rancheree they all had sixteen-shot repeaters. They had cap and ball pistols. They had .50-calibre ammunition.

The legitimate owners of the rifles and pistols and ammunition hated losing those things. They were expensive items on the sagebrush frontier. There were two ways of showing how expensive they were.

1. A good rifle might cost as much as seventy dollars once it had been sent by steamer and packhorse from New Westminster.

2. When an Indian brought a load of pelts in to trade they would be piled one on top of another in a press and squeezed down into a nice solid pack. When the pack was the same height as a standing rifle, the trade was done. Such a

heap of furs would bring in about nine hundred dollars in Victoria.

You might say that there were two ways of looking at how expensive a nice rifle was. For a white rancher it might cost seventy dollars. For a Shuswap trapper it would cost a winter's work for two or three people.

Times were tough. Money was no more plentiful than rain. But the white people were making progress. Their ranches had new corrals one summer, irrigation ditches the next. The valleys looked different every time you passed through them.

As Indian wives were widowed or abandoned, their children were left to drift through this progress. They carried European names and spoke fragments of six or seven languages. The boys carried whisky in their saddlebags, and pistols with their initials on them. They were never going to grow old.

The McLean boys and Alex Hare were nearly always moving. They knew how to live outdoors. They knew which Indian families were friendly enough to let them sleep in their buildings. They understood that there were warrants for their arrest posted at every Government building they would ever see.

They grabbed whatever they needed, horses, food, saddles, guns, brandy and whisky, blankets and boots. They stole from wagon drivers, ranch wives, Indian reserves, storerooms, bakeries and unfortunate travellers.

In Ashcroft they broke into Soo Woo's laundry and stole somebody's monogrammed dinner napkins, just for fun. While they were at it they took the Chinaman's money and pounded the piss out of him.

"Let me get this right," said Alex Hare, addressing himself to Allan McLean, leader of the feared McLean gang. "You might get shot."

"More than once. Might get shot more than once," said Allan.

"You might get shot, more than once, but a bullet will never kill you."

"That's what they say."

"That's what your voice on the hillside said."

"Well now, there's a story going on," said Allan. "Now the McLeans are getting a name in this country."

Alex was enjoying himself. Here they were, riding alongside Stump Lake, wind blowing cold in their horses' manes. There were horses' manes in the lake too, jumpy water.

"McLeans? The McLeans are getting a name? I thought this outfit was called the Hare Bunch."

"Cant have that," said Charlie. "People shoot rabbits dead as doornails. Gotta be the McLeans. The McLeans are invulnerable."

"Thank you, Mister Indian School," said Alex Hare.

When the horses moved their feet through sagebrush, the brush snapped.

"Voice didnt say anything about you boys," said Allan. There was ice in his black beard. "Voice didnt mention you boys at all. Said they can shoot Allan McLean but they cant kill him."

Cloppety clop.

"Immune," said Archie.

"What's that?" This was his brother Charles.

"Invulnerable. Immune," said Archie. "You cannot kill our leader with a bullet. You cannot arrest us."

"They got warrants all up and down the country," said Charlie.

"Dont do 'em any good. We're immune. It's just like certain people dont get smallpox."

"Doesnt include you Indians," said Alex Hare.

Anna McLean Brown got herself a London lawyer. Anna was Donald McLean's sister. She thought her brother Donald was a valiant adventurer in the New World among the Red Indians, but she liked being a wine merchant's wife in London.

Now she had a lawyer.

Because her valiant brother, dead at the hands of a half-naked savage, had left an estate. There were reports of gold, stories of fur fortunes, the northwest passage, El Dorado, the fountain of youth, peculiar opportunities never seen in Albion, or not lately.

Her lawyer told her about Sophie Grant and the earlier wife.

"I would not want to do anything that portrays less than total honour, you understand," said Anna. "I loved my brother, but, well, there it is – I am white."

The lawyer was going to be paid no matter the outcome.

"What of dear Donald's fortune? Gold?"

The lawyer explained that there were rumours that McLean had buried a treasure of unknown quantity somewhere known only to him. They had come to call the nearby community Cache Creek.

"So what is it that we will keep in the – real family?"

The lawyer told about the ranch in a confluence of two attractive valleys. He mentioned the home-made house and the other buildings, including a stable and small inn. He said that for the meantime Sophie Grant and her children had been allowed to stay in the house. The house was made of logs, one big room and a loft upstairs, where the children slept.

"Land?" she expostulated. "Am I supposed to become exercised about some soil and water halfway around the globe?"

The lawyer described the coach road that began in the Fraser Valley and led to the opening north, where the gold fields had been. He mentioned the inevitability of white settlement. He explained that this coach road ran right by the front door of McLean's little inn and stable.

Anna McLean Brown decided for familial continuity.

"It is our duty to honour the life's work of my slain brother," she said, and her chin lifted a little farther from the high collar of her somewhat costly dress. "We must not let the land he died for fall back into unchristian hands."

At the south end of Stump Lake in the Nicola Valley lay the Palmer Ranch. Its brand was the simplest in the area, as if defying rustlers with modifying irons. It looked like a big letter S.

Palmer settled in the valley in 1873. He had decided to become a cattle rancher because he could not quite do any of the things he had imagined himself doing. Once the Indians had been moved away from the lakes in the Nicola Valley the ranchers let their cows finish off the native grass and then planted hay. Their cows grew fat, and then the cowboys, Americans and Indians, drove them slowly southward, through four more valleys to the Yankee railroad.

Such cattle drives were called epic in the late nineteenth century. Why not?

William Palmer was not an epic hero. When confronted by choice he looked at the skyline. When confronted by danger he looked for help in town.

Mrs. Palmer was a termagant. She knew what she wanted. She wanted more. She wanted more out of her husband but when she didnt get that she settled for more land. She was a white woman, and she wanted more.

Mrs. Palmer had one of the most successful ranches on the plateau. Many Americanos and Indians worked for her. Sometimes the McLean brothers worked for her, and they did not ride away with any more than she would let them have.

Mrs. Palmer had a piano imported from Germany. It crossed the ocean and it arrived in Victoria. It was brought up the wagon road to the Nicola Valley. Then it was cleaned and tuned by a travelling man. No one ever played that piano in her lifetime. No one was allowed near it with a cigar. People were of the opinion that it was better than the piano in the Continental Hotel. The summers are hot as hell in the Nicola Valley, but no one ever opened a window in the piano room at Mrs. Palmer's.

One December day Palmer's black stallion went missing. A lot of sad stories are started by missing horses.

Just about every outfit in the valley had been broken into or rustled, but Mrs. Palmer had never lost anything. Now on December 3, 1879, William Palmer's best horse was gone.

He had a pretty good idea who had his stallion.

"You go and get that horse," suggested Mrs. Palmer.

"Got my brand on him," he said. "Cant imagine he'll get far."

"Go looking," she advised.

So there he was, riding from ranch to ranch and over a hill or two, along the valley. He thought he knew who he was looking for, and he was in no great hurry. He did not have a weapon with him. He was just looking for a stray horse with an S on his flank.

From time to time he ran across a neighbour.

"Used to be I thought they were just a bunch of high-spirited boys," said Richie McDonald. "But now they've just gone too far. Smashed all my wife's dishes looking for something to drink."

"Stole four loaves of fresh-baked bread," said John Stevenson.

"Broke into my house and knocked my stovepipes all over the place. For no good reason," said James Kelly.

Bill Palmer kept riding his second-best horse northward, from lake to lake. He left prints in the snow, and pretty soon he saw some other prints in the snow, five horses anyway. He didnt want to follow them, really, but he followed them. He slowed down but eventually he got there. He was in a little clearing surrounded by willows and aspens. On the edge of the clearing was the last bit of a campfire, blackened twigs with a sheen like a raven's wing, a little smoke.

Palmer stopped his horse and lifted his head, and saw that he was in the middle of an imaginary square. At each corner of the square was a boy on a horse. One of them was sitting on Palmer's black stallion. The stallion was looking at Palmer and twitching its ear. The boy sitting on his back was Charlie McLean, and he had a new-looking rifle pointed toward the centre of the square. The rifle was cocked.

At another corner sat Allan McLean, frost in his beard. He

was holding an over-and-under shotgun pointed at the rancher. It had at least one hammer thumbed back. Palmer heard a click. Two.

There was a packhorse beside the roan that Archie was sitting on. The packhorse was carrying objects that had not always belonged to this group of youths.

Palmer did not like that click. He looked in Charlie's direction and saw his black stallion lift its left forefoot, three times.

He held his hands out to the sides to show that he was not carrying anything in the way of firearms.

"Dont shoot," he said.

"You know who we are?" asked Archie. He punctuated his question with a little lift of his rifle barrel.

"Sure, you boys've worked for me."

"We do satisfactory work?" This was Allan.

"I got no complaints," said Palmer.

"What're you doing out here on such a cold day?" This was Charlie.

It passed through Palmer's mind that it might be dangerous that the Hare boy wasnt saying anything.

"I'm just looking for some strays," he said. "Stray cows."

"Do we look like strays?" asked Archie. He was the youngest, born right about when his father was killed, people said.

"Naw, I just saw your smoke, and wanted a little company," said Palmer. "I aint after you boys."

"That's a damn good thing," said Allan. He uncocked his shotgun and lowered it. The others lowered their guns too, though Alex Hare took a while to put away his monogrammed pistol.

"You boys headed for Kamloops?"

"Oh, we're headed for Kamloops all right," said Charlie, not a trace of humour in his voice.

"Mind if I ride along with you?"

"Yeah, we mind," said Allan. "We aint riding to Kamloops with you, Palmer. I mean if you *get* to Kamloops, we aint going to be with you."

"Be a bad idea to be in Kamloops when we get there," said Charlie.

Palmer saw that Charlie was having a little trouble keeping the large black horse still. It seemed like a good idea to get away from there as soon as possible without making it seem too obvious. Charlie might let the stallion's owner just ride away without any pride. He might just plug him right there and earn an entirely new kind of warrant.

He saw an empty brandy bottle shining in the burned-down fire.

"Well, I'll be riding north. If you see any cows with my brand on 'em, tell them to go home," said Palmer.

"We'll be sure to do that," said Allan. "Sorry about the guns. We didnt know it was just somebody looking for company."

"That's okay. I got nothing against you boys."

"Damn good thing," said Archie.

Palmer was now in the middle of a much smaller square. He let his second-favourite horse take a step or two.

"What you going to be doing in Kamloops?" asked Allan, obviously casual.

"Oh, got a little legal business," said Palmer, thinking as quickly as he could in the cold.

"Mrs. Palmer send you to the land office again?"

"Something like that."

Charlie leaned forward and patted the stallion on the neck. Allan moved his horse aside to give Palmer some northward space.

"If you happen to run into that son of a bitch Mara, tell him he's got something coming to him," said Allan.

"I'll do that," said Palmer.

"Tell him his brother-in-law said so."

7

W HEN THEY WERE children their parents had different ways about what some people called discipline and other people called punishment. Their father sometimes whacked them ceremoniously, a certain number of whacks at a given hour at a prescribed place. Other times he whacked them with whatever object he had in his hand, forehand or back.

When he whacked them he gave his opinion that they were little heathen or in danger of sliding into savagery.

Their mother, though, never whacked them. Where she came from people never whacked their children. They expected their children to be brave and to grow as straight as a pine tree, they challenged them to walk past their fright in the woods at night, but they never whacked them.

Alex Hare's father would let young Alex get away with murder on one occasion, and thrash him for looking funny the next time he saw him. Nicholas Hare was a busy and successful man.

He had started by looking at a pan of gold flecks on the bars in the Fraser River. When he had achieved a substantial poke he moved to the Thompson, and bought some really nice land that had once belonged to Shuswap people at the mouth of

Cherry Creek. He started a herd, and planted an orchard. He worked hard at a job in Kamloops and earned enough money to buy lumber and tools. He took a Shuswap woman who was able to work long hours in the house and in the pens.

Nicholas Hare grew and grew. Fence posts gleamed in the morning sun. Hay waved in the wind. There were horses and cows everywhere. He built the biggest piggery around. He bought a mower and rented it out to other ranchers when he was not using it. His herds grew. Wooden irrigation flumes made a big green swatch of alfalfa mixed with grass in the middle of the brown country.

His two neighbours were MacAulay and MacIvor. Nicholas Hare grew ever more successful, while MacAulay and MacIvor did not. Hare was not a popular neighbour. No one in Kamloops liked him, either. John A. Mara bit down hard every time he sold Hare a wagonload of lumber.

Once in a while MacAulay or MacIvor would complain to the Justice of the Peace about something that had been bothering them, and the Justice of the Peace would say they needed more to go on.

In 1865 Nicholas Hare bought MacAulay's ranch off him, and MacAulay started over again up the North Thompson. In 1868 MacIvor gave up too, and sold his ranch to Hare. Now Nicholas Hare had one of the biggest spreads in the Valley. His brand looked like this:

His son Alex was six years old. He could speak English and French and Shuswap. When he spoke Shuswap his father whacked him.

Nicholas Hare should have been more careful with his son.

He had acquired gold by hard work, and now he had a big spread. He wanted something else. He sent Alex to school in Cache Creek.

There he was known as Nick Hare's kid. Half French, half Indian. A short boy with a mean disposition.

By the time he was sixteen he had an SA .44 with a seven-inch barrel. By the time he was eighteen he was lying in potter's field in New Westminster, famous.

Nicholas Hare sold his whole outfit to his neighbours and left the country. There are McLeans all over the Interior, but it's not easy to find a Hare.

William Palmer was a short man. He was very fond of his black stallion because he rode so high off the ground when he was on it. He liked riding out of his yard on the black stallion, away from Mrs. Palmer.

Now he was on his second-best horse, riding down the slope into Kamloops. There was ice on both rivers, and wagon tracks crossed the thin snow on top of the ice. On the slope leading down into Kamloops there were hoofprints and pawprints. It was the coldest winter anyone could remember.

It was not the best time of year to be a desperado, or a respectable citizen riding out after desperados.

Kamloops wasnt much of a place in those days but it was the biggest place around, and there were plumes of smoke rising from buildings that were warm inside. Palmer first rode to the Continental Hotel and had three cups of tea while his horse stood with closed eyes outside. Then it was time to go and see the law.

The law was partly Johnny Ussher, and partly John T. Edwards. Edwards was a Welsh miner who had made a lucky strike in the Cariboo. Now he had one of the best ranches around Kamloops and was investing in real estate right in town. He had his eye on the Colonial Hotel. He had a lot of money in the Bank of British Columbia in Victoria. If you were a Welsh boy living in Britain you were an Indian. If you came to the land of gold and unregistered cows you could be a white man in a few years. Justice of the Peace.

John Edwards was wearing his suit and sitting next to the stove. He frowned ever so slightly when Bill Palmer came in, slapping his hat against the side of his leg.

Palmer did not notice any invitation to sit down, so he put his rump against a windowsill.

"It's them blessed thievin' murderin' McLeans."

"I never heard anything about murderin', Bill." Edwards said this with his patient superior Justice of the Peace voice.

"All right," said Palmer. "Thievin'. Today I have seen Charlie McLean sitting on my best horse, and I wouldnt be surprised if the saddle he was sitting on came from your place, John."

"Seems almost like they're part of the winter, dont you think?" said Edwards.

Palmer wasnt much for metaphysics and figures of speech.

"They werent so pleasant last summer," he said. "To get to the point, John. I come here to report a theft, and I want to lay a complaint. I want a warrant."

Of course there were lots of warrants. He wanted a posse.

"Actually, what you want to do is lay an information," said Edwards.

"What I want to do is get my stallion back. What I want to do is see those damned halfbreed sons of Donald McLean dangling from the end of a rope," said Palmer.

On the slope above Napier Lake there was a wide clearing between the trees, and in the middle of the clearing a big crippled tree. It was a Douglas fir, but not the Douglas fir you will find in the forestry book illustration. This unfortunate tree bore a few needles yet, but only on one side.

Some time ago, no one knew or remembered when, this tree had been hit by lightning, and it had been trying to recuperate as trees will do, ever since.

That was where Allan McLean was sitting, two blankets around his shoulders, his ragged hair exposed. He was sitting perfectly still, his back to the deformed trunk of the tree, his face toward the uphill slope. It looked as if there was nothing to see up there but the cold clouds that wound among the snowy fir trees. Allan sat perfectly still with his eyes open, holding the blankets up to the end of his cold beard.

The others were farther down the slope, holed up in a shed that someone had started building but abandoned before the door had been hung. Five horses stood as close as they could to one another on the least windy side of the tiny building. There was no stove in the shed, but a fire was going on the dirt floor. The smoke from the fire climbed to the flat roof and then snaked its way over to the door frame. A lot of it stayed inside the building, and the occupants coughed from time to time.

"What the hell is he doing now?" asked Alex Hare.

Charlie stuck his head out the door and looked up the slope.

"Some Indian thing," he said. "Looking for power or something."

"I got my power right here," said Alex, and he pointed the
.44 at Charlie.

"God damn it, stop that!"

Charlie did not jump out of the way. He did not twitch. He
just lowered his dark eyebrows at Alex Hare.

Alex started going through his gun-cleaning routine. He did
this five times a day. The lower the temperature got the more
often he cleaned his gun.

"You believe in that Indian stuff?" he asked Charlie at last.

"It dont matter whether I believe in it or not. It's true
anyway."

"My old man used to pound me if I did any Indian stuff.
Couldnt even talk Indian when he was around. Me and my
mother talked Shuswap, the way they do over east of here. She
used to teach me stuff and my old man used to pound me if I
talked about it."

"Our mother was a little different," said Archie. "One day
she's teaching us Indian stuff and the next day she's saying dont
forget you're a McLean."

"One time," said Alex Hare, "I let my hair grow and grow,
and I got my mother to tie it in two plaits, and they hung a
little way down behind, not long like a real Indian, but a pretty
good start, you know. My old man takes one look at me, and
then he grabs me and I'm down on the chopping block, still got
dried blood on it from the last chicken. I thought he was going
to chop my fuckin' head off, but bam bam, there goes my braids.

Later on I found out my mother went and got them and buried them. She told me once she wanted one of them shaman fellows at her funeral. Old man wouldnt allow it. No rose branches, nothing. Just a French priest talking some language."

In the fall of 1811 white men from the south arrived at what they called the Thompson rivers. There were the Shuswap people, gathering to say hello at a place they called Kamloops or something like that.

The winter of 1811 was pretty cold, and the snow was as high as a man's hips, so the white people were invited to stay in some polite people's pit house for the winter.

"We will give you anything you need if you will bring us the hair from all the beavers you can find," these white men from the south told their Shuswap friends. The Shuswap people thought they were getting a good deal.

What did they know?

"Nice country around here in the summer, I'll bet," said the white men.

"Tell you what," said the main white man from the south. "We'll build a permanent post right here. Trade you all the stuff you want."

The Shuswap people couldnt believe their luck.

Next fall the other more or less white men arrived from the east, and joined in, setting up their own trading post across the river. No problem. There were furs here, there and everywhere. People were getting rich. Times were good.

"I'm glad I lived long enough to see this," said one Shuswap Elder to his best friend.

Way back east the white men and the real white men were

starting to pound each other. They even had big ships on the lakes, shooting chunks of iron at each other.

So in the following spring the white men from the south sold all the stuff they couldnt carry to the more or less white men from the east, and headed back down to what they called the Columbia River.

All this time some real white men were starting to drift into the country. And some people they called Indians came with them from way back east where the white men and the real white men were pounding each other.

There were getting to be a lot of languages in Shuswap country.

Now the people a day's ride up the river talked the same language the people at Kamloops talked. They just said the sounds a little different. And the Okanagan people could be understood more or less if you put your hand behind your ear. All these new people talked like animals you didnt know about. But here they were, ready to make the Shuswap people rich.

In his opening address to the jury at the McLean and Hare trial, Sir Henry Pering Pellew Crease, B.C. Supreme Court Judge, said that halfbreeds got into trouble because of absent fathers and weak government.

"Quick shots, unrivalled horsemen, hardy boatmen and hunters," he said, "they knew no other life than that of the forest. They learned next to nothing of agriculture. They never went to school or had the semblance of an education and when the wave of civilization, without hurry, without delay, but without rest, approached, it met a restless roving halfbreed population, who, far from initiating, did not even understand the restless agency which was approaching them. So long as the white father lived, the children were held in some sort of subjection, but the moment he was gone, they gravitated toward their mother's friends and fell back into nature's ways. Is it any wonder then, that, remaining unchecked and uncared-for they should at last adopt the predatory Arab life which in a scattered territory is fraught with such danger to the state?"

In Victoria the Government was always made up of Hudson's Bay Company men. The old firm running the new business.

In Victoria in the late nineteenth century the biggest business led straight to the biggest government, and businessmen all through the Colony and the Province were made the local representatives of the Government.

The gold rush had speeded matters considerably. Sons of somebody else were pouring into the country, Yankees, Chinese, Sandwich Islanders, Italians, even post-Civil War black men. The sons of Britain had to firm things up, because the foreigners were not Company men. The Yankees brought lots of guns and lots of liquor, and fancy saloons appeared in the gold towns. Ordinary men working for the Hudson's Bay Company could not afford the music and dancing and whisky. Law and order were needed badly.

They needed Judge Begbie to ride around the country hanging people. He often said that he was saving British Columbia from the Yankee invasion, but when there were twenty-seven men hanged, twenty-two of them were Indians.

The McLean boys drifted south on horses that belonged in the north. When they crossed the new medicine line into Washington Territory they did not tell anyone in a uniform. They descended with the Similkameen River, and in the middle of the desert darkness they rode past Nighthawk, where the white soldiers were sleeping in each other's arms.

They rode their northern horses down the Similkameen, and where it joined the Okanogan they turned yet further south, following that river all night under the crisp round moon. They were out with coyotes and owls, drinking warm whisky and following the gleam of the water. Sometimes, when there were no fences in sight, they sang together, old French songs and coarse Yankee songs. When a coyote howled from a ridge they howled back. They threw their empty bottle into the Okanogan River.

These were warm August nights. Mice were running through the grass. Rattlesnakes were sound asleep under their rocks. The wagon road these boys were following had sleepy grasshoppers on it. Horses stepped on them. What a good time to be alive.

"It's about time we started terrorizing on the American side," said Charlie.

"Here's the way I look at it," said Archie. "The onliest thing we were ever left with was gettin' famous. So we're famous. Now, when you're famous you've got to keep on going, or people will forget all about you. You've got to – what did you call that, Allan?"

"Expand your base of operations."

"Where the *hell* did you hear something like that?" asked Hector McLean.

"Fellow was reading the newspaper out loud at the barber shop."

"What the *hell* were you doing in a barber shop?"

Just above Fort Okanogan there was a nice cattle spread on the west side of the river. It was owned by a white political man who was in Olympia, arguing with the Federal authorities his view that the Indians werent likely to put all the Indian land on the east side of the river to good use, and that it should be opened up, maybe gradually, to settlement by people with a vision of the future.

He'd left his operation in the hands of his two sons. But his two sons were over on the reservation having a good time for a night or two, and they had left the operation in the hands of their mother, who was a Kettle Falls Indian woman named Catherine.

This was the place at which the McLean boys had decided to start their American fame.

"Hey, Allan," said Hector. "You figure the old people used to sit in these caves? Maybe live in them?"

"More than likely."

"Maybe their bones are buried right under where we're sitting," said Hector.

"Hector, you got to understand something about our brother. He thinks he's an Indian," said Charlie.

"Listen, we spend our time with Indians. We sit around campfires with Indians. We talk Indian when we're around the reserve. Last I heard your brother was marrying an Indian. So what are we? Do we spend a lot of time with white society people? Been to any tea parties lately?"

Before the August sun was up over the bare hill the next morning the McLean brothers were riding their horses behind a dozen American cows, and looking for a few more along the riverbank. Catherine did hear them.

Her sons' horses were not home yet. She was in charge of

the operation. That meant getting out the side-by-side shotgun and jacking in a couple of home-crimped shells. She had done it before.

The McLeans knew they had to ford the cows across the river and get them into the hills for the long ride to Canada, and they knew the house was right next to the ford. In the dusty morning light a thousand goldfinches showed them the way. Every few minutes Archie counted the cows. Fourteen.

But there was Catherine, in a plain cotton dress, tight at the waist, sleeves three-quarters of the way down her arms, hair hanging straight down in the morning, feet in no shoes at all, toes tight in the dirt. She was pointing both barrels of a shotgun at Allan McLean's beard.

"Whoah," this man sagely required of his mount.

"I shoot rustlers," shouted Catherine.

"Ah, then we will leave your animals right here and be on our way to Chelan," said Allan, not exactly raising his arms.

"You aint going to Chelan. You're going to that marshal at Fort Okanogan," she shouted.

"Come on, squaw woman, we're the McLeans. No one takes us alive," said Archie, a kid on a big horse.

"Get down," said Catherine. The shotgun was heavy. It was a problem, holding it with the long barrels pointing upward.

Allan got off his horse and motioned for the rest to do the same. He walked toward the woman. She lowered the barrel so that it was aimed right at his breadbasket.

Now he spoke to her in Shuswap.

"Why are you protecting a white man's cows?"

Catherine spoke the Kettle Falls version of Okanogan, but she knew what Allan McLean was saying.

"These are my husband's cows. My husband's cows and my cows."

"Why are you lying down with a white man?"

"I have grown sons. I do not lie down any more."

"Put that stick down. Do not be pointing a stick at a cousin."

"You. Who did your mother lie down with?"

"A dead man," said Allan.

And grabbed the shotgun. He fired both barrels into the sod roof of the house. He started speaking English.

Who did your mother lie down with? She had asked that question, and it was worse than the shotgun. Now they unsheathed their knives and held her tightly and cut her hair all off. They used the keen edges of their blades and shaved the stubble, knicking her fairer skin and bringing dots of aboriginal blood. They rubbed Hudson's Bay Company whisky on her bare head and took fourteen cows across the river and into the hills.

Now the McLeans were wanted on both sides of the new international boundary. They made up a lopsided song about their new adventure, and sang it for a day while they rode north, and then forgot it.

The telegraph lines whizzed between Olympia and Victoria.

The McLeans got those American cows into the Province, and then they sold them for a rock-bottom price to a man with no name who lived nowhere particular in a little valley somewhere above the Similkameen River. They were careful to tell him their name but he was never going to tell anyone.

8

✳ ✳ ✳

THE WIRES HUMMED from Colville to Port Angeles, from Cache Creek to Victoria, under the sea from the Olympic Peninsula to Vancouver Island. Printing presses bit paper, and warrants made piles on country desks. Wanted posters went up in post offices all over northern Washington Territory. Summer disappeared on everyone.

In the plateau country smoke rose from burning kinnickinnick leaves. Simple drums were heard in the winter night. The poplars and cottonwoods were bare and cold in the earth. Deer came lower and lower, looking for food. They made hungry Indian people lucky. They stood in snow nearly up to their bellies, and they were easy to shoot. So were cows.

Ice on the lakes and rivers was too thick to chop through, and the fish were asleep on the bottom. Men looking for work to make coins to buy bread and tobacco could not find anyone hiring this winter. Trappers could hardly move in the deep snow. It froze clear through to China.

The Fraser was solid ice all the way up to Harrison River. In New Westminster Archie Minjus the photographer could not take his shutters outdoors. The oil congealed in his delicate black mechanisms. He would have to get through the winter taking portraits of businessmen's families.

Near Cache Creek Donald McLean's buried treasure was clenched in the grip of hard frozen graveyard earth.

J. A. Mara's paddlewheelers sat on the shore, covered with tarpaulins and snow. There was not a footprint near them.

Destitute loggers drank Hudson's Bay whisky on credit.

It froze to the stars above.

Two old old Indian men were sitting outdoors in the cold. Nobody knew anything about their earlier life, because they were too old to be Elders. These two old men never told stories to young people because they did not know any young people. They did not tell legends and they did not tell true tales. They just talked with each another. People came by and left food and ran away. People were too shy to talk to these two old men because they did not know who they were. But they were Indians and they were still alive, so people brought food and firewood and moccasins, and then they ran.

"Cold winter," said the first old old Indian.

"Eeyup, and there will be much more of it," said the second old old Indian.

They were smoking some pretty good stuff. Every time it was time to say something, the old old Indian in question would take a long slow breath out of his pipe, look with his cloudy eyes at something or nothing directly in front of him, and then say his words. It was as if they had a lot of time to kill.

"Is this here the coldest winter you've ever seen?" asked the first old old Indian.

"Well, I have seen a lot of winters, and I have felt a lot of winters," said his companion.

"This here the coldest?"

"It's pretty cold."

This was more or less the way they always talked, these two old geezers. Sometimes they went for a walk together. They would walk all the way round the teepee. They would sit down and boil a can of tea. They would get out their old pipes made of cherry wood. That would be a clue if you were an anthropologist in 1880. Where did these old old Indian men get cherry wood for their pipes?

"Lot of robbery-type trouble around these parts this year," said the first old old Indian.

"Eeyup. Never seen as much trouble as is made by those McNair boys."

"That's McLean. You remember young Donald McLean, the Hudson's Bay boy."

"Always was a troublemaker," said the second old old Indian. "Never liked anyone and no one ever took a liking to him."

"Well, he's dead. Been dead for a while. These here are his sons. Most of them from his second family."

"Ah yup. Well, troublemaking runs in families, the way I see it."

"Sh-teen," said the first old old Indian.

"McLean?"

"Sh-teen. What the Indian people around here call the devil."

"Shu-mix?"

"I was going to say something about Sh-teen and the McLeans."

"It is a complicated concept," said the second old old Indian. Snowflakes fell into the tea.

"That McLean gang. They're just a bunch of kids, except the oldest, that Allan McLean. He's got a lot of his father in him."

"Lot of Sh-teen," said the second old old Indian.

"But he thinks he's an Indian. Married to young Chillitnetza's daughter. The chief up at Douglas Lake. Got a kid."

"More troublemaking," said the second old old Indian.

"Eeyup. This Allan, though. I saw him one time. Standing on a big rock over the lake, all naked except for a piece of deerskin. Covered with paint and looked like bear grease in his hair. Bear grease in that black beard of his."

"An Indian with a black beard?"

"That Allan McLean doesnt know what he is."

"He's a halfbreed. An Indian with a black beard and no land," said the second old old Indian.

The two frail men tended to the fire together, one putting in the new twigs and roots, the other poking at it with a stick.

"You know," said the first old old Indian slowly, "every day I think about the time when I was your teacher and you were my student. Last student I ever had, and the worst. Ha ha."

"Many moons ago."

"Dont talk to me about moons. It was many years ago. Maybe a hundred. There werent any halfbreeds back then."

"There werent any white men."

"There wasnt any Sh-teen."

"You want some tea?"

History, in other words, was calling out the McLean boys.

Chief Chillitnetza would call them the last of their kind.

This would happen when they were captured and placed in iron and walked across the ice to their last place. The last of their kind. He was talking about the first generation of fur trappers' sons, trying to understand how much of the Indian person was still in them. Trying to figure out what to do with the strangers inside them.

When Allan McLean took his clothes off and put bear grease in his hair, he was trying to get the wind to wrap his body. Trying to hear a voice that was just a little too far away in the trees.

The Wild McLeans, they were called.

When people said this they were calling them animals. In many of the camps of 1880 there were dangerous-looking dogs that people said were half wolf. They talked about the call of the wild.

What if the white strangers came into your country and pushed you away from the river land, and put ropes around your cousins' necks and hanged them, and took your sister to fuck?

And what if they put themselves right inside you? What if they put themselves in the middle of your home, and then they put themselves right inside your body? What if you had to spend all your life with one of these men inside you?

Sh-teen.

John Edwards had just put another stick of wood into the stove. Now he stood with his ass toward the heat.

"Well, Bill, I think the least we can do is get your horse back off those thievin' breeds. Do you know Charlie Semlin over at Cache Creek?"

"'Course. Used to be in the Government. Good man."

"He's a Justice of the Peace. Seems Semlin got sick and fed

up with them breeds and fired off a telegram to Victoria. Got a quick answer from Walkem. The Government's offering two hundred and fifty dollars for anyone can bring in the McLeans, or at least a couple of them."

"Shit, my stallion's worth more than that," said William Palmer.

"Yeah," said the Justice of the Peace. "But are the McLeans?"

George Caughill thought of himself as a bounty hunter, but there was not much in the way of bounty in this country. He often thought of heading below the line, where the real big money was. Snaffle just one of the Clanton Brothers and you'd have a down payment on a little ranch. Bring in all of them, and you'd own the bank, start passing out mortgages yourself.

But here he was riding on a saddle edged with hoar frost, looking for some half-Indian children, with the prospect of bringing in two hundred and fifty dollars, a hundred of which he would have to hand over to his grumbling partner Jamieson.

Ussher had passed the hat around Kamloops to get them fifty bucks for expenses. It was embarrassing. He should be in Arizona, trying to find Geronimo.

Now there was a fresh pile of buns just in front of him. The green-blue flies had hardly got started. A hundred yards further along there was an enormous boulder. It was broken in half, as if by some deity's axe, and one-half of it leaned northward. Each half was the size of an Indian's shack.

"I think we got us a robber," said Caughill, addressing an absent readership.

Now some tactics were called for. First he reached down

and cocked the hammer of his rifle, leaving it in the scabbard. Then he checked his hand gun. He tried to spit but his mouth was dry. His horse plodded on.

"Yep, got me a McLean," he said, quieter this time.

He neck-reined the horse to the right. He would ride around the boulder in a counter-clockwise pattern, make sure there werent any hoofprints continuing away from the spot. This way he would not be facing into the sun until he had circled the whole thing.

He got around to about twelve o'clock before he realized his mistake. He should have been going around clockwise. If you are circling a rock you have to have your horse sideways to your target, but if you go around clockwise, and if you are right-handed, you can face the rock with your weapon drawn, without having to rise in your stirrups and twist yourself around. Caughill was just considering turning around, and just beginning to figure out whether he should turn his horse in a right-hand about-face or a left-hand one, when he heard Charlie's voice.

Not from the shadow of the huge rock. Charlie was standing in the grass sixty feet away, and he was holding what appeared to be a sixteen-shot rifle. It was pointed toward Caughill's chest.

"Dont."

"Dont what, Constable?"

"Up to now you boys aint ever shot anyone, at least not dead."

"You aint got your hands up, Constable."

Caughill put his hands up.

"Things would go a whole lot worse with you boys if you killed anyone," said Caughill. His mouth was really dry now.

"Was you thinking of shooting me today?" asked Charlie. "You kind of look like you was thinking of shooting me."

"Never crossed my mind," said Caughill.

Charlie pointed the rifle at Caughill's head. Then his leg. Then his chest again.

"I'm trying to make up my mind," said Charlie.

"You're a robber, not a murderer, Charlie."

Charlie put on a pretend expression of surprise and recollection.

"Oh yeah! Thanks for reminding me. What have you got that I can rob off you, Constable?"

Shit, thought Caughill.

"What size boots you wearing, Constable?"

They were not brand new, and they were not old and scuffed. They were just nicely broken in. They had little shiny metal strips around the points of the toes.

"I got pretty small feet, Charlie."

"Give me the boots, Constable."

When the transaction had been made, Charlie decided to bring the afternoon's entertainment to an end.

"I'm going to let you go, Constable."

"Thanks, Charlie."

"Under one condition, Constable. You forget about the McLeans. You get yourself a nice job at Mr. Mara's sawmill. That a promise?"

Caughill did not like the feeling of cold stirrup irons.

"All right, Charlie. Would you consider quitting your wild ways in exchange?"

"I'll give it some thought," said the boy. Then he made that horse-encouraging sound that depends on a supply of saliva.

John Tait was the local boss for the Hudson's Bay Company, so he was interested in local politics, or, as he called it, law and order. There had never been a McLean that he much liked. When Sophie McLean's little pension ran out after five years he had explained law and order to the clerks in his store. No more credit for Mrs. McLean, if that's what she wanted to call herself.

Now he heard about William Palmer's black stallion, and he heard about the Premier's two hundred and fifty dollars.

"The Hudson's Bay Company will match the Government's money," he said to the small group of hairy-faced men in his office. "And if the Company thinks I am being rash, then I will guarantee the money out of my own pocket."

He was looking straight at John Ussher, the constable, jailor, Government agent, tax collector, court clerk, registrar, mining reporter, rancher, saw-mill operator and prospector. Ussher was a skinny man.

"I'm throwing in fifty dollars of my own," said Ussher.

John Edwards looked at William Palmer, who was working on his cigar.

"What about Mrs. Palmer?" he asked.

"I'm throwing in fifty dollars," said Palmer.

So now the McLeans were worth six hundred dollars.

The McLean boys had a sack full of Hudson's Bay whisky. The bottles had been gathered, some full, others half-empty, from various parlours. Alex Hare had found a pewter goblet in someone's house. While the others gulped from the bottle, Alex sipped from his goblet, whisky with a handful of snow melted in it.

"Ought to be eating something," said Charlie McLean. "If we just drink this rotgut on an empty stomach we wont be in any condition to pursue our occupation."

It was morning. This would be their second day at this camp. The fire was large, and thick sage smoke curled up through the pine needles. The good thing about pine trees was that you could find more or less bare ground under them. The bad thing was that once in a while a big dollop of snow would fall from a bough and hit you when you werent expecting it.

Archie was using his Bowie knife to hack strips off a bacon he had found in someone's root cellar.

"Willy Palmer said he was going to Kamloops, didnt he?" he asked.

"Eeyup," said Alex Hare.

"Figger he'll be back with some friends, looking for that horse he thinks is his?"

"That there is *my* horse," said Charlie. "Possession is nine-tenths of the law."

"Oh yeah, we got the law on *our* side," said Allan, and took a swig of whisky. Today he was being a white man.

"What are we going to do when they come?" asked Archie.

Alex Hare and Charlie McLean might have been twin brothers. They both reached at the same time, and pulled out their .44s and said, "Bang!"

Allan laughed at them.

"What's wrong with you, oh great leader?" said Charlie. He staggered just a little as he stuffed his long-barrelled pistol back under his belt.

Allan took a swig, then wiped his beard with the back of his glove. He watched Archie's knife as thick strips of bacon fell into the pan. His eyes were just about black and deep in his skull.

"I have been sitting here doing some arithmetic," he said.

"Always hated arithmetic," said Archie, and spat into the fire just next to the pan.

"Doing some arithmetic," said Allan. "Figure there's about four of us."

"How many James brothers was there?" asked Charlie, brash.

"How many is there right now?" replied Allan.

"Well, we aint the James brothers. We're the Wild McLeans," said Archie, slicing bacon.

"How come they dont call this here the Hare Gang?" suggested Alex.

"Arithmetic," said Allan. "There's roughly four of us, five if you count Hector. There's likely a hundred men that would like to see us finished around here. Them aint good odds."

"Odds dont bother me," said Archie. He was fifteen years old.

"Well, you're not too bright, then," said Allan.

The bacon writhed in the pan.

Alex Hare poured a little more whisky into his goblet and passed the bottle back to Allan.

"All right, tell us about adding and subtracting," he said at last.

"Go ye four and multiply," said Allan.

"I aint sure you got that right," said Alex Hare.

"Nobody asked you," said Allan. "What's the picture of the future look like for people that are half Indian and half white?"

"You're looking at it," said Charlie.

"So why dont we just decide to be white men? Get a little sawmill? Go into politics?"

"Hardy har har."

"Okay. Why dont we go to the reserves, go four and multiply? Maybe them Scotchmen made a bad mistake creatin' us kind of people. Maybe we're just what the Indians need to help them ride off the reserves and take their land back."

"Hardy har har har."

"I'm serious," said Allan.

Three of the outlaws took bacon from the pan. Allan was looking out over the white slope.

9

ALL THROUGH MY childhood and whatever it is that comes later, I spent a lot of time alone in the Valley and especially the hills.

There were certain things I liked to do over and over again when I was alone in the hills. I liked to lift and peel moss off big rocks. I liked scaling cliffs. I often buried things I had brought with me, a baseball, a hunting knife, an old locket. Burying things here and there you didnt mention to anyone, especially your parents, because they would have asked useless questions. When the irrigation ditch was drained for the winter I often walked a few miles down its length and discovered things that had been underwater all summer. Once I found a small pistol. Once I found a necklace made of Dutch coins.

I really liked running rock slides. These were usually made of old shale with thin hard algae on it. The pieces were usually more or less flat, from as big as you to as big as your foot, and in their millions formed huge fan shapes. You had to go a little faster than the sliding rocks. You had to take a giant step before you knew which rock you were going to step onto. You had to go faster and faster. The only part I didnt like was at the end. By the time you reached the bottom you were really going, and when you took a step onto unmoving ground, you were pretty sure to bang your knees hard or you would pitch forward onto your face, or your head if you managed to roll, and find a space between single rocks and cactuses and so on. You never thought about that part when you were standing near the top of the slide, looking out at the beautiful valley and getting ready to step into space.

One time I was catching my breath at the bottom of a slide, sitting on the brown grass and looking up at the shale. I was trying to recreate my downward path. Sometimes you would come more or less straight down, and sometimes you came down on a slalom route. I always thought you should be able to see your track, but the dark grey rocks just looked thousands of years old.

Near the bottom of the slide, where bushes and grass gathered between the last rocks, was a funny shape, a not-quite-natural heap of stones, flat on top of flat. I started removing stones, throwing the pieces of shale to left and right.

More rocks were falling into the space I was making, so I had more to do than I had thought I would. If I had had to do this much work at home, I would have had to make up a game to pass the time. Here I was just reshaping the end of a shale fan.

Then I saw a thin bone.

I picked the rocks out carefully now, and saw more bones. I saw a skull, separated from the other bones, which seemed to be in what was once a kind of little circle. The skull was pretty small in my hands. It was a human skull and it was brown like something from under the earth. I put it back as close to where I had found it as I could.

I saw a shape and picked it up and scraped it. It was a

medium-sized seashell. I had not seen many seashells then, except the ones some people used for ashtrays. I put the shell back with the thin bones.

Then I put pieces of shale back. I figured out how to place the first ones so that the skull and the thin bones and the shell would not have rocks lying right on top of them. I worked another hour in the hot afternoon sun, building a pile of stones. This time they would look just like the natural end of a rock slide.

John Ussher was feeling pinched by something, pinched by history or a story, or if that seemed too grand a picture, pinched by the demands made on both sides of him, and pinched by time.

He started out of Kamloops with Bill Palmer by his side, blinking in the winter afternoon light that came shooting around the corners of balled-up clouds. Johnny Ussher had always liked the McLeans, or at least he had not feared them. He wanted them to survive their wild teen years and grow up to be ordinary men, like some of their half-brothers.

But now he had a bad feeling. Time seemed to be pushing things too close to the end of some story. This time he would have to get all four of the gang and get them inside that log jail, and hire some guards to sit there with shotguns all day and all night. Even if he had to pay for all this out of his own pocket, again.

Palmer and Ussher rode into the snow-covered Nicola Valley and followed tracks they were not interested in, until they came to Amni Shumway's little spread beside a frozen lake. Shumway was a famous tracker around those parts.

Shumway didnt want to go.

"I am a freighter," he said. "I carry goods to people who need them. I save a little money and pay off my land a bit at a time. I do not catch murdering savages."

"They havent murdered anyone, Shumway. They stole Bill's horse is all."

"They've got more guns than you can shake a stick at."

"I've known these boys for years," said Ussher. "They wont point any guns at me."

"They got more brothers than you can get inside that flimsy jail of yours," said Shumway.

"First thing we did this morning was get Hector McLean and stick him inside," said Ussher. "With a guard."

Shumway grumbled. He groused. He pleaded business pressure.

"I know where I last saw them," said Palmer. "I figure you can take us straight to them."

"I havent got a saddle horse," said Shumway. "A man aint going to track no murdering savages on the back of a dray horse."

But it didnt work. Shumway got into his winter boots and winter coat and winter gloves and rode on the ass of Ussher's horse till they got to the next ranch, where his neighbour was only too glad to lend him a mount and saddle. Shumway grumbled that he never should have left New York State. Johnny Ussher refrained from telling him that he'd heard Shumway had had no choice in that departure.

So they rode, and it was not long till Shumway found the prints they were interested in. It looked as if the boys were looking for the old fur trail, which led right to the reserve at Douglas Lake. Then it curved back down to the Forks, where the Nicola River and the Coldstream River came together.

The bacon was gone, but there was plenty of Scotch whisky.

They were all sitting around the big fire. The smoke went up thick and curled into the pine boughs overhead. Far above, the ceiling was made of uniform white-grey cloud, with one clear white circle. Brightness off the surface of the snow made a man squeeze his eyes to slits.

Alex Hare was full of whisky and it was only morning. He could see all right, as long as he was not looking straight at the snow. He could stand up and walk all right if he had to. He would be able to lift his rifle and shoot a rabbit jumping in the opposite direction. It was just thinking that was hard to keep level.

"If we're supposed to decide to be Indians, eh, if we're going to throw in with the Noble Red Man, how come we're eating bacon and drinking whisky from across the big lake?"

Allan was with them. Sometimes he went whole days without coming back out of his dream. This morning he was ready with humour and patience. He had a little bacon grease shining in his beard.

"That's an easy one," he said. "Instead of gathering and preparing winter food all summer, we were gathering other stuff. I suppose you could eat a hand-tooled saddle with pewter conchas, but that aint purely Indian food."

"Any time my mother tried to get near me with Indian food, my old man would pound her," said Alex Hare.

"Our old man didnt give a shit." said Allan. "But onliest time we got Indian food was when we were playing at someone else's place."

"I dont remember much playin'," said Archie.

The early morning wind had died away to nothing, and there

was no snow falling. They should have been moving down the old fur trail, but they were sitting.

"If we were pure Indians," said Allan, as if he were taking up an earlier line of discussion, "we'd likely be dead by now, all except Archie, I guess."

"They cant kill a McLean," said Archie.

"That's what I'm talking about. You were born two years after the biggest part of the smallpox."

"I was born smack dab in the middle of it," said Charlie. "So was Alex."

"That's what I'm gettin' at," said Allan.

They were really listening now, feeding the fire and listening. Sometimes they made jokes about Allan the outlaw leader, and he *was* older than them. He had a black beard and a wife who was directly descended from Chief Nicola.

"Okay," said Charlie.

"In the big smallpox epidemic the Indians were dying like grasshoppers, but the white people weren't dying. The white people had needles made them all right. The Indian doctors didnt have any dances for smallpox. Smoke lodge never heard of smallpox. Indians died on the ground."

Nobody was drinking now. The bottle was standing on the ground.

"I heard about Indians getting the needle," said Alex Hare.

"Some of the Indians got the left-over needle in the Kamloops Reserve village, that's all," said Allan.

Charlie McLean spit into the fire. He lifted one side of his ass and farted. He spit into the fire again. They knew he was getting ready to say.

"White men say the smallpox was a good thing. Only way they could get the Indian population down in this country. Across the line they shot more than half of them. Up here they had to let the bug do it."

"Arithmetic," said Allan.

"Hated arithmetic," said Archie. Now he reached for the bottle.

"Could be making people like us was the worst mistake them Scotchmen ever made," said Allan. "Could be, making people like us gave the Indians another chance. Get some white man blood into them, the smallpox bug cant kill them anymore. They'll have to think of another way of killing us."

"Us?" said Charlie.

Johnny Ussher and William Palmer and Amni Shumway rode the icy wagon path into the McLeod brothers' sheep ranch above Shumway Lake. They werent looking for a sheepman. John McLeod had been a policeman in Victoria, and before that he had been a policeman in Glasgow. He had been a policeman when he was eighteen years old, so he knew about outlaws that were not twenty years old yet.

Johnny Ussher was not crazy about John McLeod, but so far he had a victim witness and a tracker. He needed a policeman. John McLeod said he would go with them in the morning. He had a few guns around the place, but nothing you would want to carry after the Wild McLean Boys. He went to a neighbour and borrowed a shotgun and a bag of shells. When he joined up with the posse he saw that Bill Roxborough had joined up.

Roxborough was a mule-wrangler for the Canadian Pacific Railway surveyors. He never stopped talking, to people or mules or whatever god it was he had in his head. Shumway looked at the ground and figured out the story. He didnt need a story-teller at his ear.

Shumway leaned over and read the ground. The tracks were clear. They didnt need him. The boys were riding uphill last night, looking for a place from which they could see anyone in the valley.

"Even if we do get my stallion back," William Palmer said.

"We'll get him," said Johnny Ussher.

"Even if we do get him, he'll probably be ruined. Let an Indian ride your horse for a while, and he's ruined for riding."

"We arent riding after Indians," said Ussher. "We're looking for the McLean brothers, and we arent looking for trouble."

"Might as well sell him to the Government," said Palmer.

"I'll take him off your hands," said Roxborough. Then he started a long story about horses.

They had a smokeless fire going. The trouble with a smoke-less fire is that it is not very warm except right next to it.

"You better lay off that rotgut for a few hours," Allan said. "I got a feeling about today."

"This here firewater is the only thing's keeping us warm," said Archie. He was kicking his boots together, leaning from leg to leg.

Alex Hare thought about shooting Mara all the time. He saw Mara buttoning up his clothes, coming out of Annie McLean's tiny room. Alex shot him between the buttons that were done up. Between every pair of buttons.

The Cheyennes had a saying. "A nation is not conquered until the hearts of its women are on the ground."

Allan was sitting the way he always did these days, his back straight, his long hair straight behind his neck.

He was looking at four little horsemen who were making their way up the slope. Whoever was telling him things had told him that there would be five. He hated arithmetic when this happened. The fifth man was nowhere. Unless he was behind them, in the trees, on the back side of the hill.

The Yankee was in front, reading sign that any idiot white man could have followed. There was Mrs. Palmer's husband, on his second-best horse. McLeod the sheepman on someone else's animal. And John Ussher, their old friend.

If there was a fifth man, he would like to know his name.

Allan watched the posse climb the snow for a while. Then he went back to the camp for a decision. To the whisky drinkers.

John Ussher was looking for a successful end of the story. He had a feeling about today.

They had been riding single file, with Shumway in the lead. Now without any command, they fanned out a little, and rode uphill toward the horses. Ussher wished that they were not riding uphill.

"I dont see my horse," said Palmer.

"I see a couple that dont belong up here," said Ussher.

Then they saw the camp, the smokeless fire, the bags of food. All four horsemen stopped and waited.

Shumway was over at the remuda, reading scars on horses.

John Ussher got off his horse and walked up to the low fire. McLeod and Palmer sat in their saddles, clouds coming out of their mouths.

Johnny Ussher knew they were being watched from the trees. He looked at the glowing fire and spoke to it instead of the trees.

"All right, Allan, let's go. We're here to take you to Kamloops."

In Victoria Premier Walkem was thinking about lunch. Roast beef. Perhaps today he would have a little horseradish. For protection against the winter air. This afternoon he had to go outside, down to the edge of the sea. He had to make a speech and there might be wind off the water.

Allan McLean's voice came from behind some trees.

"Ussher, go back where you came from. There is nothing for you here."

"McLean – "

"Go back, Ussher. Leave us be."

"You're a bunch of horse thieves," shouted Palmer, sitting on his horse.

"Palmer, shut your face," said Ussher through his teeth. "I will do this."

"A bunch of horse-thief kids that wont grow up." Palmer was going berserk. "Your mother must be very proud!"

"Oh shit," was all Ussher had time to say.

William Palmer had a thick black beard full of ice. He felt a bullet ripping the bottom of it off.

He knew the bullet had been aimed at his beard.

There was blood on the snow.

The bullet that had taken hair off Palmer's chin entered barefaced McLeod's cheek and went out the other side, missing his teeth entirely. No halfbreed could shoot that good. McLeod fell from his horse and into his own snowy blood.

McLeod was trying to get his neighbour's shotgun out from under him. He felt a bullet breaking bone in his knee. He heard the horse above him grunt as bullets thudded into its ribs. Gunshots echoed back from the valley.

The McLeans could knock a squirrel out of a pine tree with rifle or revolver. But none of these white men was dead.

Palmer had his rifle out now. He was trying to sight a McLean. He swung the barrel from smoke to smoke but there was never a horse thief there. Long Indian yells came from the smoke where there were no McLeans.

Amni Shumway had no weapon. He stood bent over a little behind some horses. All he wanted to do was stay alive and haul freight. If he had had a gun he would have thrown it at the campfire.

John Ussher left his constable's pistol in a belt hanging from his saddle, and walked a little uphill toward the fire. He could have been dead with any step. He walked until he stood beside the long grey ashes. He was looking straight at Alex Hare. Alex had a pistol in one hand and his goblet in the other. He walked a little downhill toward Johnny Ussher.

"Damn it, son," said Ussher.

"I'm nobody's son," said Alex.

Johnny Ussher wanted to save these boys from history. They had a wounding charge now, but this was cow country blood.

"Alex, what's got into you boys? You never shot anybody before."

"Get used to it, Constable."

Alex Hare tossed his empty goblet toward Ussher's boots.

"You know me, Alex. I have always treated you boys all right."

"You come up here with ranchers, John."

"I can smell the liquor on you, Alex."

Alex Hare smiled, and his face got younger than its seventeen years.

"Good stuff, too. We picked it up at one of your friends' place. Got some bacon to go along with it."

Ussher did not like the look in Alex Hare's face. The boy's eyes were not looking at him. The boy was seeing somebody else he hated. The pistol was not pointed at the ground.

John Ussher took two more steps, and reached out to touch Alex Hare.

10

At kamloops the bones lie under rectangles of grass, differing patchwork colours joined, some lower than others, one stone in the grass. The other stones are gathered in a corner of the park, the "Pioneer Cemetery, 1876 - 1900."

Some of the names on the stones are John Latremouille, Rev. Harding, B. Newman, P. Fraser, J. Woodland, J. Peterson, D. Wily, A. W. Hull, V. Guillaume, J. Hancock, Archie McKinnon.

There are no yew trees here. The park is bordered with elms and pines. It faces the river. Behind it is the biggest bottle recycling warehouse in the city.

One week in the late seventies there was a big powwow at the border country, where the Shuswap people and the Okanagan people met. For years the Shuswap people and the Okanagan people had not been the best of friends. They did not go to each other's salmon catches. Once in a while a little party of Shuswap people would steal some horses or shoot at a few Okanagan men. In Okanagan country a story-teller would tell a true legend of how three brave Okanagan youths had outsmarted the Shuswap warriors and saved an Okanagan winter village.

Now at the border country north of the big lake the

Shuswaps and the Okanagans had a big meeting. There were no French priests there.

The meeting went on for days. The Chiefs spoke and the Elders spoke. The doctors spoke and the spirit men spoke. The French priests had their spies there, and everyone knew who they were, but the people talked for several days. At night they played their drums.

The white people were scared shitless. They didnt have cavalry soldiers with bugles in the Interior of the Province of British Columbia. They liked it a lot better when the Okanagans werent talking to the Shuswap people.

A lot of white people asked John A. Mara for prices on rifles.

But there was no Indian uprising. White people could concentrate on the weather and the price for beef and lumber.

Then the damned McLean gang began its ride.

Sophie McLean was thinking about her daughter Annie. The question of Annie and J. A. Mara was a disgrace. The boys were a problem, but not a disgrace.

When Annie was thirteen years old, Sophie did not teach her about blood and womanhood. She did not tie up her hair and send her out for her fast on the mountain.

She had taught Annie about the sweat lodge. She had always intended to teach her about the blood and to prepare her for her fast on the mountain. What had happened to the time, that before she had even been prepared to be a woman, Annie McLean went to work for J. A. Mara?

Sophie McLean was nearly six feet tall, and she was a strong working woman, but she felt ashamed about Annie. She thought she should be able to handle the story better.

When a white man's baby came out of a Shuswap woman the baby had to wear a white man's name. If the white man disappeared the baby would wear the white man's first name. If the father stayed around the baby could wear the white man's last name.

Shuswap names were disappearing, like everything else.

Most of the new names were from France, and then they were from Scotland. But some names came from China.

In Kamloops there was a famous person named John Chinaman. He wrote poems about the Shuswap people and the white people he saw every day. He wrote on home-made paper with a brush and ink. No Scotchman would ever read these poems, and no Indian would ever read these poems.

"Work like the devil, them Chinamen," said one passerby.

"You got to hand it to them," said his companion.

Johnny Chinaman cleaned his ink brush and left the poem to dry.

"There's a thing I could never figure out," said a white man who was sitting inside the Dominion Hotel having a mug of some beer made right there in Kamloops. The grain was imported but the hops were grown locally, and picked by Indian women.

"I figure there's a good number of things you cant figure out," said the second beer-drinking white man.

They were sitting at a scarred table, and in the local fashion drinking beer without removing their hats.

"I been thinking of horses and donkeys," said the first white man.

"Forget it. There's a law against it. But I heard John Mara's going to be bringing a bunch of unattached women up from the coast soon as the road is passable."

"That there road is never passable. Negotiable, maybe, but not passable."

They were smoking long narrow cigars as was the custom in such places.

"You get a horse and a donkey to do it and if everything goes okay you get a mule. Works hard and dont eat nothing but cactus and sagebrush."

The second white man sneezed loudly, and beer went up his nose. After he recovered he spoke with a little difficulty, which he hoped to assuage with more beer.

"I always wondered about mules. I mean who's the dam and who's the stud? Or does it matter?"

"All you got to do is watch 'em."

"You watched 'em?"

"More'n once."

"So which one was on top?"

"I forget."

They were both married men, and their wives, they thought, were under the illusion that they were at work.

"So what were you thinking of mules for?"

"Well, it's a famous fact that mules cant have any offspring."

"Lucky for you, even if they were legal."

"Then I was thinking about white men and klootches. Seems as if the same rule should prevail."

"You lost me already," said the second white man.

"You going to let me finish my thought?"

"I'll give you two hours."

"Well, when you cross a white man and a squaw you get halfbreeds."

"Lots of 'em."

"Now, if the same rule prevails, them halfbreeds shouldnt ought to be able to produce any whelps."

"Nature is always amazin' us," said the second white man, using a huge handkerchief to dab at the beer he had spilled on his lap.

The second white man drained the foam from his mug, said a loud ahhhh, and peered significantly at the breast pocket of his lodge brother.

"I reckon we cant rely on nature to solve the halfbreed problem for us," he said, peering at the other's chest. "I figure we have to put our faith in Begbie and the other hangin' judges. It's only a rope's going to keep them from having descendants."

Now he looked back and forth between the gleaming bar and his partner's chest.

By 1870 everyone knew that the railroad was coming. Times were tough. The Provincial Government was next thing to useless. The gold rush was just about petered out. The railroad would bring a lot of workers and a lot of businessmen. A subtle man had to think about one of two things. He could get his hands on some land as close as possible to the tracks, and in the meantime use every resource at his disposal to find out where those tracks would be laid. Or he could establish himself in some business the railroad would find essential, a monopoly if possible.

There would be a lot of gandy dancers who wanted to eat

cows. There would be a lot of hauling that required horses. There would be foremen who shouted for great piles of timber. The rivers would have to be scoured for salmon, and the beverage rooms would have to be well stocked with beer and whisky.

There would have to be a lot of clearing. Right of way. Titles. Indians.

Two desperados from the old southwest were taking a vacation from the hot weather down there, and trying to enjoy a kind of busman's holiday on the great plateau. They had run into a little botheration in Fort Brewster, Washington Territory, and come up north looking for entertainment and a bit of travelling money.

Now they were sitting on their horses behind a big rock that stood alone beside the coach road between Cache Creek and Kamloops. The big rock had Indian paintings on the sides and snow on the top. The two desperados were new to the country, so they had no idea that this geological phenomenon was named Holdup Rock. People around there thought that was pretty funny. Turkey Doolan and Billy Magee hadnt had a smile on their faces for three days.

"Jesus Murphy, it's colder than a mother's kiss," said Turkey Doolan. "What the hell are we doing in Alaska when we could be eating chicken fajitas in Rosy's place?"

Billy Magee was shivering, but he was proud. There was snow on his hat, but he was proud.

"You're a hopeless stick-in-the-mud yellow-chicken tenderfoot, Turk. All the time want to do the same thing. D'yever read anything? Life's an adventure. The open road beckons. There's gold in them hills."

"There aint shit in them hills, and you know it, Dingus. And I'm beginning to think there aint any fiazackin' stagecoach coming along this here open road, either."

The sun fell out of a long streaky cloud and light bounced off miles and miles of snow. Both horses flinched. The two desperados were momentarily blinded. But it was a silent day, and they could now hear in the distance the creaking of wood and leather and metal. It was eerie. There were no hoofbeats in the soft snow.

Turkey Doolan had to take his glove off in order to pull his neckerchief over the bottom half of his face. Then he had a hell of a time getting his glove back on. Billy Magee didnt bother. They'd be heading back down south before anyone could get a wanted poster printed anyway. No sense having a frozen hanky against your mouth.

The stagecoach was in view now, and their eyesight was back.

"I just thought of something," said Turkey. "What kind of money do they have up here? They got Unitey States cash?"

"Shut up," said Billy, who had not thought of this problem.

Then the stagecoach was a hundred feet away. Four horses with clouds in front of their snouts jogged along, enduring an unpleasant job. The two brigands eased their mounts out onto the road and fired their peacemakers into the air the way highwaymen traditionally did back home. They were almost run down by the contraption with snow on the top. But the driver up top finally woke up and said whoah, yanking on the reins and grabbing for the brake.

"Jes' keep them hands in the air and you wont get drilled," shouted Billy.

The old fart in the driver's seat had rheumatic shoulders but he did the best he could, holding his thick gloves as high as possible.

"Throw down the strongbox," said Billy.

"Aint any strongbox," said the driver.

Turkey, as he had done in rehearsal, got down off his horse and opened the passenger door. There werent any passengers.

"There aint anyone inside," he reported to his senior partner.

"Shit for breakfast!" Billy expostulated. "Well, have a look around inside. See what you can find's worth something."

"Aint nothing worth – " started the driver.

"Shut the fuck up," Billy instructed him. "Check out the mail-sack, Turk."

"Aint any mail," said the old fart. His shoulders were killing him.

"You want a hole in your face?" enquired the young man on the horse.

Turkey was rummaging around inside. There was no mailbag. There was no cashbox. All he could find was a small batch of Victoria newspapers and eight rolled-up Oriental carpets.

"I hate to say this, Dingus, but there aint nothing here but a bunch of rugs," he said, his head poking out of the stage-coach. The frozen neckerchief had fallen below his chin.

"You boys the McLean gang?" asked the old fart up top. "You look a little pale to be McLeans."

"Shut up and empty your pockets," said Billy. He had moved his horse up close and had the peacemaker pointed right at the man's face.

"Can I take my hands down?"

"Jesus Murphy, dont be so goddam stupid. Of course you

can take your hands down. Get them mitts off and empty your pockets."

The old gink emptied his pockets. All he produced was a plug of chewing tobacco and a wallet with sweet bugger all inside it.

"Aw shit. Give me them mitts," said Billy Magee.

Turkey Doolan walked up to Billy's horse.

"Nothin' but newspapers and rugs, Dingus," he said.

For five uncomfortable seconds the horseman stared at his satrap. The old fart put his bare hands as high as he could. Turkey squeezed his neckerchief and it cracked.

"All right," said Billy. "Pick out one of them rugs and get in on your horse. And you, you sorry excuse for a syphilated rattlesnake, you get into that town whatever you call it, and tell them we think this is a poor scrabble-ass excuse for a country. Tell them we got shit-houses more worth heistin' than this whole fiazackin' country."

The old guy with the cold hands shouted nonsense syllables at his horses and whacked them with the frozen reins. As the coach disappeared, creaking out of earshot, the two robbers could not look one another in the face. Turkey carried a carpet to his horse and tried to figure out how to tie it on. Billy stuck his sheepskin mitts into his almost empty saddlebag.

The two horses kept their silence, prudent animals.

Margaret McLean was embarrassed to be married into this family. She had been born in Fort Kamloops, she was the daughter of Caesar Vodreux, and she was having a hard time leaving that pride behind. She was thirty-three years old and married to Alex McLean, a bad half-brother. She looked around at

Alex's immediate family and saw respectable halfbreeds edging their way into the new world.

Alex should have been one of Sophie's brood. He was a decade older than Allan, but as much a young heller as any of that bunch. There was nothing Margaret could do. She put on her high collar and walked on the wood outside stores. She did not like the present but the past was gone. She had seen the future and it was just like the present, only longer.

She did not know how long that future would be. That she would be for half a century Granny McLean. She would live to be one hundred and two years old and depart in 1948, a matriarch in the newspapers. She would go to the graveyard with a letter from the King of England.

Ten years after the Wild McLeans were hunted down at Douglas Lake, Alex McLean ran amok on the Kamloops reserve. He punished his horse and clobbered everything in sight. He shot a man to death and wounded others. He was an Indian killer like his father.

But there were still enough Indians left to grab him and hold him.

Chief Louis could have handed Alex over to the white police across the river. But he did not want the whites to hang any more McLeans. He ordered a trial and an execution on the reserve. Then he had Alex McLean taken to the sweat lodge for his last words. Then he had him shot.

Chief Louis went across the river and told all this to the white law. The white law performed an inquest, but the white law would not have to hang any more McLeans.

Granny McLean had fifty-nine more years to live.

11

✳ ✳ ✳

ALEX HARE'S PEWTER goblet lay on the ground behind John Ussher. In his hand where the goblet had been was a big knife named after a violent Texan.

Maybe John Ussher meant to touch Alex Hare in order to reassure him, but for Alex Hare that extended hand was the law. It was the hand of Matthew Begbie. It was the hand of a policeman who had gone into business with J. A. Mara. If he could kill Mara in the snow on the top of a bare hill he would do it, quick.

Alex Hare screamed something in none of the languages he knew, and went at Johnny Ussher with both hands. He slashed with the big knife and the long pistol. Johnny Ussher's face opened like red beef. His heavy coat took slash after slash. Ussher fell backward and the pistol hit him in the eye. He kicked as best he could but the knife got him again, opening his forehead. Blood was slippery on Alex Hare's fingers. He slashed with both hands, hitting the ground more than Ussher. Ussher's left boot was in the embers of the fire. Alex was afraid the man with the red open flesh would get up and take him. Maybe he was all alone.

"*Maudits!* Give me some help!" he shouted. He felt Ussher's knee in his crotch. It was not strong but it was desperate.

Archie had his pistol pointed at the head on the ground. His eyes were enormous. There were tears on his face. Archie should have been in school, putting teeth marks on his pencil.

Johnny Ussher's face was ugly. The flesh was open in flaps and there was blood in his hair. One eye was nowhere to be seen. The other was looking through bloody lashes at Archie McLean.

"Dont do it, Archie," he said. His voice was full of blood.

Archie could not make himself understand everything. He had too much morning whisky in him.

"Dont kill me, son."

Archie's mother told him he was the last son of a brave man. He heard a voice shouting at him in words he could not understand.

Ussher twisted as much as he could, and half of Alex Hare's blows landed on his head and shoulders, the rest in the reddened snow around him. He heard a voice calling from the trees.

"Kill him, you chickenshit little coward!"

Archie looked into Alex Hare's strange face. Alex was staring right through Archie's eyes deep into his brain. Alex's eyes were the most frightening thing of all. They turned from Archie's face toward the sliced face of Ussher, and back again.

Archie thumbed the hammer and squeezed the trigger. Johnny Ussher disappeared behind smoke, and the two boys smashed at him with their pistols, smashed and smashed the face of a dead man.

What could the unarmed Shumway do? He stayed with the horses, listening to guns. He could not see what was happening to Johnny Ussher but he heard the pistol shot that killed the leader of the posse.

William Palmer was still on his horse, trying to get his ancient weapon reloaded. He saw Allan McLean stand up behind a rock and aim a pistol at him. Palmer swung the rifle at last and got off a shot. He saw McLean's body turn quickly. I got him, I got him, he thought.

But Allan stood there and fired at him. He saw the other McLeans now in the open, shooting. Why wasnt the whole posse dead? Palmer gave up on the rifle and turned his horse.

John McLeod emptied his handgun and threw it away. Bullets and pieces of rock made geometry all over the campsite. Blood fell down his throat as he stood up and ran for his horse.

The McLeans and Alex Hare were firing shots like crazy but not hitting men or horses. They watched as the three horsemen drew closer together while racing down the snowy slope. The four victors put their heads back and made a high-pitched ululating sound as they stood side by side watching the posse retreat. They emptied their guns into the air after the fleeing ranchers.

Bill Roxborough heard the shooting on the other side of the hill. He had a nice little bunch of mules tied nose to tail, but he was a posse member. It was time to ride. He walked his horse through the snow in the direction of the shooting.

In a little while three horsemen were riding as fast as they could down the hill, but Roxborough did not see them or hear them. The shooting had stopped. That could mean a lot of different things. Maybe someone was dead. Maybe the McLeans were in custody again. Roxborough's horse kept its pace. Roxborough saw what looked like two sets of mule tracks in the snow, headed off on a right angle. He took a mental note.

His hat came off.

Then he heard the report of a pistol, sounded like a .44.

He thought about getting his own sidearm out.

He saw his hat bouncing over the snow. Someone was shooting it again and again.

His horse was just a cowhorse. It whinnied loudly and danced around. Roxborough worked the bit and looked around in every direction as the horse turned and turned.

He left his sidearm where it was, inside his overcoat.

Bullets spanged off a big nearby rock. Snow jumped around his horse's hooves. The horse turned its wide-open eye toward its rider.

A man with a big black beard stood on top of another rock.

"My name is McLean!" this figure shouted.

Another voice came from another direction.

"My name is McLean, and I have shot my man!"

Roxborough kept his silence. Whatever had happened to the posse, the McLeans were still free. It had to be his duty to carry this news to Kamloops.

Two more voices rang out, but Roxborough could not understand what they were saying. He put knees to his horse and slacked the rein entirely. He forgot the free mules. He listened to four dark men laughing and shouting and he did not take the time to flinch at the sounds of their guns.

Johnny Ussher's body lay on its back beside the dead fire. Its face had been replaced by a jumble of red-black flesh with an eye in the middle. Someone had stripped the lawman of boots, jacket, and belt. Alex Hare had a pair of shiny handcuffs dangling from his belt. There was not a penny in John Ussher's pockets.

Alex Hare had retrieved his goblet. He filled it to the top with whisky and passed the bottle.

"You done it, Arch. You're a man and a dead certain outlaw and killer. You're famous. I'll drink to that."

"*We* done it," said Charlie. "That son of a bitch lawman from back east turned traitor on us, and we stood up for ourselves."

Archie drank as much whisky as he could at one time. He looked at the bloody corpse. He saw himself aiming the heavy revolver and he saw Johnny Ussher's eye asking him to quit. Johnny Ussher was a father. Archie felt the vomit reach his throat, but he forced it back down.

Allan was feeding the fire that had almost disappeared. He put in some sagebrush, some old grey pine cones, and then larger pieces of dead old wood. From the pocket of his saddlebag he brought some dried kinnickinnick berries and sprinkled them over the whole collection. There was probably no magic involved, but right then the new flames burst up through the middle of the heap. Allan stood back and stared into the flames. Then he reached into his breast pocket and brought out a regular white man's pipe. This he stuffed with tobacco or something, and began to smoke.

But as he took a step backward he stumbled a little, and the face above his beard looked like a clay cutbank.

Charlie had been watching Allan all this time.

"What's the matter with you?" he asked.

"Nothing."

"Dont go Indian on me right now, Allan. What's wrong?"

"Oh, I just hate to waste all that ammunition those Nicola Valley ranchers were so kind to give us."

Allan smoked his pipe.

Charlie poked around in Allan's clothing. He unbuttoned his coat and pulled one side of it away. He opened Allan's deerskin jacket. So he saw what he was looking for. There was a widened stain of blood on Allan's shirt, and not all of it was dry.

Charlie looked for bullet holes. The coat and jacket would have slowed the rifle slug down, and if there were no holes in the back the slug would still be inside his brother. Allan knew what Charlie was looking for. His flat grin made a hole in his beard for a pipe to fit into. He held something between his fingers and thumb in front of Charlie's eyes. It was a clump of metal.

"*Merde*," said Charlie.

"That Bill Palmer got lucky," said his brother. "Let's not discuss the matter with the boys for now."

"Allan — ?

But Allan spoke to the others.

"Get a whole lot of wood, good stuff full of pitch. Make this here fire skookum. Pile the son of a bitch up. Make a fire people can see from Kamloops."

Now the outlaws and killers were boys again, running under the pine trees and gathering firewood. They piled it up higher than their heads. They uttered war whoops and hunting cries and sheer pointless yells. Allan sat on a rock where he did not have to look at the corpse of his brother's jailor, and held his elbow against his side. The boys skipped and hollered and competed to see who could fetch the most outlandish firewood. Soon they were throwing in everything, spare saddles and blankets, the boots Alex Hare had been wearing before he got the expensive new pair from Johnny Ussher.

"Okay, that's enough," said Allan, allowing a laugh in his voice.

There was a lot more smoke than there was fire, because of the sheer weight and height of the wood piled on top. But it was wood that had been dry for a few years, or that had thick veins of pine pitch in it yet. There would be a hill of flame.

"All right, *mes enfants*," said Allan, "saddle up."

"What are you saying?" asked Archie, who was still puffing from his exertion. "We just got us one hellation of a campfire, and you want us to light out? What the hell did we do all this for?"

"Need a big fire to keep Constable Ussher company till the next posse gets here. Wouldnt want them fellows to arrive to cold ashes."

This time the posse was made up of twenty men, and this time they were all armed, except for the tracker Amni Shumway. John McLeod took his bleeding mouth and broken knee to Dr. Trump, but William Palmer still wanted his stallion. He decided to ride nineteen places behind Shumway. He thought about his wife and how he could tell this story to her, Bill Palmer, frontier lawman. Had his beard trimmed by an outlaw bullet.

The new posse was captained by J. A. Mara, who understood that you get rich by owning the politicians or buying political office yourself. That way you can figure out when the next new thing is coming to town, and at the same time make sure that you own the land it's coming through. J. A. Mara owned the whole east side of Kamloops and held a lot of signed papers in his big iron safe. He didnt need any outlaw racial degenerates destabilizing the territory.

His second in command was Justice of the Peace John Edwards. He didnt look comfortable on a horse, and his clothes looked a little too fine. He had a cigar clamped between his teeth, and his whole beard smelled of cigar smoke. He wished that he had thought to ride in the sleigh, a Hudson's Bay blanket for his knees.

But as the twenty horsemen and the sleigh reached the high flatland after the climb out of Kamloops, Amni Shumway spoke once.

"And power was given unto them over the fourth part of the earth, to kill with the sword, and with hunger, and with death, and with the beasts of the earth," he said, his voice in rhythm with the soft footsteps of his chestnut gelding.

"What's that?" asked J. A. Mara.

"Sometimes I just say out loud what I'm remembering. It's a way I have of trying to keep warm."

"We are going to make it altogether too warm for those degenerates," said the Justice of the Peace.

The Wild McLeans were riding too, southward through the Nicola Valley. The sun was out now, having at last burned its way through the high cloud, but it would soon begin to fall toward the fir-covered outline of the hills on the west side of the valley.

They had one pack horse now. They were carrying only their food and blankets and the best of the weapons. The rest of the stuff they had thrown on the giant fire, and they had set the extra horses free to wander in the snow. Johnny Ussher's horse was now carrying Archie McLean, so he had the second-best mount in the gang.

This night Allan might go and sit beside a rock painting, but for now he was their tactician.

"We have some collecting to do," he shouted. "We will go to every spread between here and Douglas Lake, and get every gun they've got. Every gun we get is one less gun they can use against us. Second, we need a big arsenal for the Indians."

"First we've got to get Palmer," said Charlie. "We've got to kill that bastard. Bastard shot my brother."

The other boys looked out of their headaches at their leader, and their eyes were full of accusation, accusation and respect.

"Shut up, Charlie," said Allan.

Everyone shut up and rode south. After about a mile Alex Hare spoke up, continuing the line of argument.

"I aint going to get myself into any Indian politics until I get to kill that cocksucker Mara."

"That's part of it," said Allan the leader.

"That's all of it, far as I'm concerned."

"Shut your face now, Rabbit," said Allan.

They rode in silence again in the dead cold air. They were excited and they had headaches, but they knew where every hawk was in the sky and they saw every line of smoke rising straight into the bright chill.

"I am going to enjoy this," said Alex Hare at last.

"When they see what we did today, our people will be itching for war. There will be paint on their faces before the winter dance. One day soon there wont be any more ranches in the people's valleys. There wont be any railroad, and there wont be any white men's schools. This morning we fired the first shots of the people's war."

"So you settled it, eh?" said young Archie.

"What? This is the true story."

"So we aint the James gang. We're the Indians," said Archie.

"We're the Indians and the breeds," said Charlie. "And we are going to have all the guns this time."

They were not very drunk now. They had headaches, and they were no longer troublemakers. They were soldiers.

Matthew Begbie, the hanging judge, was a Scottish book reader among the mountain dangers. He was haughty and often angry, and his presence was a mirror of Donald McLean's presence. Each had killed his man, each was a tough Scot in a peculiar country filled with Indians and strangers.

He wore a necktie in the Cariboo, and when he sat on a horse he did so in clothes that were cut perfectly. The USAmerican miners thought he was a dainty British sugarfoot, unlearned in the fractious ways of the goldstream.

But Scottish judges were like French priests. They expected to be all alone in very strange country. They knew that they were precursors of something much larger. Begbie was the scourge of the USAmericans. He once hanged a man with his own hands. The regular hangman was lying on a bunk somewhere with microbes squandering his blood. Begbie jumped off his horse and onto the condemned man's shoulders. He signed the papers and rode out of town.

Once a mountain man found guilty of clubbing his sluice partner to death said to Judge Begbie, "I did not have a fair trial. There was no one to defend me."

Begbie had a slow look around the little schoolroom that was for a few days a courtroom.

"In that case," he said, "I shall send up your case for a new trial – by your maker."

Here was a difference between Matthew Begbie and Donald McLean. Begbie had a Scottish sense of humour. He had the humour of the powerful. No one ever took a shot at Matthew Begbie. He was wearing a strange armour.

James Kelly was a head and two hands sticking out from under a thick plaid. He was sitting on a flat rock in the cool sun, watching his sheep forage in the snow for the stiff brown grass underneath. He held some kind of Scottish flute to his mouth and made weird music in the winter air.

A couple hundred feet away was Kelly's plain cabin. There were no weapons in it. The boys had cleaned it out earlier in the week. There had been no weapons in it then, either. This fact had displeased the McLeans, so they had felt constrained to rearrange the mean furniture. If there had been glass in the windows they would have smashed it.

Kelly kept on playing his flute as the four horsemen approached him. He watched his sheep but he had the corner of his eye on the McLeans.

The horses stood next to Kelly's rock. Steam came from their mouths.

"If you're looking for a job I havent got any," said Kelly.

"We could use some gauze and cotton," said Charlie.

Kelly put his flute away in a pocket. He took his watch out of the pocket and looked at its big face. Then he put the watch back in the pocket with the flute. This is called "business" in the theatre, but here there wasnt any audience, only a few hundred sheep, pushing their faces into the snow.

"They have got a plenitude of gauze and cotton in Kamloops," said Kelly. "If I be giving you my gauze I'll soon have none for my own needs."

"Maybe you'll need some for your head, sheepman, after we are finished here," said Archie the shooter.

"Were it you boys that wrecked my home the other day?"

"We are only sorry that you were not here at the time," said Allan McLean.

"What kind of a rat would deny bandaging to a wounded friend?" asked Charlie McLean, a deep sneer in his voice.

"Nobody here is a friend to this Scotchman," replied Allan. "And I would appreciate it if you could keep quiet about wounded people."

But Allan was leaning forward with his hand on his saddlehorn.

"And how did you come to be wounded, lad? An accident on the job, was it?"

"Let me send this son of a bitch on the road with Ussher," said Archie.

But Allan was thinking of his Indian uprising. He wanted to get to the next ranch to look for supplies.

"If anyone should happen to ask," he said to Kelly, "you havent seen us. We didnt come this way."

"Then who left all those horse tracks in the snow?" asked the sheepman.

"That's it," said Alex Hare. "We have to shoot the bastard."

He had his beautiful .44 out now, aiming it at the man on the rock. He wanted a notch on his pistol. He was eager for a big noise.

The air was still and sometimes a sheep could be heard

speaking in its accent. Kelly knew there was something wrong with the timing here. He reached inside his plaid, for his flute or his watch. It gave Alex Hare an excuse.

Two enormous explosions met one another in the cold. One started in Hare's gleaming .44, the other elsewhere nearby. James Kelly's feet were lost on the flat rock. His body needed those feet, but now it was sliding, and his face scraped on the rock as Kelly slipped to the snow underneath. He was alive and suffering his horrible stomach. His face was now in the snow, his mouth biting for air.

Charlie McLean stepped his horse around the rock and put a bullet into the side of Kelly's head.

Now young Archie got down and put his hand inside Kelly's plaid. He found a flute and a watch with a golden chain, and a hopeless little .21-calibre pistol. A woman's gun. Archie put all this stuff into his own pockets. Allan watched his little brother take coup.

Hector McLean was in jail. He was the first prisoner of war. There he had been, standing in his sheepskin coat beside the frozen river, smoking a cigar that had once belonged to a Cherry Valley rancher. He had recognized the two riders and watched as they placed their mounts between him and his hungry gelding. That dumb fart Palmer and Johnny Ussher. Well, here we go again, thought Hector.

"You've been pretty busy the last week or so," said Johnny Ussher, in a friendly way, or so it seems.

"I aint been doing anything special," said Hector, and he used his little finger to flick away a cigar ash.

"Breaking into houses and stores," said Palmer.

"Let me do this," said Ussher to him.

"Nothing special. Helped a friend find his pony."

Johnny Ussher smiled and leaned down from his saddle, kind of casual. It didnt look as if Hector was wearing any iron.

"Seeing quite a lot of your brothers lately, I think."

"Oh, it's been a while."

"Tell you what, Hec," said Johnny Ussher. "Why dont you just come with us for now, and we'll see whether we can come to some kind of agreement with the magistrate."

And now here was Hector sitting in jail. He heard the commotion when Palmer and his friends rode back from Stump Lake. He heard the new posse riding out, men yelling and horses making sounds from their bellies. He was going to miss the first part of the war.

The second posse arrived in town with John Ussher's frozen body on the sleigh. It was dark by then, but J. A. Mara sent a rider west, because this could be the first day of the war. The rider changed horses three times on his way to Cache Creek, with a wire message to the Premier. The wire message was longer than most wire messages, and it was filled with narrative. Mara figured the way to get the Premier's attention was to say big things, use big numbers, say bloody and murderous and savage. Say halfbreed.

Premier Walkem was planning to write a book when his days in Government were finished. He knew about books, especially books in the wild west. You wanted scalps and guns and forthright premiers. He called in the Superintendent of the Provincial Police. He called the newspapers.

12

IN MEXICO THEY WERE called *mestizos*, and they were the largest number of people, Mexicans. In Quebec and Manitoba they were called *Métis*. Mixed. On the great plateau of British Columbia and Washington they were half-bloods, half-breeds, or simply "breeds."

They were always dangerous because they gave evidence of where they came from, the sexual union of native women and hairy-faced men from outside the world. They were horse-riding consequences of dark guilty fucking. They were the tag ends of Scottish families, and they would never go back to the Old Country to see their relatives.

The Indians and the white men had different reasons not to like them all that much. They were better than their white folks and they were better than their native progenitors. Each side saw them as a degeneration, though. Tag ends. The Indians saw them as the children of lost women. The white ranchers saw them as reproof of their younger days.

They were dangerous because they were made from desperation sex, and there was a score to be settled somewhere. There was a darkness that would not stay down in the basement of history.

Early in the afternoon the four riders came to the house where Tom Trapp lived. Like a lot of local ranchers who got there early he had a lake named after him. Trapp Lake is still there, still gets ice on it in the winter, but there is no McLean Lake.

The riders must have been quiet in the snow, because Tom Trapp did not come to the door until Allan McLean banged on it with the heel of his revolver. Three of the boys were standing at the door, while Archie sat on his horse and moved his fifteen-year-old eyes back and forth. The three big dogs in Trapp's yard had not raised their usual ruckus. These must have been magic riders.

"We are collecting guns," said Allan, "for a good cause."

Trapp knew who these young fellows were. Everyone in the valley had hired at least one of them from time to time. Trapp didnt have any boots on. He was standing in his long underwear and a Hudson's Bay blanket. It was going to be hard to bargain with halfbreeds working for a charity.

"It looks to me as if you have just about enough artillery already," said the barefoot rancher.

"We want your rifle, your shotgun, and your revolver," said Allan.

"I suppose you'd like all the cartridges on the place too."

"Glad you mentioned it, Tom," said Allan.

"I'm afraid I need them firearms, boys," he said, as calm as he could get.

The cold air was filling up the house, but Trapp could not close the door. The Hare boy was holding a long pistol with the hole very visible to the rancher's eye. Trapp could not step outside in his bare feet. His dogs were lying down near the strange horses.

Now there was a very big knife in Hare's other hand. Alex turned it so that Trapp could see the winter light on the metal.

"This here knife aint afraid of people like you, Trapp," said Alex. "It has already been inside John Ussher about ten times."

"What you done with Ussher?"

"We sent him to the happy hunting ground," said Charlie McLean. "You can go too, if you like."

"Or you could donate them firearms of yours to a worthy cause," said Allan.

Trapp stepped backward as Charlie and Alex moved past him into the house. Allan stood at the door and Archie sat on his horse, his eyes moving.

Charlie scooped up the guns while Alex dropped cartridges into a pillow case. There was mud on Tom Trapp's carpets.

"You really killed Constable Ussher?"

Charlie let out a loud yell inside the house. It sounded like a war whoop. Alex Hare did a little dance in his new boots.

"He was the first to go," said Charlie.

Now Trapp was learning to be afraid of these boys.

"Look, I've known you boys since you were shavetails. I dont know what you're planning to do with all them guns, but I'd have to say it's a bad idea. The way I figure it, you've got two chances. Either you ride down to Kamloops and try and make a deal — "

Charlie and Alex laughed like people with no happiness. Allan spit into the house and then looked to see whether he was spitting red. Archie had one of his pistols in his right hand.

" — or if I was you — " said Trapp.

Alex laughed again, like a sad piece of wood.

"We're four men and you're one short white man with no boots," he said, waving the thick knife in front of Trapp's face.

"Alex if I was you, I'd be headed down the Similkameen, get across the border as soon as I could," said Trapp.

Now Allan came inside.

"It's too late for all that," he said. "It's started today. Ussher was the first. There's going to be lots more."

"What about me?" asked Trapp. He was truly frightened now. He could smell the whisky. But there was something else in the air too. It was blood, probably blood, but what kind of blood? Trapp thought he might die in his bare feet.

Every once in a while in your life you are reminded of the camels that were let loose in the dry middle of Australia, and of the camels that were let loose in the dry middle of British Columbia. Back in the nineteenth century, with all this new land just sitting there waiting for people all over the world, men did not have much consideration of the patterns made by what we much brighter people call the gene pool.

Everyone knows about the camels, or comes to know about them. Some bright bozo in the British Empire got the idea of importing camels to haul stuff up to the established gold fields and the land that was going to be developed because of them. But camels did not like rafts and snakes and cliffsides, and Cariboo horses did not like camels. Cows could stand the smell of them. A lot of people got spit on and stepped on, and a lot of camels got things thrown at them. Finally, the provisioners turned the camels loose. They were not about to take them down past Hell's Canyon again, and there was not a big market for camels at the Coast. In the Interior there was not a single friend of the camel. There were no bedouins along the Thompson River.

But the Wild McLeans knew what it was like to be a camel in cattle country. And they had a warped sense of humour. They knew where to find loose camels, and just for the fun of it they learned how to ride them, even how to make them run like hell with their flamboyant camel hurry. Indians like to bet and white men like to race, so these half bloods ran their high humped beasts across the gopher plains. They often fell off at first, but McLeans are tough. After a while they were the best camel riders in the western hemisphere. They smelled bad but they were brothers.

Allan and Hector and Charlie and Archie, Arabs of the Great Plateau.

But if you were going to go to all that work, learning to ride those awkward smelly animals, and falling on medium-sized rocks, there had to be a reward. And no one was about to buy a used camel from a Kamloops Arab.

One Monday in late spring a bunch of ranchers on the south side of the river hired a bunch of wranglers and got together for a huge breakfast, and then headed out into the range country to round up strays. They would get them into one nice big round herd, and along about Friday they would start sorting them out. First they would snaffle the ones with coded scars on their skin. An awful lot of them had a scar that looked like this:

They belonged to John Tait, a man who had got in when the getting was good. Then they would start negotiating about the cows with no initials, or with highly ambiguous markings. Every once in a while it would look as if some editor had been trying to change the story and then given up.

On Thursday morning the clump of dark reddish-brown cows was pretty big, all of them with their noses to the ground in a big flat clearing nearly surrounded by dark green lodgepole pines. Cowboys were already out in the higher hills, looking for whitefaces. There were about a half-dozen men with the herd, some of them guarding against jailbreaks, the others messing around the coffee pot.

Then there was a hell of a surprise, as four weird animals came flapping out of the trees, and men on them yelling Yeeee-hah! Ayayayayayay! Whooooooooup! Ahahahahahah!

A horse jumped up and landed right on top of the coffee pot and scattered fire and tin all over the camp. Other horses opened their eyes wide and screamed and broke things. The cows lifted their heads and looked at the other moving animals. Horses ran into the forest, trailing harnesses. Cows followed, scattering uphill or downhill depending on their neighbours.

The Wild McLeans hollered some sentences nobody could understand, and then they were gone.

Then the McLean boys did the town they hated. They waited till Sunday in Kamloops. It was late on a spring morning, and the good citizens were standing in the famous May sun, warm inside their sleeves, talking about the sermons they had heard, mentioning the weather.

And along came the camels, thundering from churchyard to churchyard. Women and horses screamed. Well-dressed husbands and bachelors shouted racial imprecations. There was dust everywhere, and it would settle on Sunday clothes.

A McLean on a camel clattered on the porch of the Colonial Hotel. A Chinese laundryman dropped his gleaming bedsheets and ran in his wrapped legs. Nobody was going to form an Arab-chasing posse because there werent any horses around.

The wild brothers raced out of town and let their improbable animals go free. They sat around on rocks beside the river and laughed their heads off.

"I like those camels," said Hector McLean.

"I've been wondering how we got camels," said Allan. "I figure the white men brought horses with them and the horses interbreed with bears."

"You've got a strange imagination," said Hector.

According to the stories a few other people have told, the killers of John Ussher and Jim Kelly arrived at John Roberts's place in mid-afternoon. They were gunmen on the loose now, so they rode down on the place with rifles and shotguns in their hands.

John Roberts was a crusty man of middle age and tough muscles. He could lift a half-grown hog and throw it over a rail fence. When the gunmen rode up he was out in his yard with his two oldest sons, killing pigs and dunking their carcasses in boiling water. He had a big pot hung over a huge fire, and a warm pig carcass hanging over it from a pulley. He was just about to dunk the pig. His sons were holding the rope. They did not let go when the guns arrived.

The fire was so hot that there was no snow in any direction for ten yards. Sweat was in the hair over John Roberts's ears. He was holding a bristle knife in his right hand. A rifle pointed at his head, and he seemed calm as he stuck the knife into a block of wood with dark blood stains on it. His two sons held on to the rope. Nervous pigs crowded the far side of the lodgepole pen.

"Kla-howya, boys," said Roberts.

"Dont give us that weird white man's language," said young Archie. "Talk English, Roberts."

"Something I can do for you?"

Roberts gestured to his sons and they cinched the pig on the rope. It hung there upside down, steam around its snout. Roberts took out the makings and rolled himself a crooked little cigarette. He offered the makings around. Charlie balanced his rifle across the leather in front of him and started making a smoke.

"Well, we got plenty of bacon," said Allan, and his brothers laughed.

Up at the house Mrs. Roberts and the rest of the kids would be looking out the windows. It was just about time for afternoon coffee.

John Roberts smoked his thin cigarette.

"Why dont you get down and ease up to this fire?" he asked. It was as if he didnt have guns aimed at him.

"We're used to the cold," said Charlie around his cigarette.

"We'll be getting plenty of fire soon enough," said Alex Hare. But already the snow was melting on his wide hat.

"Fact is," said Allan, who was holding a hand to his side while he leaned forward in the saddle, "we're looking for some people, and we might want to use your cauldron."

"We figure that fat bastard Mara might just fit in that pot," said Alex Hare. He was thinking about John Mara just about fifty times a day now.

"First we'll boil him. Then we'll pull him out and shoot him full of holes," said Archie.

John Roberts was brave and tough. He had pig fat under his crooked fingernails. The only thing he was worried about was his wife and kids up in the house. He wanted them to stay there, and he didnt want the McLeans in the house.

"We already killed John Ussher," said Alex Hare. He held out his wide knife and turned it in the diminishing light.

"We already shot a sheepman," said Charlie. "Sheep stink worse than pigs." Charlie had a big grin made of brown teeth.

John Roberts felt a change in the weather. The heat from the fire fell and the cold came down off the lodgepole ridge behind his house.

Allan McLean saw this.

"Dont worry, John," he said. "We aint fixing to shoot you. We dont even want your boots. Have a look at Alex's new boots. Pretty, eh? We figure you got a big family to take care of, and it's the coldest winter anyone ever saw around these parts. But there's a war starting today, and if you want to survive this war, you better stick to pig-killing."

Allan did not usually put that many words together.

John Roberts felt the cold down off the hill. But he had pig work to do. If there was going to be a war he wanted to be a hog farmer with a big family.

"Why dont you boys go and look for Mr. Mara? Or better yet, why dont you head for the border? I got work to do."

"John," said young Archie. "We aint boys. We are bad men. We are the bad dream of the Hudson's Bay Company. And we aint heading for no border."

A fifteen-year-old halfbreed with four guns can scare any Welsh rancher. John Roberts nodded his head in the cold.

Allan McLean made a noise with his teeth. The four gunmen danced their horses away from the fire and rode away in the darkening snow. A horse with the Government brand followed them, loaded with weapons and food.

In Victoria John Tod was an old man living with his daughters. He was always contacting young newspaper reporters and filling them on stories of his derring-do during his years as fur factor in Kamloops.

The older newspaper men never warned the young fellows about old man Tod and his stories. According to John Tod, the white people of the Hudson's Bay Company had lived on the edge of the precipice. At any time the fierce redskins could have taken a notion to go around and collect some scalps off the brave but outnumbered Scotchmen.

But the stories always turned out to be very similar to stories that found their way up from the other side of the medicine line. If a Yankee fur boss in Oregon managed to face down a dozen feathered warriors at the edge of some creek down there, John Tod stood resolute against two dozen of Chief Nicola's fire-eyed braves on the shores of the Thompson River.

The older newspaper men had a good laugh when one of John Tod's old stories found its way into print again. But when news of Johnny Ussher's killing reached Victoria, all the stories John Tod had been telling for thirty years took on a certain historical light.

John Tod felt bad for Ussher's family, of course, but he welcomed the news. He sent a message to a new young reporter, that he was willing to give his advice to the Government. He was only disappointed that his great age made it impossible for him to saddle up and ride those miscreants down.

The outlaw gang rode from ranch to ranch through the afternoon, cracking ice in rutted yards, gathering weapons for the army they would raise, boasting about their deeds of the day, showing dried blood and new boots. Every time they left a ranch a rider would leave too, in the direction of Kamloops, to warn the men whose names had passed the lips of the Wild McLeans. The afternoon descended, and Allan McLean felt his body stiffen where Palmer's lucky bullet had passed through.

When they rode the path through the snow that led to William Palmer's door, Palmer's prize stallion tossed its mane and snuffled, lifting its front feet high and banging them down.

"Now here's the place I've been waiting for," said Charlie McLean.

"S'pose he's in there?" asked Archie.

He had his shiny pistol in his hand. Like a small boy he pointed it at the house and made explosive sounds with his mouth, yanking his hand to imitate the kick of a hot revolver.

"I see some tracks, but they aint Palmer's," said Allan.

The tracks led around the back of the house, to a pinto with a blanket on its back. This horse belonged to a middle-aged

Shuswap man named after a large animal high in the berry fields. He was inside with the woman who was generally considered the boss of this spread. He was drinking English tea and lacing up his boots. The woman, Jane by name, had messy hair. Well, she wasnt going into town or anything.

"I havent seen him since early this morning," she was saying to her visitor. "He went out looking for that damned horse of his. Everyone knows where that horse is. I just hope he doesnt come home lying on a buckboard."

Her visitor straightened his back and reached for his tea. He could not get his finger into the delicate cup handle, so he grasped the whole cup and brought it to his mouth. He did this instead of talking.

They heard boots being stomped free of snow on the porch. Mrs. Palmer took a step to the door, but then the door opened by itself, and there was a man in a black beard, with a small painted feather in his hat. There were two boys with him, and they all came inside.

"At least close the door," said Jane Palmer.

One of them closed the door. The others looked at the Shuswap man but did not address him.

"Your husband aint to home?" asked Allan.

"He'll be on his way home about now," said Mrs. Palmer. "He's been out all day looking for stray horses."

"Oh, we know where Bill Palmer is," said Charlie.

So they told her the whole story, all about the first meeting with Palmer, and the arrival of the little posse, all about the gunfight. They said they could have shot Palmer between the eyes but they'd decided to scare him instead. They did not mention how much whisky they had consumed through the morning. They described the shooting of James Kelly, the musical sheepman. Archie dangled Kelly's watch and let it swing. His eyes reflected its flash in the light that came from the stone fireplace.

Mrs. Palmer did not sit down.

"You got some more of that tea?" asked Charlie.

Mrs. Palmer turned and walked into the large kitchen. Charlie followed her, looking at her messy hair.

While she boiled the water and shook out the tea leaves, Mrs. Palmer talked to the seventeen-year-old gunfighter. She talked to him with her back toward him.

"Why are you out there drinking and putting knives in people? You are still a boy. You should be thinking about your mother."

"I'm thinking about my father. He died with a bullet in him. Died on the ground in the Chilcotin."

"Charlie — are you Charlie?"

"Charlie McLean."

"Charlie. Your father worked hard all his life and raised a big family."

"Two families, Mrs. Palmer."

"You should be thinking about your family, Charlie. Your family name, and what you're doing to stain it."

Charlie walked around and stood in front of the woman. He bent over a little and tucked his revolver into his midsection. He had some hair on his face and his eyes were bloodshot.

"Listen, lady. Us McLean boys, we already *are* a stain. We're a stain you white people made, and you're never going to be able to get us out."

Jane Palmer put the teapot and some flowered cups on a

wooden tray. She leaned forward too, and looked straight into Charlie's red eyes.

"What do you know about white people? What is white and what is not white? What do you think you are? Are you an Indian? Dont make me laugh! Do you think your father was a white man?"

"Ah, you're crazy," said Charlie. "Begging your pardon, ma'am." His speech was as mixed up as anything else.

They all drank tea in front of the fire. Archie went into the kitchen and came back with a mug. He filled it with hot tea and took it outside for Alex Hare.

"My, aint this nice," he said, when he got back inside. "We ought to come calling on folks more often."

He looked over at the Shuswap man and laughed.

Allan stood up slowly and walked over to Mrs. Palmer. He grabbed her upper arm and pulled her to a standing position, then pulled her toward a door in the back of the building. The Shuswap man made as if to stand up, but settled again when he saw the hole in the end of Charlie's revolver.

In the bedroom Jane Palmer tried to straighten up her hair with the palm of her hand. The room smelled warm and there were triangles of snow in the window panes. Allan looked at the bed with the slightly crooked comforter, and he looked at the mirror on the dresser. He could see a black beard and red eyes and the back of Mrs. Palmer's hair.

She looked him right in the red eyes.

He did not reach out.

"I want to tell you you have nothing to worry about from us," he said. "I will handle the boys. You hand over all of

Palmer's ammunition and some food. Sugar, tea, stuff like that. We will take your Indian friend's horse and leave you be."

"What about Mr. Palmer?" she asked, no weakness in her voice.

"We'll leave him be."

"You shot at him before."

"Do you think we cant kill what we want to kill with a gun?"

She was still looking at the eyes above the black beard. There was still defiance in her own eyes and in her straight spine. Allan McLean understood what people said about Mr. Palmer.

"There will be another posse," she said. "A big one. And Palmer will be in it."

"Then," said Allan McLean, "if he rides into my sights, I will put a hole through him."

When Allan and Jane came out of the bedroom, Archie rolled his eyes. Charlie whistled through his teeth. Allan glared at them and walked out into the snow.

The sheepman's frozen body was on the sleigh now, headed for Kamloops, where the bodies were taken in this war. Thomas Trapp rode between the sleigh's tracks, thinking about his own body. He was lucky he didnt have bullets in it. He was lucky it wasnt him lying face up under a rough Hudson's Bay blanket on that wood. The halfbreeds had let him live. Now Trapp was wearing his old boots with the holes in them, and he knew that he was going to be a soldier in the first war on this side of the medicine line. All he wanted was his ranch, and his lake, and springtime. He would need a new pair of boots when the mud came.

Donald McLean had created the first family ranch at Hat Creek in 1860. Now twenty years later the Nicola Valley had been settled, as they used to say. It was the last ranch country to be grabbed. The original bunchgrass was just about all eaten by the new animals in that country. Overgrazing, we call it now, left a landscape of speargrass and cactus and sagebrush. Now in December it was under snow. In the high country the snow was picked up by the hand of the wind and thrown sideways against anything vertical. If you were an animal it would be a good idea for you to know a burrow, or at least a rock with a leeward side.

The low country was "settled." Where there had been fishing camps there were now water rights. The recently arrived white people were comforted by the fact of the Indian reserves, that the Indians were assigned a place where they might be watched. The reserves kept getting smaller and farther away, but then look around – how many Indians are there anyway?

The recently arrived white people did not like halfbreeds much. They might be necessary when it came to hiring extra hands at certain times of the agricultural year, but the rest of the time these people were loose. The recently arrived often spoke of damnation as a fate for the mothers of these drifters.

The Nicola and Kamloops Indians had been around for longer than their stories, or their stories were here before they were. When the river valleys were settled, the Indians were assigned a little bit of land and encouraged to change their lives to fit into these enclosures. These enclosures were sometimes pretty crummy. When halfbreeds came onto them, some of the Indian people did not like them much. Sometimes they referred to them as ammunition created by their fathers, shame entering the land and poisoning the roots of the recovery food.

The McLean boys did not own the Hat Creek ranch. And there was no reserve land for halfbreeds. They had to carry a Scottish name and all their belongings on horseback.

While they were around Indians they spoke white. When they were in town they spoke Indian. They spoke French, but never when there was a priest around. Allan McLean spoke Okanagan when he was absolutely sure he was alone with his wife and son.

When he could feel the track of the bullet through his side he cursed in French. It was the language of the Oblate fathers. They were instructors in pain. They would be there till the end. They would be on the scaffold when the circle game was played.

13

✴ ✴ ✴

IT WAS THE MOST important afternoon of Allan's war. Earlier in the day the McLeans and Alex Hare had been talking with young Nicola men at the reserve on the edge of the large frozen lake. The young Nicola men listened to their stories of the first battle and the war trophies they had taken. These young men would have liked to get their hands on some rifles that worked, and some bags full of ammunition. Bullets are nice and heavy in the hand, and the bit of oil on them feels good. The young Nicola men wanted to go to this war. They did not want to remain in this prison camp any more. They knew what the white people knew – that if an Indian man gets his hands on a new rifle, it is only a matter of one day, and he can shoot better than a white man can learn to shoot in years of practice.

"You have seen what the white people have done so far," Allan McLean told them in a mixture of Okanagan and Chinook. "They have taken our rivers, they have taken our animals, they have taken our land, and they have taken our women."

He spit on the ground.

"They have taken our health," said his brother-in-law.

"They have taken the health of our old people," said Allan.

"And now, what do you expect of the white demons in the future?"

"Sh-teen."

"They will take our dance. Shnay-wum. They will take our songs. They will take our stories."

By the time of the Council with the Elders and Chillitnetza, Allan McLean with the pain in his side had recruited a young army, the beginning of the white man's fear.

The reserve at Douglas Lake was on high ground, not the highest ground about, but not in the river valley either. There was open country between clumps of fir and jackpine, and in the winter of 1879 any night in those rolling plains was the last night before Hell. The Indians did not have many cows. They liked horses. So while some of the white men's cows were freezing solid on their feet in the open country, the Indians were keeping their horses close to one another, and as many as they could under roofs, behind walls.

And they went to ways their families had known before the white men brought horses back again to this land. Allan's brother-in-law Saliesta went with snowshoes around the edge of the lake until he found the deer he was looking for. He chased them as fast as he could go on snowshoes, and they moved more slowly than they wanted to, just where he wanted them to go, into the deep drifts against the edge of the dark trees. There they foundered, and Saliesta approached them on top of the snow. They ceased to thrash about and stood with only their heads and light brown backs showing out of the snow. Saliesta looked into the brown eye of one buck with five years of antler rising above the drift. He killed the buck quickly and then went back for his sled. This was very difficult work, and his breath froze like a waterfall all over the front of his clothes. The other deer turned their heads at first while he worked, to see their fate, but then they gave up. They stood still and felt the snow all around them. They smelled some warmth. This was the momentary blood of the deer that Saliesta wrestled out of the drift and onto his sled.

When Saliesta the lone hunter arrived in the village with his frozen deer he was asked why he did not follow the usual custom, why he did not leave the carcass for the women to retrieve with their knives and sleds. Saliesta said he did not want the women to go there in this weather. There were wolves in the open country. He could hear them. He listened to their story, and their story was about women.

The people ate this animal, and it was warm again.

Saliesta forgot about the deer heads sticking out of the snow.

The Council was not looking much like a war council. Allan forgot the pain in his side while he struggled with his father-in-law. He spoke his best Okanagan. He punctuated his speech with Chinook. He made gestures with his left hand because he did not like to raise his right hand above his waist.

"What my brothers and I have started you can fulfill," he said. "Those people with sick skin have been in our valleys for sixty summers. For sixty summers you have seen your land get smaller, your animals disappear, your sacred places mourn behind the fences of the cow people and the sheep people."

There was no expression in the faces of the Elders in this log house. They had their meeting faces on, these intelligent democrats. Anyone who wanted to speak could speak here, but you had better not take any decisions or actions that the Elders would not approve. Allan's young army was ranged around the perimeter of the large room. Allan stood at the end of the long table. He was the oldest person in his army.

"The white men have not killed us the way they did below the medicine line," said the large man in the place of respect at the table in his own log house.

"When I was a boy they killed us with their smallpox. They killed half of us, and they made the rest of us weak." Allan took a chance, adding, "They made some of us too weak to stand up and protect our land and our stories."

Chillitnetza scowled his famous scowl.

"What is smallpox? Did you ever see smallpox?"

"Did you ever see Sh-teen?"

All the Elders scowled.

"The white people have not made war on us. They have brought many things to us. They brought things that we can eat in winters such as this, when we cannot even find famine food," said the Chief of the Nicola. "They brought weapons to help us bring down the deer from the high country."

"Before the white people came the deer were in the low country," said Allan. Small sounds of agreement came from the edges of the room.

But there was no war at the table of the Elders.

"We have land," said Chillitnetza. "The white chiefs and their policemen and their priests have made nothing but peace with us. They leave our land to us, and they make work for us when we want to work for them. They live beside us and they do not kill us with their army."

Allan did not like the way the Elders were sitting. They were a lot of thinner Chillitnetzas. If he could not get his wife's father to agree with a war, his little army of four men would be nothing but outlaw murderers. The people who killed them would not be another army but only white justice. The leader of the Wild McLeans tried to remember the words he had heard under the lightning-charred pine tree.

"You talk about your land? The chiefs of the white people give great gifts of land to the cow people. But to the Shuswap and the Okanagans they give small hillsides where no beavers can find water to build a dam, where horses cannot walk, where Coyote could not stand still enough to have a piss. They do not give land to people who need the wild animals. They leave what is left over, and if one of them finds gold on it, they will take it away too, and send you to the moon."

The voice under the tree had said something about the moon. But it was hard to translate it into these languages at Douglas Lake.

"There are already Indian people on the moon," said Chillitnetza. Some of the Elders looked a little surprised. But they knew that Chillitnetza held knowledge they could not look into unless he opened the bag. "But we are living here above the valley the white people have named for our greatest chief. The white people will grow to understand us. Sometimes they live with us. Sometimes they marry among us."

Allan did not see where the Chief was leading him. What did Allan McLean know?

"Do their women marry our young men? No. Only one time has this happened, and the white men hated that woman. You talk about marrying among us? Just as often the white men take our young women and destroy them. Have you seen what

happens to the women who are not married to your wonderful white men? Have you seen my sister?"

Alex Hare banged his gloved hand against a log in the wall.
He was not allowed to say anything aloud. None of the Elders
turned to look at him.

Chillitnetza was the Chief of the Nicolas. There was no
expression on his face. He showed Allan McLean who had
stepped into whose argument.

"You are right. The white people have not given us as much
as they have taken. They have given us these little holes in our
faces. They have taken the ground beside the rivers. They have
come among us and taken away many of our women. Your
father took the fields and hills where two streams met and made
the first cow ranch in the people's country. Your father took
two women from the people."

"You are my father," said Allan. And he tried to imitate the
plain face with no anger in it.

"No. Your father had red hair, and you are named McLean.
You are another McLean who has taken one of our women."

Chillitnetza's black eyes were intent on a McLean. One of
the eyes was anger. One was sorrow. Allan McLean knew that
he would never be able to do that with his eyes. He felt the
pain in a wave through the side of his body.

"I have not taken her away," he said. "She lives here among
our people."

"Your people live in the other world beyond the sky," said
Chillitnetza.

"My children will live here," said Allan. "I am a man, and a
man's heart tells him what he is. I am an Okanagan. What did
my father's people give me? Unless I am an Indian, I have no

land. My heart lives with my mother's people, and with the people of my wife. My brothers have killed white men and they have killed the white blood in their bodies. We have begun the war that will return your land and your soul."

Allan McLean could have been a great orator. But he was talking to a man who did not have suicidal dreams. Chillitnetza told him that the answer was no.

Allan told him that some of the young men wanted guns.

"I will not allow them to go to their death," said Chillitnetza. "You are not warriors, Allan McLean. What you have done is kill a policeman and a shepherd. That is murder, and it is murder in the white men's world. The Nicola people will not kill policemen and shepherds."

Allan McLean began to make the proper movements of departure. But Chillitnetza spoke more.

"Your mother was one of the people, and you cannot do anything about your father's blood except suffer for it. We cannot join you in murder of your other blood. But you may stay in the village this night."

Now the meeting was over.

"Jesus, thanks a heap," said Archie McLean, in English and under his breath.

They gathered up the pile of guns. Allan took his bleeding body to his wife. The others had enough friends among the young to find beds indoors.

In the rolling hill country around Douglas Lake you will see many sparrow hawks in the sky. They are fast and small and they can see anything that travels in the air or shifts position on the earth. They can hear anything that moves under the snow or under the ground. In the winter they feed on small creatures that are not asleep. In December of 1879 the sparrow hawks had to call upon their greatest skill, but the sparrow hawks were not starving above the white drifts.

In Victoria, where there was also snow, the lawyers flew from building to building. There was ice in the little harbour. There was beautiful ice in crystal landscapes on all the windows in the capital. The lawyers warmed their naked hands at busy fireplaces and picked up their pens again. The Province was made largely of land you would seldom see human figures traverse, but the people who were there were trappers and miners and ranchers and aborigines. The lawyers lined their offices with books that explained the law in Britain. The huge stony frontier was an interesting challenge. The lawyers in the capital were eating good big Victorian meals at nightfall.

Somewhere in the upper country there is a little low-roofed shack that used to be a cabin. It is made of big planks and squared logs that were hand-axed out of local trees that are not there any more, probably giant cottonwoods. There is space between the planks and darkness inside. It is surrounded by high grass, and nearby there is a stream that does not wander but flows slowly into a big lake. The shack is owned by an Indian man who keeps tools and feed in it. Next to it is a chicken run. Hanging on one of the end walls are three branding irons from the old Palmer ranch.

It was in this shack that Alex Hare and three of the McLean brothers were resting up in December 1879. They had a stove to boil their coffee and warm the little streams of winter air that came in between the planks. They had a big pile of firearms and ammunition against one wall. They had a lot of portable food, and they had one bucket with which they could bring water from the stream.

When the wind turned around it brought a sift of fine hard snow inside with it. But no snow could get anywhere near the iron stove. The little lines of snow would slowly darken and become part of the earthen floor.

There was no whisky. The young males inside the dark cabin had headaches where the alcohol had done its work in the blood vessels of their brains. But Allan's headache was the worst because it came from the waves of pain in his wound made by the lucky William Palmer. The night before his wife had cleaned it and wrapped it with white cloth, and now there was no blood in the cloth but there was something brown, a kind of dark yellow brown. Allan knew about this liquid. He had seen it before.

Out back of the cabin their horses did whatever they could in the ventilated stable. There was a bale of hay on the snow for each horse. No one inside the cabin knew how the hay got there.

Alex Hare was wearing gloves and drinking coffee out of his pewter goblet.

"Allan, you heard what the Chief said. Those assholes are not going to join your army," he said.

Chillitnetza's son-in-law was lying on one of the two bunk boards that hung on chains off the wall.

"Some of the young ones will enlist," said Archie.

"You're a dreamer," said Alex. "I think you have to be a dreamer to be a McLean. We're the whole fucking army, Allan."

"Maybe we'd better forget about the Indians," said Charlie.

"Maybe that's what being a breed means. Maybe we have to have an army of breeds."

"Chillitnetza will go to war against the breeds, too," said Alex Hare. "He's trying to be a good Indian. He's trying to suck the asses of the whites."

"Shut up," said Allan. "Shut up."

It was a good idea. Allan had a piece of red cotton tied around his head. He got it from his wife. Allan could not go and sit under some blasted tree, but he had a cloth around his hair.

The boys were becoming more expensive all the time. Now the Provincial Government was offering a thousand dollars, and the Hudson's Bay Company was still offering two hundred and fifty. A man could dig post holes and skin pigs for three years and never come away with that kind of money.

George Caughill was still on the trail. He had notices out everywhere. He gave his ear to every rounder and go-between in the sage country. At night he dreamt about his boots on McLean feet. When he got finished with this murderous band he would take a little trip to New Westminster and buy himself the best pair of English-made boots he could lay his hands on. But right now he had his eyes on a lone rider who was approaching pretty quickly through the drifted snow along the stage road.

This was Sammy Simpson, a halfbreed that no one knew, but who was always around. Some people said he lived at the Douglas Lake reserve, but the people there said they thought he lived down in the valley. Sammy Simpson had big ears and open eyes, and he was never seen to be working. No one ever saw him buy anything, at a store or a bar. He was not a ghost, because you could touch him. People hardly ever did, except to shove him away.

Sammy Simpson was looking for George Caughill. Sammy Simpson thought he wouldnt mind trading words for dollars. He mentioned dollars as soon as he got his horse next to Caughill's, nose to tail.

"A hundred," he said.

"You'll get what it's worth," said Caughill. He had the reins lifted in front of him. He was ready to go.

"A hundred," said Sammy. "I know where they are."

Actually quite a few people knew where they were. All the Indians at Douglas Lake knew, and Sammy Simpson was not the only horseman with the information. He had to make his deal quick.

"Give me the information first," said Caughill, holding the reins a little lower. "If it's what I want you get your hundred."

Sammy Simpson sat up straight and made as if to ride on into town. Caughill put his big gloved hand on Simpson's chest. That was an example of people touching Sammy.

"A hundred?" asked Sammy.

"All right."

"History will remember us for this."

The hand became a fist. Sammy told what he knew.

"The four of them are in a little rancheree just outside the Douglas Lake village. They have about a hundred guns. Allan's got a bandage around his ribs. The walls of that thing are two feet thick."

Caughill took his fist down. He was getting ready to ride.

Sammy put his skinny arm up. He wanted something in writing.

"You're a good citizen, breed," said Caughill. He had messages to send. He was thinking about Charlie McLean with the
new boots. He wanted to see Charlie McLean's bare feet in
the snow.

Alex Hare looked at his leader getting weaker on the hard bed.
He did not like the looks of this war. He could have used a
small flask of Hudson's Bay rum.

"Here's what I think."

Allan McLean looked at him with black eyes.

"Here's what I think," said Alex. "We are not going to get
an army here. The only young guys I talked to that wanted to
fight were from across the line anyway. I figure that's where
we want to go. Get across the line and rest up for a while.
Get you to a doctor. Give us time to round up a regiment. It's
a three-day ride, maybe four with the snow," said Alex.

"My brother cant ride four days like that," said Charlie.

"He's Allan McLean," said Archie, the youngest.

Allan swung his feet onto the dirt floor. He was ready to
talk. He looked at Alex Hare for a long time. Then he looked
briefly at his little brothers. Then he looked back at Alex.

"Hare, you can do whatever you want. Ride down to Washington, okay. You're a free man. But Charlie's right. I have to
rest up. I figure a few days, I'll be all right. Hector and our brother
Alex will be down pretty soon, and they'll bring some Indians
with them, I know. We have enough guns and ammunition to
hold out here for a few days. We have horses that will get us out
of here when we're ready to go. We've got more firepower than
all the white ranchers and deputies in the whole valley. You,
you go to Washington, we wont say anything about it."

"Shit," was all Alex would say now.

He went to the door of the cabin and opened it. He could see the shacks and tents of the Indian village, but no one was out in the cold. Alex went out for a piss. He saw a small ratty coyote walking diagonally down across a big white slope. Alex stomped backward through the roughed-up snow and took a leak, marking off their territory.

The coyote walked across the snow on top of the creek.

George Caughill was having trouble figuring out his legal position, and it was a cold afternoon. He pulled his hat down as far as it would go. He pulled off his sheepskin glove and sucked on his fingers and put his glove on again. He was not going to get a sheepskin finger into a trigger guard. He was not going to get the thousand dollars if he was a special constable. But if he was not a special constable he would have to take the McLeans alone. Allan McLean, even with blood dripping out of his gut, could shoot his hat off from five hundred feet away. Caughill had got himself sworn in, so he was an employee of the Province. Maybe he could get the two hundred and fifty from the Hudson's Bay.

He sent a messenger to John Clapperton at his ranch just outside Nicola. Clapperton was the Justice of the Peace. He would sign the paper and gather his friends. He sent a messenger to Kamloops. He was going to need a lot of men with horses under them. He was going to need rifles. He was probably going to need dynamite. He had heard about dynamite but he had never seen anyone use it. There was talk about the railroad using dynamite. Maybe the first charge ought to be set at Douglas Lake.

He sent a messenger to Douglas Lake. Any Indian that went near that cabin would be shot with a Government bullet.

George Caughill forgot about the thousand dollars. He sucked on his fingers and thought like a white rancher. When the news of the killings made its way through Indian and breed country, it was going to bring the fur back. Indians were going to put paint under their eyes and go and dig up their guns.

He thought about the Chilcotin uprising. Every white person in the Interior was haunted by the Chilcotin uprising.

The McLean brothers' father was killed in the Chilcotin uprising. Maybe they were going to kill him again.

When the McLeans rode into John Roberts's yard, Roberts was spattered with pig blood. Allan McLean had his own blood on his jacket. Charlie and Alex had John Ussher's blood on their sleeves and steel.

John Roberts saw blood every day in his yard. There was blood under the snow. When things got really cold for a long time, the coyotes went to places they remembered and dug up frozen blood.

The McLeans had European blood and Indian blood. Their mother's family did not know them, but they would have called them half bloods. When Archie McLean had a leak he never allowed anyone to see his nakedness. He did not want other people to see his red pubic hair.

There was an Indian at the door. Allan nodded, and his brother opened up. The visitor was the same age as Charlie and Alex, and he had news for the army. Cowboys and ambitious drifters were arriving along the trail of packed snow that led up out of the Nicola Valley. If the McLeans were going to slip away they had better do it right now, in the starlight.

"Did you bring any whisky?" asked Alex Hare.

The Indian repeated his news, and then he left. Charlie held the door halfway open and looked up the slope across the road, scanned the trees, saw a sky filled with white stars. He heard a little metallic clink. It was from the mouth apparatus of a horse.

Northwest along the snow road there was another cabin, and this was where the first hunters were waiting for reinforcements. A wagon of supplies had just been emptied. Dark-eyed Scotchmen were drinking tea out of tin cups. This was the quiet beginning of the siege.

Clapperton and his posse were spending the night at his ranch. They counted their ammunition and counted it again. Everyone was hoping that there would be a wagon full of rifles and ammunition coming from Kamloops. No one knew how much ammunition the McLeans and the Indians had. Some of them wanted their favourite weapons back. Most of them had shot animals. They knew what dead eyes looked like.

In Kamloops the Chinaman's store was open late, and a wagon was pulled up under his lantern. His family was loading blankets and food, and writing things down. Young men were knocking at old people's doors, asking for rifles and cartridges. John Edwards was waiting for a rider to return from the telegraph office at Cache Creek. He expected to stay up all night and ride at the front of a column of patriots well before sun-up.

Archie felt the bale of the bucket cutting into his gloved hand. They should have made sure they had three or four buckets. If they were going to stay here they were going to need a lot of water. He had had to come back for the axe and go and smash the ice in the creek. Now the bucket was full. Archie was a water boy but he had a small bottle of whisky hidden away. It was in case they werent going to make it. It was for spiritual reasons. He took a mouthful of water from the top of the bucket. Looking up the snow road he saw light leaking from the other cabin. He heard someone hammering wood.

The young Indian man stood in the snow at the edge of the trees. He knew how many men were at the other cabin, and he knew about Allan McLean's pain. He knew that this was the night they could ride away to the medicine line. The posse had begun to arrive, but they had not set out any sentries to watch the McLeans. They would do that tomorrow night, but tonight they had not learned to make a siege. There were a few men keeping warm and fixing walls in the other cabin, but south of the McLeans there was nothing but an Indian village and starlit road. The young Indian man was not interested in war, but he did not want the whites to kill people in his country.

He thought about going to their door again. He took a few steps. But then he went to the village. Tomorrow he would not work for anyone.

In Cache Creek the telegraph operator had a busy hand. Other men were tapping in Clinton and Spences Bridge and Ashcroft, in New Westminster and Victoria. As they wrapped the long wires with stories, the uprising grew in the sleepless heads of government and business and press. In Victoria sallow men picked metal alphabets out of their slots. Men with military decorations resting on velvet answered the whispers of their

————— GEORGE BOWERING —————

favourite memories. Premier Walkem's eyes were ringed with moisture as he thought about the thousand dollars someone would have to carry up the brigade road.

At Douglas Lake Allan McLean's wife lay under two blankets with her baby. Her father had not asked her what she might be thinking, and her husband had not invited her to speak. No other woman in the village said her husband's name. Her baby was asleep with a forehead shiny with sweat. Outside the pit house the black air was pierced by white stars, but down here the fire's light was red. Her father was speaking low words with the smoke. Allan McLean's wife had another human being inside her. He would one day become the greatest warrior ever born in British Columbia.

Now his uncle stood watch at the door of a cabin with snow in the walls. His father could not sleep. He had a hole in his side.

—174—

14

THE SHUSWAP PEOPLE and the Okanagan people did not know as much about arithmetic as the white people did. The white people had a law in arithmetic that said that two things could not be in the same place. They had another law in arithmetic that said one take away one equals zero.

One white man and one normal woman could have all the babies they wanted to, but they would all be zeroes, and zero times ten is still zero. The white half was adding and the Indian half was subtracting. A half take away a half equals zero.

Arithmetic was a way of making sure there would be enough space in the valleys for all the white people. They tried to teach arithmetic to the halfbreed children in the school at Cache Creek.

But taking and fucking and arithmetic were not the only interchange between the white people and the normal people.

The normal people were also artists, and it did not take long for the white people to notice. They did not want to call it art, exactly, but they wanted it. What they called art was likely to be a big gold-painted scrolly frame with a dark brown and black oil painting of their parents. They had used valuable space in carrying these heavy things over the sea and over the continent. To go to all that trouble you had to care a lot about art.

John Mara had a lot of art. He even had a piano in case any of the women in his family or his social circle could finger a ditty. As far as he knew there was never any music in this country until the white settlers brought it. Music would smooth the mountain tops and gentle the river. Music would keep the white man from falling into savage ways.

The Shuswap people made imbricated red cedar-root baskets. You could fill them with water and drop rocks from the fire into the water and make the water hot enough to cook with. Families had baskets that lasted for years, and they made new baskets every year.

The white people began to buy these baskets, but they did not make hot water in them. They arranged them. Later they put them in their Indian museums. They said tribal people make baskets and white settlers make oil paintings. That is the difference between popular art and fine art.

The Shuswap people also made finely cut buckskin clothing. They decorated this clothing with coloured hair, and on special occasions with the scalps of red-headed woodpeckers. When the Chief of the Kamloops people went to meetings with red-headed Donald McLean in the old days, he liked to wear woodpecker scalps. Indian humour. Donald McLean did not get the joke.

Later the white people introduced some nearly worthless coloured glass beads to the fur trade, and the Shuswap people made finely cut buckskin clothing with beautiful beadwork.

Soon the white settlers noticed that they looked a little dowdy standing beside a Shuswap person in buckskin art. So they found ways to get the buckskin clothing. Sometimes they bought it. Sometimes they stole it. After a while they tried to make it themselves. But when white settlers made things they tried to make them as cheaply as they could and sell as many as they could for as much as they could get. After a while they enquired of poor people in Asia whether they would make a lot of Indian clothes. They said they look sort of like this.

But the Shuswaps never sold their rock paintings. Most of the normal people did not even know who made the paintings. Rock paintings were sometimes hard to find because they were in high places where the people went every year to pick berries. Years later other rock paintings were hard to find because the thin lichen would grow over them. The unknown artists always painted their pictures on very big rocks, so the white settlers could not take them home.

So they sent their schoolchildren out to find the rocks. Then they supplied their schoolchildren with paint to paint white settler art over the Shuswap or Okanagan art. Sometimes they painted words commanding people to get to heaven by believing in the Lord. Other times they painted amatory subjects. PF LOVES DM, for instance.

In the schools these white settler schoolchildren went to, arithmetic was very important. For the first few years art was important too, but then it became a frill. Once the schoolchildren were finished with school they did not see much room in their lives for arithmetic or art.

Ana Richards, the schoolteacher with no husband and no child, was one of the few people in town who did not know that Allan McLean was in a dark cabin with his brothers, waiting for gunfire. Ana did not know that Allan had a wife with a fetus inside her in a pit house at Douglas Lake.

The schoolteacher looked into a cloud of fine snow blowing off the bench above town, and she saw Allan McLean's glistening beard. She saw the buckskin gloves on his hands. They had no bead work but there were small red feathers hanging from their edge.

She had spoken to him only once, late last summer. They were walking in opposite directions on the wooden sidewalk in front of the Dominion Hotel. Piano music came through the open door while a stockman held it open, finishing a conversation with someone inside.

Allan McLean stopped walking and unexpectedly addressed himself to her.

"What's that?" he asked, indicating the music.

His body had turned toward the music.

"A mazurka," she said. Now she was stopped.

"What?"

"Chopin."

He was tall. She could not understand what age he was. His eyes met hers for only a second. They were black, and the sun looked at them, looking for a shadow.

"Mazurka?"

"I do not know what number," she said. "Probably six."

But he was gone, his big boots walking the way she had come, and she could not hear them on the wooden planks.

She was a schoolteacher with a child in the ground.

In the morning John Clapperton looked down the white slope at the little cabin. There was a little smoke coming from the roof, but that didnt mean there were killers behind the square log walls. He asked around, and nobody had seen any signs of life. There were two weeks till Christmas, and everything looked peaceful except for the turmoil of horse tracks up here on the light slope and down there on the road and all around the cabin.

The Justice of the Peace was worried. He thought the killers had ridden away in the dark. They could be in the high country on their way to the Okanagan. He thought about sending someone to look inside the stable, but if there were three McLeans and a Hare in that cabin he would have another dead man on his hands.

Clapperton waited. Someone came with a bucket of coffee and they had breakfast in the trees. Back in the other cabin there were women making biscuits. Thick smoke came from that roof.

Clapperton sent for the Chief of the Douglas Lake people.

There were some McLeans in the cabin. They had spent the night wrapped in blankets, feeding the fire a little at a time. Allan had a hard time making his first body movements of the day. Archie and Charlie were putting cartridges in most of the rifles, leaning them against the four walls. Alex Hare was looking through the slits between the logs, brushing away thin snow and peering at the treeline.

"How many?" asked Allan.

"I counted eighteen," said Alex, "but there's bound to be a lot more. Some Indians."

"Nicola or Shuswap?"

"Both, Allan."

"Siwash," said Allan.

Allan was stuck inside a cabin with a low roof. He could

not go and sit by the river or under a tree. There was no one to talk with except his brothers.

"Shit!" said Alex. "Will you look at that?"

They all bent to peek out between the square logs.

There was an Indian sitting on a pony in the middle of the road, carrying a stick with a white flag on the end of it.

"It's your wife's brother Johnny," said Alex Hare.

"His name is Saliesta. He was in our army," said Allan, bitterly.

"Well, he's out there now, waving a white snot-rag."

"Find something," said Allan.

They looked around, dug under the food on the shelf, poked behind the stove. Finally Allan reached inside Charlie's clothes and pulled out his undershirt tail. He ripped off a piece and stuffed part of it into the muzzle of a shotgun. The flag was not white, but it was not black, either. He handed the shotgun to Charlie, and Charlie poked it out the door. There were a lot of white men out there somewhere – it was dangerous to open a door.

Saliesta's pony took small slow steps toward the cabin, and Saliesta waved the flag. He did not really believe that his brother-in-law would shoot him, but his brother-in-law had a bullet wound in him, and he had wild teenaged brothers. Saliesta the lone deer hunter was in the open. He had the promise of a hundred dollars from the white man Caughill. He had his father's decision that there would be no Indian war.

The pony stopped in front of the door. There was a shotgun with no rag in it aimed at Chillitnetza's son.

"Stay right there," said Charlie. "Between them and the door."

"Kla-howya," said the man on the pony.

Three McLeans stood in the little doorway. Alex Hare brushed snow between square logs on the creek side of the cabin.

"They send you, brother?" asked Allan.

Saliesta held a piece of paper in front of the pony's fore-head. Then he leaned down as far as he could. Charlie took a step forward, grabbed the paper, and stepped back fast. Saliesta was still leaning forward. He had a pencil. Charlie stepped again.

Archie waggled the end of his rifle. The pony took a few steps back.

"Alex," said Allan. "Schoolboy, read this writing from the enemy command."

Alex waited till Charlie had taken his place at the other side of the cabin. Then he read the message.

"McLean brothers and Alex Hare, are you ready to surrender quietly? If you are, throw all your weapons outside and walk out. I guarantee your safety. If not, we will burn your house. John Clapperton, J. P."

"Clapperton! We should have killed him and burned his ranch," said Archie.

"What other white friends you got out there?" asked Allan of his brother-in-law.

"No friends," said Saliesta, who hated being here. "John Edwards. Caughill. Palmer."

"Tell Palmer his horse is all right," said Archie, trying to sneer.

"How many white men out there now?" asked Allan.

"Hundred," said Saliesta. "More coming. Some Indians."

"Yeah, we know about the Indians," said Archie.

"Indians on one side. White bastards on the other side. Look who's in the middle, as usual," said Alex Hare.

"They want you to write an answer," said the man on the horse.

"Tell them to get fucked," said Archie.

"Shut up," advised Allan. Allan took the paper and pencil and handed them back to Alex Hare. "Tell them no in a proper way," he said.

Alex Hare wrote on the other side of the paper. No one there could read what he was writing.

> *Sir: The boys say they will never surrender. You can burn the house and go to hell. — A. J. Hare. I wish to know what you have against me. If you have cause to arrest me, I wish to know the cause.*

Saliesta took the note and rode away in the marked snow. Behind him he could hear a shout before the cabin door closed. It was the kind of shout you could hear at the Indian horse races.

The boat left Victoria for New Westminster with a dozen police and volunteers. These were men who had killed Maoris in New Zealand and black men in Africa and *Métis* on the prairies. They had wagons loaded with rifles and revolvers. They had ten thousand cartridges. In New Westminster there were special constables waiting, men who had notches on their hearts. They were tired of looking at telegraph poles. They wanted to sight dark faces with their Government rifles.

The men who had been sent to close off the border crossings were told to ride north to Douglas Lake. At Ashcroft Manor the famous Senator Cornwall left his big stone fireplace and rode at the head of a posse gathered from north and west. He rode his Arabian horse, and he wore his sabre. The corners of his coat were turned up.

Everyone remembered the Chilcotin Uprising.

All the Catholic priests called in their Indians and told them their duty. God and Premier Walkem wanted the McLeans in jail. Any Shuswap or Okanagan who sided with the McLeans would be hanged, and hanged again and again in Hell.

The whole Province was excited. But there was ice everywhere. The Fraser River was solid up to Harrison Lake. Posses converged on Douglas Lake, but they converged slowly. Horses fell on the ice. Wagons dropped into ravines.

Ten men from the Kamloops Indian Reserve rode their hairy ponies over the Brigade Road toward the battlefield. They all had bad memories of the McLeans, and their families had bad memories of the Okanagans. These ten men were not wearing any colour on their faces. They were wearing heavy coats the people bought from the Hudson's Bay Company. They were carrying single-shot deer rifles.

Bullets thudded into the wall. Bullets came through the cracks. The boys put their faces to the dirt floor and covered their heads with their arms. Bullets clanged off the stove and fell as flat slugs of metal near someone's ears. They could hear faint sounds of gunfire from outside. The main noise was here between these log walls. A bullet passed through the water bucket and water fell on Archie's leg.

Bullets thudded into the wall in clusters, loud fists that would kill a man and then spray him to pieces.

They wanted to get up and return the fire, squat at a chink, at a slightly ajar door, and pick off posse members who put their heads too far to one side of a tree. Bullets were pounding into the wood, and then bullets were hitting the embedded bullets. A small piece of metal hit the barrel of Archie's pistol and sent a numbing message up his arm.

A horse was wandering toward the cabin, reins dragging in the crumpled snow. There was no shooting now, so lighter individual sounds made their way through the cold afternoon air. A clink of cold iron. In the distance a bell clanking three times. Metal in winter. Never put a tongue to it.

"Aw shit," said someone behind a tree.

And then John Stevenson was walking toward the horse and because of that decision, also walking toward the cabin where the uprising was contained. His riding boots slipped on the packed part of the snow. But he reached the horse, bent over and picked up one loose rein. The horse twisted away before he could get the other. There he was, a man holding a strip of leather with a stupid animal pulling in circles at the other end.

Not an easy shot.

"Who gets this one?" asked Charlie.

"You can have him," said Allan. "For the time he shorted you a day's roundup money."

Charlie hefted a big Henry rifle no one had used yet, and stuck its evil nose between two cottonwood logs.

"Where should I do him?"

"Shoot him through the fucking head and get it over with," said Archie.

"Give them one chance," said Allan. He was not bleeding at all now, but every movement he made cut into his torso.

Stevenson was dancing with his horse, a turning centre of a turning world of horse heads and careless oaths.

"What do you figure? Two hundred feet?"

"Charlie, just shoot him. Hit him in the knee."

Charlie squeezed the metal once, and then yanked the big rifle out of its hole. He didnt even look to see. He smiled and gestured with his hand at the slit in the wall. The others had a look. Stevenson was lying in the snow, trying to lift his shoulders. The horse was heading home.

The countryside was racked with thunder and lightning. Five hundred bullets banged into the cabin walls, some outside, some inside. The McLeans put their faces to the dirt in the corners. A section of the stovepipe came loose. Flames jumped in the stove.

The growing posse enjoyed a target bigger than a man's knee.

"Christ, them Breeds can shoot!" said one of the two men who were dragging Stevenson over the snow.

The days went by and so did the nights, and it was cold by day. By night the cold was dark. A faint light emanated from the cabin, as the boys fed whatever wood they could find to the stove.

The newspapers carried nineteenth-century headlines into the Interior of the Province, and along the streets of the capital. "Murders" and "outlaws" were their favourite words. Telegraph wires carried the story eastward and south. The boys in the cabin were becoming the centre of a widening doom.

The editor of the Victoria newspaper liked the idea of a war. He pointed out that there in the harbour the Government of British Columbia possessed some wonderful rockets that had been used to good Imperial purpose in various parts of Africa. The explosive shells that had turned clusters of proud Zulus into chunks of meat would blow one little cabin into sticks of wood stained with mixed blood. The McLean problem could be blasted into history by men in tidy uniforms, and Indian counsellors would warn their disaffected tribesmen against any manifestations of anger toward the legitimate stewards of peace and enterprise.

The editor of the Victoria newspaper was just one of many who understood why Indians were forcefully invited to witness the hanging of dark-skinned lawbreakers.

Inside the cabin the outlaws had to dig a hole to shit in. They pissed in the hole, but not much, because the water bucket was empty. They threw empty cans into the hole. But they drained every bit of liquid out of the cans first, and then they tipped the empty cans to their lips again before tossing them at the shit.

They put sticks out the holes in the wall and after a while pulled them back in, hoping for snow on the sticks. There was no snow left on the ground anywhere near the door. Archie picked up the bucket and looked at the bullet hole in it. He stuffed a piece of torn shirt into the hole.

"Where you going?" asked Alex Hare.

"Goin' to the creek to get us a drink," said the kid.

"You'll get yourself killed."

"More'n likely."

"Dont do it, boy. We dont need no water."

"Cover me."

Archie beat it out the door, while his brothers and Alex Hare filled the night with loud explosions. He slid and stumbled down the little slope toward the creek. The snow was jumping all around him. A bullet bounced along the ice in front of him. Archie drove his boot through the ice and scooped up a bucket of water. How did I do that, he asked himself, as he dodged bullets on his awkward way back. The bucket became lighter as he neared the door he loved. When he stepped inside, someone slammed it and there was a terrible knocking at the door.

"Your drink," said Archie, nary a bullet in him.

They all looked at the bucket. There was a tiny bit of water in it. They shared it, less than a mouthful each.

"*Calice!*"

"*Tabernac' et calice!*"

Alex Hare went to his favourite chink in the wall and stuck a Nicola Valley rifle out. At school they had called him Rabbit. If he were a rabbit he would have scooted away from here two days ago. He would have scooted until the shadow of a hawk fell across the snow before his little eyes. He wasnt a rabbit. He was a halfbreed outlaw with a problem in mathematics. He squeezed off three shots. They made a little grouping in a jackpine, shaking the tree and spilling snow down Senator Cornwall's neck.

There were McLeans inside the cabin and McLeods outside. McLeods and Campbells and Fergusons, Muirs and Gordons and Frasers. There were pieces of plaid between the trees. The white people's army shouted in a Scottish accent. They were the grandchildren of men who had swung clubs and swords and empty muskets in the bad light of a Hibernian raid. In the cabin up the road the women made a tureen of oatmeal porridge.

The McLeods and Frasers and Gordons wanted to shoot the McLeans. Get rid of the Hudson's Bay Factor's mistakes. Scottish boys with dark skins and feathers in their clothes. McLeans, indeed. There should have been a law that said they had to take their mother's name. But their mother's name was Grant.

They should have started the law right from the beginning.

They hoped the halfbreeds would not surrender.

It was approaching evening, and the snow was coming down thick. There was no wind now, and the small hard flakes fell on eyelashes and the ears of horses. Each flake was different from all others. Yet there were millions of snowflakes falling on the high country around Douglas Lake. The snow was thicker and thicker, and these Scottish riflemen pulled their hats down tighter, ducked their necks down into their collars. Everything was turning white, but it was nearly night now. Everything that was not white was already black.

Then there was a yell that came up from dozens of throats at once. The cabin door was open, someone said. There were muzzle flashes from outside the building. There was a lot of shouting in the trees, and all kinds of guns went off.

"They're making a break," said a Fraser.

It was so noisy that some men would not be able to hear a normal conversation for the next two days.

"Fill them devils full of lead," suggested a Ferguson, but the guns were speaking more loudly.

There were two McLeans at least, just outside their door, living through the fusillade, but where were the others? The falling snow was so thick that bullets had to cut their way through it. The McLeans were firing shotgun blasts, and pellets were hitting trees and men.

A McBride down by the creek held his fire, looking as best he could through the falling snow. He wanted to stay out of range of the lawmen's fire, but he had the job of watching the horse shed. He hunched his shoulders and forced his eyes to probe the darkness and the snowfall. And there it was, a boy on a horse, riding straight at him. The McBride stood so that he could lift his rifle over the dead grass in front of him. The boy on the horse was leading another horse and turning now, shouting something. The McBride aimed for the boy on the horse and missed. He aimed for the horse.

Archie let go the reins of his own mount and pulled out a long pistol with his left hand. From the saddle of the twisting horse he turned, still holding the lead of the other terrified animal in his right hand, and shot the McBride, first in one arm, then in the other. The McBride screamed unintelligibly, and Archie threw a curse his way. Then he cursed the horses, and headed back toward the front of the cabin, bullets chasing him in the dark and the pearly spectral white.

Shoving the animals back into the shed, he prepared himself to take bullets in the back. He did not know that they had already made holes in his clothing.

They were all four inside the cabin again. Allan was lying on the floor. The walls were still being pounded, and a few slugs bounced around them.

"Anyone hit?" asked Archie.

"Some asshole got lucky and nicked my elbow," said Charlie. "Allan?"

"They will never kill me with a bullet," said Allan.

They lay where they had fallen. They did not hide in corners with their faces in the cold dirt. The big cottonwood logs could absorb ammunition until they were made largely of metal. The McLeans looked at the dying light in the little door in the stove. They watched the fire go out. They did not care about fire. They cared about water. Maybe with the stove out they would not be so thirsty.

At the other cabin there were two men who did not look like anyone else. They had hair that was black with a shimmer of blue in it, like a raven's wing, but so did many of the Indian men and women. They had skin that was some shade of medium brown, but not that much different from the skin of Soo Woo and his family. A hint of gentility to their faces and bodies, an intimation of softness, smoothness, as if they should have been round, like some sort of human plum. No, that was going too far. Perhaps they were from a race of people who always looked young, especially in comparison with wind-chiselled Scotchmen or the Salish. The white people always said the Indians were leathery, and no one knew whether they were referring to colour or texture.

These two young men were from what the English called the Sandwich Islands. Here in the Province they were Kanakas. The white people did not know that the word means human beings.

The Kanakas came to work in the logging camps and then the railroad. These two men were in the country to do joe jobs for the railroad survey crews, but this cold week in December they were doing joe jobs for the big posse.

"Hey, Joe," someone would shout. "We need lots of water in here. Much water, chop chop, savvy?"

"Comin' up," Joe would say, one of the first local phrases he had learned. "Fuckin' idjit," he would whisper once he had got through the door.

The heavy snow and the deep unrelenting cold were interesting to these chaps. They seldom went out into the cold except when they had to, wrapped in a lot of local clothes. But they were both glad they had added snow and cold to their experiences. When Kanakas went back home they were expected to bring stories. Now they were going to be able to bring back the story of the Wild McLeans.

"How many men are inside the cabin?" asked the first Joe.

"One man and three boys," said the second Joe.

The first Joe held up all the fingers of one hand, and folded the thumb out of sight.

"Okay. How many men coming to shoot guns at them?"

"Hundred. Hundred and twenty," said the second Joe. "More coming all the time."

"Have you ever seen those McLean boys?" asked the first Joe.

"Nope." It was the second Joe's favourite range country word, nope.

"But they are just kids, arent they?"

"Yep. So I have heard."

"So why does it take a hundred and twenty men with guns to kill them?"

"And more coming."

"So?"

"How old are you?"

"Ah, well – "

"I think even you must remember the white men coming to the Islands."

"Ah, yes, the Sandspirit Islands."

"Close enough," said the second Joe.

"I think I see the point you are laboriously striving for," said the first Joe. "But I must say that it does not really answer my question."

"I think you'd better peel that potato," said the second Joe.

15

✳ ✳ ✳

INSIDE THE CABIN it smelled too bad for the dignity of a war. With the stove out and the cold air rolling in between the square logs the odour was not as bad as it had been, but to hold off the siege in dark air that smelled like shit was just another insult in a lifetime of insults. Allan minded most. He was the oldest son in the younger family. He had a responsibility to his little brothers and a greater responsibility to his people. But his people were not here with them in the shit.

Once in a while they heard a sudden burst of gunfire outside the cabin somewhere. There would be undecipherable shouts in the distance, then more gunfire. Bullets were buried in horses. They sliced through fir needles. They burrowed into the snow. If the boys in the cabin had had warmth and water enough they could have waited while their adversaries shot each other into the ground.

Charlie lay on a board, with his back against the south wall. He had two coats on but he was cold. You had your choice: be cold or be asleep. Sometimes you thought you had to stay awake so that you would not have to worry about whether you would ever wake up from the winter. Charlie looked at Archie, who was using an old shirt to clean his pistols. Who could tell what was inside a child's head? Archie had never touched a woman's bare skin, but he was probably going to die at Douglas Lake. They never told stories of boys like Archie in those books at school. Romans and Englishmen. Talking animals. Charlie had once known how to read. Alex Hare could still read, but what does he read? Letters from white men who are trying to kill halfbreeds.

Alex Hare was thinking about Annie McLean. He saw a businessman named Mara pulling his belt out of his trousers, and he saw Annie McLean. He did not see her naked because he had never seen her naked. He should have spoken to her instead of waiting. Now he saw John Mara. And behind Mara a long line of white men. Alex Hare had a long pistol that never ran out of cartridges.

Archie used his skinning knife to open a can of compressed meat. It was thick with salt. He was thirsty and he was almost as hungry as he was thirsty. He ate the meat with the tip of his knife. He grew thirstier. If there were only some shooting right now he would not think of meat in a can.

The inside of the cabin was a mess. Half-empty cans lay on their sides, clothing was strewn on the earth floor where wooden planks should have been. Rifles and shotguns had once been stood against walls but now they lay on their lengths, crossing each other. Boxes of ammunition without lids were the only signs of orderliness. On the east wall there was a picture of Jesus with a bullet hole through his long light brown hair.

A thought flew slowly around the room. How did we get here? How did all this start? The way it will end is more certain. Was this all certain from the start?

Fifteen-year-old Archie was asleep with a smile on his face

and a knife in his gloved hand. In his dream he had a black mustache and a thick black beard. He was doing something with a woman but what was he doing? He was doing something with a woman.

John Clapperton and his partner Alexander Robb discussed Alex Hare's letter. They decided that if Victoria was not going to supply some heavy ordinance to blast the cabin to matchwood, they would burn it down.

Nicola Valley settlers feared the burning of their own barns and houses, but they loved to watch low crawling flames work their way through grass and brush, clearing the soil for potatoes and the like. The low flames left behind an intricate network of blackened grass and twigs, and a man with a rake in his hands could stare at this transformed landscape for hours at a time.

Clapperton and Robb supervised the loading of a wagon. No one told them whose wagon it was. It probably belonged to an Indian. Clapperton and Robb stood side by side, arms folded across their sheepskin jackets, while hands piled the wagon high with bales of hay. They smiled under their facial hair while coal oil was poured all over the hay.

"Light it," said John Clapperton.

Matches flared and were thrown onto the wagon. The hay had been sitting outdoors, under a mantle of snow. It would not flame. The coal oil soaked into the hay, and the hay held the idea down to thickening smoke.

Match after match went into the wagon. A man with a torch made of burning rags thrust his arm over the side of the wagon. The hay offered smoke, and an occasional grin of orange fire.

"All right, we will smoke the bastards out," said Clapperton.

Four men got behind the wagon and four less lucky got behind the wheels, and they pushed the smouldering cargo toward the McLeans. They laughed and encouraged one another and shouted things such as "Haw there!"

Bullets sounded like strange winter bluebottle flies in the air. Bullets pounded into the hay and the wood of the wagon. The men faltered.

"Push that damned thing," shouted John Clapperton.

A bullet hit one man's boot heel and spun him ninety degrees. He fell full length on the snow and stayed there, his arms around his head. He saw his hat tumble over the surface of the snow as bullets ruined it.

For the fifth day pieces of metal flew between cabin and trees.

When things quieted down a little Clapperton and Robb ordered more coal oil. Three more times the foolhardiest young men shoved at the wagon. It got a little closer to the cabin. It looked for a moment as if the hay would catch flame, but there must have been only a puny dry patch.

Clapperton ordered the smoking hay removed from the wagon. The new idea was to get the wagon itself burning and run it up against the cabin, thereby roasting the murderers inside, or obliging them to leave the building, arms in the air or loud rifles in their hands.

"We'll give it a try tomorrow morning," said one of the wagon men.

Here is what happened to Palmer's favourite horse, the lovely black stallion.

Horses, after they have worn leather for some time, will put up with many unpleasant things. They will walk down steep hillsides they would never walk down if they were alone and naked. They will run very fast straight at other working horses that are running straight at them. They will move about with precision inside a railed enclosure that is crowded with large animals equipped with horns.

Now these McLean horses were not tied to anything. They were standing next to some loosely shaken hay under a broken roof. They were wearing leather, and no one had rubbed their sides after the short excitement with all the noise.

One of them had jangly synapses, and this was Palmer's favourite, the large black stallion. The reins touched the frozen mud below his muzzle. He lifted his long neck and snorted, and steam drifted out of a cloud in front of his face. His eye on one side saw the back of the cabin and his other saw the snow sloping to the creek.

Palmer's black stallion left the other horses standing with their necks bent to the scant food, and walked toward the creek.

Palmer's black stallion had prominent veins on the sides of his long head, but there was no one to notice them as he walked through the snow to the creek. There were willows along the side of the creek but he wanted to reach the other side. He wanted to go somewhere where the other mammals were not making so much noise and smoke. He walked until the willows stopped, and then he was walking toward a wide flat whiteness in the dark. This was the lake in winter.

He was still wearing leather, and when he lowered his head the reins trailed in the snow, but he was making his own decisions now. He decided to walk on the wide whiteness, around the buildings and tents of the Indian village. He did not know about Indian villages. To him this was another place where the other mammals slept. He stepped onto the untracked flatness. He knew nothing about story. He was a large horse who stepped deliberately away from where he had been.

Some mammals were watching him now. They were interested in whether he was alone.

The willows did not follow the creek all the way down. There was a wagon road at the edge of the lake, and a little bridge made of planks, covered with snow and the snow covered with moonlight. Palmer's black stallion would never walk across a bridge unless there was a mammal on his back. He stepped out onto the lake.

There was thick ice on the lake, and snow on the ice. There were footprints half-filled with drifted snow all over the nearby surface of the lake. But there are currents of differing water in this lake, and sometimes these currents will come to meet the water entering from one of the numerous creeks. Where Palmer's horse was now walking there were no footprints on the lake. He stepped and stepped, his head down, his ears bent forward.

Some men were more or less watching him. They were watching the cabin with the McLeans in it. But they looked from time to time at this horse. They were interested in where it might be going, because sometime soon someone would have to go and fetch it.

Now the stallion heard what he had been listening for. It was the echoing sound of a crack in the ice. He stopped walking and listened. He shifted a front foot and listened. The sound of a crack in the ice can be close or distant, and it is difficult to tell which. He stepped again, and stopped. He stepped again.

One of his back feet went through the ice. One back leg was in the water and the other was bent double. His front legs slid out in front of him, and his chest was on the ice. He would have to get back up on the snow. He tried to step on water, but then his other back foot went through. His eyes opened very wide, white in the moonlight, but there was no one close enough to see them.

He made the sound of a stallion discovering trouble. In the Indian village they could hear him, even the people in pit houses, but the Douglas Lake people had been told that all these events of this week were someone else's story. Let them tell it, they were told. Let them tell their story badly.

Palmer's black stallion lifted his long neck and grabbed at the ice in front of him with his front legs, and then the back portion of his large body flowed forward. He slipped off the ice and fell underwater in the darkness. He thrust himself up into the air again, and fell again, his long thin legs swimming and reaching for the ice. Moonlight gleamed on his wet black body, but he was not a creature from the lake. He did not know that men were carefully hurrying toward his place on the lake. He did not know how far he was from the shore under the snow. He floundered in a hole of water. He slipped out of sight under the ice.

Now the men he could not see were looking through the darkness and the moonlight at the black hole in the white lake. The horse appeared again, but now he was upside down. They were close enough now to see his shape. They could see the underside of his long jaw.

The black stallion saw the sharp white stars turning above him. His front legs found ice again but it fell toward him when he heaved at it. There were chunks of ice turning with him while he fought the cold water.

One of the men on the snowy shore hollered insanely at the others, but no one was going to crawl out to the edge of the breaking ice and grab for a rein on a heavy horse under the ice.

The horse was fighting more slowly now, but his dangerous feet whipped the night air. He was consumed with the desire for surface, for his lifetime habit. He shrieked again, but the water filled his throat. The underside of his long jaw and then his huge teeth could be seen now. The men were not that far away. They could see now, and now the horse was slowed in the dark water. The current pulled at the heavy body, and the body fought back. The stallion knew that this black hole he was captured in was his only hope.

The shadow men on the shore had their own idea about his only hope, all but one of them, the one who importuned.

The men on the shore had been stuck here in the December cold for five days, trying to do something about four half-breed outlaws. They had been shooting rifles at a log timber cabin. Now in the moonlight on the white lake they could turn their minimal thinking elsewhere.

Bullets nosed very fast into the snow and skittered off the ice, their echoes making a somehow familiar undersea pinging sound into the distance. There was a rifle report, and another, and then there was a familiar terrible noise on the edge of the lake. Some of the riflemen walked out onto the lake, where there were already footprints, and then they all advanced, except the one man without a rifle. The rest were shooting at a large horse in a black hole. The target was black in black

under the darkness lit by moon and stars and surrounded by
the moonlit snow, an idea of white, a memory of day.

Bullets struck the water and slowed as they fell. Bullets made
deep holes in meat. Bullets were like axes in the deep chest of
Palmer's favourite mount. His back feet still churned the water
beneath him and his front feet broke ice away from the edge
of the black hole. Bullets went through his long neck and
removed part of one foot. Bullets went deep into his belly, and
finally two bullets bounced off his skull. After his churning
legs dropped under him the bullets continued to enter through
his black skin and find crooked pathways inside him. He was
entirely silent. His long tail floated in the water. Bullets broke
ice around him and bullets smashed the bones of his long face.
If anyone had been close enough to hear those bones shattered
he wouldnt be able to name what it was. He would never turn
this night into a story.

Either the currents of Douglas Lake pulled the black stallion under the ice and away, or the animal was an irregular
shape in the thin new ice that spanned the black hole in the
dull light of morning.

In the morning light the McLean brothers and Alex Hare saw
a man sitting on a spotted horse in front of the cabin. The
man was John Leonard Jr., whose mother was a Shuswap. He
was not carrying a rifle but rather a stick with a filthy handkerchief tied to the end of it.

Charlie rummaged among the junk piled everywhere and
came up with their truce flag. He opened the door a notch and
waggled the cloth. John Leonard Jr. stepped his pony up close.

"What do you want, you fuckin' halfbreed?" asked Charlie.

"They want to know if you're ready," said John Leonard Jr.

"Your father send you? Your father out there getting prepared to shoot us down, John?"

"Mr. Edwards sent me."

"Oh, *Mister* Edwards sent you," said Archie, who was standing now in the notch of the doorway too.

"I havent fired a shot, Charlie," said the youth on the horse.

"Well, *I* have," said Charlie. "And if you're up there in the trees you stand just as good a chance of getting plugged as your father or *Mister* Edwards or that bastard Mara or anyone."

"Mara aint here."

Charlie shut the door. John Leonard Jr. sat quietly on his spotted pony. In half a minute the door opened again, a notch.

"Here's our message for *Mister* Edwards," said Charlie. "Tell him we will come out peaceful if you give us our horses and a quarter of a mile. If you catch up to us you can shoot us or hang us. One of us is shot and the rest is thirsty and cold. That ought to lower the odds against you."

John Leonard Jr. rode back to the trees. In ten minutes he was back outside their door, carrying his filthy flag.

"They say no deal. They say this here is a matter of the law."

Charlie threw his dismal flag on the ground in front of the spotted pony.

"Then tell them the law is welcome to come and get us."

The door slammed shut, and John Leonard Jr. neck-reined his pony. It stepped patiently back to the line of siege.

The Victoria *Colonist* kept the Outlaw story on the front page day after day. The *Colonist* said that this uprising was a challenge to the new Province, and that the proper response was the

Provincial Police. Indians, said the *Colonist*, are deeply impressed by white men in uniform. They are impressed to the point of superstitious fear.

Allan could hardly move. He kept asking his lieutenants what was going on out there. He could hear Charlie cursing under his breath.

"What?" he asked, leaning back on one elbow on his board.

"They are making something," said Charlie.

"Be a little more descriptive," said his oldest brother. There was a white hair in his thick black beard.

"They're putting logs up on another wagon. Across the front. Got it aimed at us."

"Get yourself another flag," said Allan.

John Leonard Jr. was there again, sitting on his spotted horse fifty feet from their cottage door.

"Get down and come over here," shouted Charlie.

John Leonard Jr. turned his head and looked up at the tree-line. He looked back at the cabin. He saw a shotgun barrel. He looked up the slope again.

"Get down, John, or you'll never get up again."

John Leonard Jr. got off his horse and walked in his father's old boots. He stopped twenty feet from the cabin full of guns.

"Come to the door, John."

Now he could see Charlie standing in the slit of the doorway. There was a long revolver in Charlie's hand.

He kept walking till Charlie spoke again.

"Not inside, John. This is our house. No halfbreeds allowed inside."

"You boys are just as much halfbreeds as anyone," said John Leonard Jr. He was filled with fear, stuck in the middle again. What would they do with him up there? What would happen with him here?

"What did you say, John?"

"You are."

"What, John?"

"You're breeds, same as me."

"We're dead boys, John," said Charlie. "Famous dead boys."

Allan had pushed himself up and was now standing against the wall beside the cold stove.

"Business," he said.

Charlie pointed his pistol at John Jr.'s head, then at his stomach, at his groin, back at his head. John Jr. did not know how heavy the pistol was in Charlie's hand.

"What are they doing with that wagon, John?"

John Jr. turned his head to look behind him, as if he was for the first time hearing of the subject. When he looked back he saw that the door was open a little wider. There was absolutely no expression on Charlie's face. There was a little smear of light whiskers on his chin.

"Logs," said John Jr.

"We can see that, John. We have keen vision. We inherited it from our mother's people."

Charlie was jeering, and this made John Jr. much more nervous.

"Coal oil," he said.

"Be a little more descriptive, John."

"They're going to ride down on that wagon and throw coal oil all over your shack — "

"Our house."

"They'll be behind them logs. You wont be able to do any-thing about it. They'll burn your – "

"House down," said Charlie.

"Can I go now, Charlie?"

Charlie steadied the pistol at John Jr.'s face. The shotgun barrel between the logs aimed at his body.

"Sounds like it'll work, this coal oil stuff," said Charlie.

"I got nothing to do with it. I aint fired a shot," said John Jr.

"Why dont you get a seat in the wagon?"

"Can I go now?"

"Sure. Tell them to burn our house down. Tell them to use whisky instead of coal oil."

Charlie jerked the end of his pistol upward, and John Leonard Jr. walked back to his horse. He mounted it from the left side.

Ana Richards had seen men riding out of town with pack horses, but she did not know their purpose. Ana Richards did not like the news. She was no longer interested in history.

But she was thinking of Allan McLean. What was it about his eyes or his beard or his mouth or the way he walked? The small feather in his hat? It was not that he was a man. She was no longer interested in men.

It was not an eye or a beard. It was the high air, the sky, rolling back on itself like a fist, like a snake being skinned alive, the air tucking into itself, high, making space or power for a gash of lightning. To bring a tree to its knees. To make space for thought. To bring it to an end.

They didnt send John Leonard Jr. this time. He was gone, probably, gone in the cold to some place where his father did not live, some place where people were not going to be shot on the frozen ground.

They sent Fred Ruck, a farmer nobody knew anything about. He was not a friend of Clapperton's. He was too small. He walked behind a heavy horse in the spring. He chased crows in the late summer. In the winter he repaired things. No one knew where he was from. The Wild McLeans never knew such a quiet man.

Now here he was without a horse, standing in front of the cabin. He was the sorriest looking emissary anyone ever saw. It was clear that he did not want to be there. He was a dull mortal in the wrong place.

He was holding a piece of paper in his woollen glove.

Charlie McLean opened the door a crack and shouted at Ruck.

"You a friend of Clapperton or a friend of John Edwards?"

Ruck shook his sorrowful head.

"Get over here."

Ruck shuffled toward the door. He stopped. Charlie gestured with his gun. This happened three times. Charlie reached out his arm, and Ruck leaned toward it, nearly falling. Finally he put the paper into Charlie's hand.

"They just about got their coal oil wagon ready?"

"Uh, yup, just about," said Fred Ruck.

Charlie handed the paper to Alex Hare, who read it in an overloud voice.

"McLeans. Come out and lay your arms on the ground. We will guarantee your safety."

"Never mentioned me," said Alex Hare. "Is that good or bad?"

Allan McLean walked slowly to the door, the upper half of his body bent forward. He rested his hand heavily on his brother's shoulder. He stepped into the doorway, a white hair in his beard, and Fred Ruck took a step backward on the frozen rutted ground.

"Tell your bosses we want an hour to talk it over," said Allan.

Fred Ruck was stiff. He could not blink his eyes in the cold afternoon air.

"Git," whispered Archie.

Fred Ruck shambled up the slope. The McLean brothers could see the log wagon. It was aimed down hill.

Outside the cabin there was frozen water on the ground, blowing through the air, hard snow that would lie on the palm of your hand for a minute before it melted. A hundred paces from their door was a big lake covered with ice and the ice covered with snow. But they were crazy with thirst. Archie had already drunk something he would never have thought possible.

Up at the line of trees there were a hundred and fifty men with water bottles and whisky bottles. Would I trade my Colts for a tin cup of water, Allan asked himself.

He looked out between two logs. The log wagon was aimed straight at them.

"We had some good times, didnt we?" said Alex Hare.

It was time for that kind of talk. Their voices were strained. The odour in the cabin was terrible, and only the cold kept it from driving them out into the death waiting there.

"How many times did we get out of Ussher's calaboose?"

The boys tried to laugh but they had barbed wire in their throats. Allan McLean was sitting on the dirt, his back against a wall. He was opening a beautiful sixteen-shot rifle, count-ing shells, easing the mechanism. He held it to his face. He had always loved the oily metal scent of firearms. He was think-ing about his son, asleep or awake in a pit house a few minutes' run from the cabin.

"I suppose you boys want to shoot your way out," he said.

"Our only chance," said Archie, his voice a hard whisper.

"No chance," said Allan.

"Think we'll ever look back on this as one of the good times?" asked Alex Hare.

"No chance at all," said Allan.

"We'll be dead tonight," said Charlie.

"They'll remember us," said Alex Hare. "A hundred years from now people will be coming to this here shack to see where we got it."

"Not if it's burnt down," said Charlie.

They all stopped. They could hear a shout from the posse's position. It was quiet inside except for what Allan was doing with the repeater.

"We'll get loose again," said Allan. He was thinking about his son and his son who was not born.

"Allan, we're going to surrender?" Archie had a pistol in either hand.

"We are going to escape from somewhere warm, somewhere that's got water to drink. If we burn to death right here in this Indian shack, our friend John Mara will go scot-free. We've got business with Mara. And a couple others. It aint surrender."

They all looked at Allan McLean in the weak afternoon light.

"That idea come to you in a dream, Allan?" asked Alex Hare.

Archie saw Fred Ruck standing in front of the cabin.

16

* * *

THEY CALLED THEM The Queen's People. There was a certain ambiguity, one supposes, in both that term and the feelings that were behind it. Something like God's mark on Cain. God said this mark means that you other people had better not work out your feelings on this boy, because vengeance is mine. But wherever he went, people would ask Cain: where'd you get that mark? Are you the boy that killed your brother? We know when we grow up that Cain was picked to be the bad brother because he grew grain, just like the Caananites or somebody, the enemy on the other side of the hills, while Abel slew sheep like a good local boy. So when the Indians and the halfbreeds were called The Queen's People, it meant that they were under her protection, but it also meant that no one else could have them. They were her property. She could put them wherever she wanted to. In the next century queens would have Corgi dogs instead. Little troublemakers.

I wonder whether, when Victoria died, she willed her people to her old son. Did they then become The King's People?

Nowadays the British monarchy is known in British Columbia largely through the stories told in the brightly coloured newspapers that specialize in sex scandals and miraculous cancer cures. So the present-day Queen doesnt have much time for her Indians and halfbreeds. She lets the local governments take care of them. You're our people, for all intents and purposes, say the local governments.

That's their story.

We know whose people these are. We know how they got here. It's an old true story. True story or legend, same thing now that we're this old.

Coyote met the great huge monster from the east. Jumped inside his belly and cut his heart off, let all the animals out. Then he chopped up that monster and flung him in every direction. That's where all the people got started. Washed his hands and dripped the blood and water on the ground. That's where the locals came from.

Queen's people, my ass! Coyote's people.

People's people.

Fred Ruck handed Alex Hare's note to Justice Edwards. Edwards tilted it so that he could read the pencil marks in the afternoon light that found its way between huge grey balls of cloud. His mind wasnt made up. He was a lawman and a businessman on the frontier. Words were precious. There was wind in the tree boughs.

"They say they'll come out if we dont iron them."

Clapperton opened his mouth, but Edwards raised his gloved hand, and Clapperton sucked at food between his teeth.

"And if we let them ride horses to Kamloops. No wagon."

Now Clapperton spoke.

"No irons, ride horses. They'll break, first chance they get."

"They're not going to get away from a hundred men, John," said Edwards. He could feel history welcoming him.

"Why should we give them any conditions? We've got them. I say start your little rolling fort, and lay the coal oil on that roof."

History Edwards kicked his boot against a jackpine trunk, knocked the packed snow off the sole. Took his gloves off and reached a cigar out of his inside pocket. Lit the cigar. Put his gloves back on. Justice of the Peace for the whole region.

"Mr. Clapperton," he said, as if he were sitting on the *banc*, "if we turn that cabin into a torch, we will be making Her Majesty responsible for its replacement. We will set Indian relationships back fifty years. The famous one-thousand-dollar reward will go up in oily smoke. There will be a mess that will not be brought to order with despatch. The widow Ussher will be deprived of visible justice."

"And you, Judge, will not be seen riding into Kamloops with the McLeans in your charge," said Clapperton.

"We have an offer of surrender," said Edwards. "I think it's the best we will see. Happy Christmas, Mr. Clapperton."

And he signalled to the reluctant farmer Fred Ruck. The pair strode side by side down to the cabin. They stood together in the rutted snow and frozen mud in front of the low building. There were over a hundred gun barrels aimed past them in both directions. They did not tell each other, but each man was feeling an unfamiliar urge in his bladder.

I went to elementary school with Kenny McLean. I dont remember seeing him around in high school. Maybe he went to high school in Penticton. Maybe he quit going to school. I never heard of him again till he got famous.

Kenny McLean was the bronc riding champion of the world.

On the highway just outside Okanagan Falls they put up a hand-carved sign: HOME OF KENNY McLEAN, BRONC RIDING CHAMPION OF THE WORLD. I dont know what happened to the sign, but it isnt there any more. Someone told me they heard from someone else that Kenny got into some kind of trouble after his last bronc broke his leg or hip or something. Maybe they took the sign down then. Maybe he did. People say they dont know what happened to him. But I know that he's living on the reserve in Penticton. Maybe I'll work up the nerve to go and see him this summer, find out what *his* story is. He's probably never heard of me. It would be interesting to find out whether he knows any stories about his great-great-grandfather.

Two men stood on the hard ground facing him, their hands hanging by their sides. Allan McLean could see the terror in their eyes. He was a defeated general standing straight as he could with blood in his clothes. He had a pistol in one hand and Palmer's shotgun in the other. Allan McLean moved his eyes, but then he settled them on John Edwards. Edwards did everything he could not to take a step backward.

Archie McLean stepped outside. He had no hat, and he looked like a waif in a thick serge coat that was several sizes too big for him. In the afternoon winter light Fred Ruck and John Edwards could see a trace of red in Archie's short hair. He was carrying two long pistols that looked as if they were weighting his arms. He would never be able to lift both those pistols at the same time.

"Are they going to throw those guns down, or what?" asked a wrangler in the trees.

"They're going to get plugged good if they dont," said his foreman, a rosewood stock smooth against his cheek.

Alex Hare stepped outside. He was the only one who looked nervous. He was carrying a beautiful pistol with his initials on it, and a pewter drinking cup. There had been nothing in the cup for days. He had put on his black hat with the wide brim and leather strap. He coughed as he stood beside the McLean brothers. He coughed, and tried to stop coughing.

Then Charlie McLean stepped outside. He stood beside his brothers and Alex Hare. No one could figure out how long it was that no one said anything. Charlie McLean looked out from the shadow of his hat, and Fred Ruck took a step backward. He stood awkwardly then, one foot back. A farmer without a gun.

The wild McLeans were in a line, black against the black and white. The hunters in the trees could have knocked them down like silent bird targets at a country fair.

John Edwards was trying to think of the right words to say. What were these people in front of him? He had seen them all many times. He had employed two of them on his land. But there was something else here.

The dangerous boys looked right through John Edwards. He felt himself becoming something he did not want to be. The eight eyes looked out of some kind of darkness. John Edwards was not afraid of these thirsty men in front of him. He was afraid of something else, and he did not know what it was. He would never seek to learn what it was. He was only glad that it was not behind him.

Now Allan's army raised all eight arms into the air. Edwards and farmer Ruck staggered backward a step or two. Frustrated men at the treeline wanted to mow them down, but Clapperton had told them that they were to do nothing until he gave the word. These were not soldiers. Some of them had been soldiers. Some of them had killed Indians, and the Indians they had found in other countries. Some of them had killed white men, or French-speakers from back east. Clapperton had his hand raised.

Allan's army began shooting the sky. Gun smoke obscured their faces. The huge noise of the shotgun in Allan McLean's right hand could be heard like sudden pain in your bones. All over the Douglas Lake country winter birds hid.

The McLeans had their mouths wide open, teeth like monuments. They were wailing, a high-pitched sound that came from a darkness Edwards knew would always be there. The McLeans' voices were as loud as the guns they were emptying into the sky.

On the little ridge at the edge of the trees the dirty men in heavy coats were disciplined and amazed. Except for one old geezer who fired a lead ball into the open doorway of the cabin.

Alex Hare fired his long monogrammed pistol into the sky, and with his other hand he held the pewter goblet high. When he brought it down at last, what would be in it?

The long high voices of Allan's army climbed and merged. These voices had once frightened some camels that galloped through a roundup party and scattered horses and hearts in every direction. Now they spooked a lot of cold begrimed men who were unsettled among the trees now that their mission was nearly complete.

"What in God's name are they doing?" shouted one man to another at his elbow.

"Indians always do that when they are giving up. Break their bows or empty their guns. Indian cant surrender while he's got a weapon left to fight with," said the other, a man with no ear on one side.

"But, shit for breakfast! They aint Indians. All the Indians are in their holes or sidin' with us. Them fellows is not Indians, Ian."

"Might as well be," said the man with one ear, "for all the good it's goin' to do them."

The McLeans were finished shooting the sky. They were not shouting any more. Archie pointed a pistol at Edwards's head and said goodbye. Then he laughed and threw the pistol as far as he could into the snow.

Justice of the Peace John Edwards would never forget that big pistol aimed at his face from fifteen feet away. The boy should not have been large enough to hold that weapon. He should not have been able to hold it above his head and discharge its bullets into the air. What was he, thirteen years old? What was he?

He would wake sweating from a dream of that gun and that face for the rest of his life. He would always be standing without a weapon of his own in front of that boy's terrible youth. Sometimes he would be clouted with bullets before he could wake up, sweating and alone in his cotton bedclothes. Long after that boy's small bones had been buried and browned, John Edwards would dream him alive again and standing in front of a deep cavern. What was in there?

Now there were a hundred men running down the slight slope toward the McLeans. A few men ran out into the snow, looking for the pistols the boys had thrown. The first steps of winter darkness had approached too, and a few of the men noticed them. Fred Ruck disappeared behind the crowd of dark clothing. John Edwards did not step toward any of the outlaws. He had seen the darkness before anyone else.

Senator Cornwall and the Cache Creek posse heard the shooting as they were approaching Douglas Lake under the birdless sky. The posse did not know what the shooting signified, but they were hoping for a fight they could win. They had come a long way. They were more interested in history than geography.

A muscular Scot rammed his shoulder against the wound in Allan's side, and Allan was the first McLean to quit fighting. They cursed in four languages. The McLean boys were experienced scrappers, and before they were subdued they gave a good account of themselves. Anger nearly melted the snow. The small figures were finally in the grasp of three or four men each.

"Decorate them," said John Clapperton.

Special constables shackled the captives' wrists behind their backs. It was not an easy task, with the McLeans twisting and cursing and moving their boots.

Except for Allan. Allan was leaning the top half of his body forward. He was sweating around the eyes. The temperature of the air was zero. In one of those peculiar silences that can cut its way among a hundred roisterers, Allan's voice came steady.

"This is how the white men keep their word."

There were Indians in the crowd, and halfbreeds. But most of the men there would call themselves white men.

"You broke the law, Allan," said John Edwards. He was thinking about politics.

Charlie McLean took a step forward, used his whole body like an *atlatl*, and gobbed in John Edwards's face.

"Is there a law about that, judge?" asked Charlie.

Three men pounded Charlie while John Edwards got his handkerchief out of his pocket.

George Caughill looked at Charlie McLean's feet. He saw the bits of metal around the edges of the toes. Those boots were more than broken in now, but George Caughill knew he wasnt going to get any of the thousand-dollar reward.

"I see you aint been taking good care of my boots, Charlie," he said.

He knocked him to the ground, where four others held him while Caughill pulled the boots off. Charlie moved his feet as much as he could with agricultural workers sitting on his legs.

Caughill took off the ratty boots he had been wearing for a few months and replaced them with the metal-tipped ones. He did not offer the ratty ones to Charlie. Charlie would be barefoot in the snow.

Now Sammy Simpson stepped out from behind someone. He nodded at Alex Ware's feet.

"Dont them look a lot like John Ussher's boots?" he asked.

The mob became, or seemed to become, furious.

They jumped all over the handcuffed people, pulled off boots and belts. They got the key from Justice of the Peace Edwards and unlocked the handcuffs. They pulled the coats off Charlie and Archie and the French boy. They took away everything they thought was stolen. Then they put the boots to the small outlaws until Clapperton and Edwards asked them to stop. They put the iron back on their wrists and forced the four people onto mules. They started the march back to Kamloops with the boys shivering on the backs of saddleless mules. Allan McLean felt every step of the mule under him.

The Chilcotin Uprising was over again.

Some wise people say that stories never end. Stories are open like doors, and no one can ever shut them. Stories stay open for hundreds of years, and grandchildren stand in front of an open door, learning to tell.

But maybe stories end more than once. End, again and again. The enemy dies, and there's an end to the story. The enemy prevails, and the story is over. The enemy puts a waxed rope knot under your child's ear, and the story just disappears. Someone is always turning to look at you one last time, to say goodbye.

When Premier Walkem got the telegram that told him the McLean Uprising was ended, he said, good, there's an end to that.

They stayed overnight at William Palmer's ranch. The victors liked back-country irony. They got a lot of chains and manacled the prisoners to the woodwork in the stall where Palmer's favourite stallion had spent most of his nights. There was a stove in the barn, and Palmer's hired hand kept it smoking all night because the barn was full of posse members. The stove was pretty close to the McLean boys because William Palmer had loved that horse, now gone somewhere under the ice. But two of the boys had no boots, and three of them had no coats. They made do with bad-smelling horse blankets that some kind cowpoke had found hanging over a railing.

It was a cold night, but Archie and Allan and Alex Hare were asleep. Their stomachs were full of water. Charlie McLean sat with his back to a wall and his knees drawn up. He had the old blanket wrapped around his feet. He didnt have a gun. He had thick black hair and he was surrounded by darkness except for the nearby glow from the front of the stove.

There was another boy sitting just outside the slats of the stall. Charlie could see only a shape in the gloom. He might have recognized the boy from some ranch he'd worked. He didnt care.

"Hey, Charlie," whispered the boy.

They were both seventeen, but one of them was the son of a ranch owner. The other was a McLean. They were not the same age at all.

"Hey, Charlie."

"That's my name. Dont wear it out."

He had to talk and shiver at the same time. He had been too cold for a good part of his life. But usually he had had a horse, or he knew where to get one.

"How many men have you killed, Charlie?"

"Enough."

The boy was hunkered right up against the slats. Firelight

picked up his face and made it even younger. There was no sleep in his eyes.

"You're going to be famous. All over the world."

"No fooling," said Charlie. Why was he bothering to open his mouth to this kid? I should have had more Indian in me, he thought.

"Get your name in all the papers. They're going to write books about you. Kids will learn about you in school," said the seventeen-year-old at the slats.

"You're a lucky boy to be sitting here right next to me. What's your name?"

"Billy Fortune."

"Why dont you give me your boots, Billy?"

"Ah, no."

There, now it will be quiet. I can sleep like tetwit Archie. Wake up and it will be just about Christmas. Get all excited about my presents.

"I never took a shot at you fellows."

He's back. This was going to be the price of fame. Snot noses in the middle of the night.

"That's what they all tell us," said Charlie. "Seems like there was a few rounds sent our direction, but it's awful hard to find anyone that fired any. Like looking for a priest with hard hands."

"Well, I never shot in your direction once," said the boy.

"Yeah, well, I reckon if you had, I wouldnt be here to tell the tale."

Billy Fortune did not understand sarcasm. He didnt know whether Charlie was joshing him or insulting him or passing

the dark part of the night with him. But there were not many
famous outlaws on the north side of the border, and this might
be the last chance he would ever have to talk with one. It was
not that he wanted something to tell his grandchildren. He
never gave a thought to having grandchildren. And even if he
did it would be an idle thought because grandchildren arent
that much interested in old stories.

"Did you ever meet Jesse James?" asked the very young boy
at the slats.

There was more light than heat coming out of the stove now.
Charlie understood that this boy was supposed to be awake all
night, putting wood into the fire.

"How the hell would I meet Jesse James?" said Charlie. "Jesse
James is a white man."

"Your father's a white man."

"My father is a dead man," said Charlie.

"White," said the boy at the slats.

"Feed the fire, or you're a dead man," said Charlie.

That was exactly what the boy had been waiting to hear.

It got colder and colder as the end of the year approached.
The geese were by now a long way south. They had made their
peculiar whistling as they crossed over the Columbia River.
People had heard them in the otherwise still air and wondered
how they were making that sound.

The salmon were far out at sea, their flesh tight in the winter
Pacific. They remembered how to get home, and many of them
would. There were Indians waiting for them. But there would
be boulders dumped by the railroad people into some of their
streams.

The colder the winter became in the Plateau country the farther down the hill slopes came the deer people. The black bears and grizzlies were asleep in their secrets. Moose horns came into sight between the bare branches of willows along the streambeds under the snow. The last caribou gave up their sweet muscles to hungry and clever men with old-fashioned rifles.

There were tracks in the snow, and tracks of something else following the tracks. It was the hungriest winter anyone could remember. Children who had acquired pocks on their faces fifteen years ago were now old people who could not walk with snowshoes between the cold trees.

There were some frightful tracks in the snow. They looked like the prints of a giant man without shoes. This was the passage of Tsi-wa-Nye-tum-wa. He is a giant fellow with thick hair on his body. He eats whatever he can find. He cannot sleep all winter without eating. Some people would like to enrol him in their plans for revenge, but he does not know revenge. He knows hunger. People have seen how little he leaves in the snow after he has eaten what he wants. No one picks up what is left. If he leaves behind a perfectly good goat's horn, no person will pick it up.

It may be that Tsi-wa-Nye-tum-wa was watching from a slope while the party of successful lawmen led the Wild McLeans and Alex Hare along the compressed snow that was the brigade road to Kamloops. He saw these men shivering on mule-back, their feet tied together under the animals' bellies, their hands manacled behind them. Their faces were lowered by exhaustion, not by shame. Their slumping bodies looked like history. Arithmetic was being combined with history in the Nicola Valley. The shaggy creature up the slope knew nothing about arithmetic. Most of the white people in the region had never heard of him, and most of those who had did not believe that he existed.

They had studied the British Empire in school. And adding and subtraction.

On December 14 and December 15 the white people in Kamloops performed two pageants that began the story. The story would be told with steel and burnished hardwood and wet stones and new rope with wax rubbed into it. There would be powerful men from the British Isles, dressed in thick dark cloth, sporting manly beards. They would devise the forward motion of the story. There would be darker-skinned boys in hastily sewn deal cloth, their hair hacked off raggedly and their hands connected to one another and to their feet by metallic contrivances. They would be the subject of the story. If they managed to slip away from the steel and stone and find their way into the low patches of cloud that drifted between the hills above the Thompson River, they might live forever. If they fell through the new resinous floor near that other river at New Westminster, no one would ever let them die.

On December 14 there were two popular funerals in Kamloops. When James Kelly the shepherd was given to the ground, he was spoken about in accented English and Latin by an Oblate father. Kelly's silver watch, rubbed and oiled and ticking the seconds away, lay in the coffin with him. When the new hero Johnny Ussher was laid to rest in the little park beside the river, his service was read by Senator Cornwall of Ashcroft manor.

Senator Cornwall said that John T. Ussher had given his life in the defence of Canada. The new Nation had to be protected against those forces that would set anarchs and satans loose among the peaceful pioneers of Christian order.

Shovels clanged against stones. The wind blew thin snow and turned the air grey. Women held up arms bent at the elbows, gloved hands on their hats.

The next day was colder. Two valleys meet at Kamloops, and a hard wind came down either valley, one from the east and one from the north. The rivers that came down those valleys were back in the ice age. They were glaciers. It was ten days till Christmas, and some people were wondering whether they would make it.

In the Kamloops Court House the stove was glowing red through the iron. A hammer could have banged it into another shape. People were happy that the stove was there, but no one wanted to be the person closest to it. Every time someone came through the outside door at the foot of the stairs a river of cold air flowed into the courtroom. Ana Richards came in once, and departed once. She did not know why she did either.

Four McLean boys and one Hare were facing their preliminary hearing. Every man with a suit was there, and nobody was in doubt regarding the outcome of the hearing. Their nascent fear had been replaced by something like triumph, but who could feel triumph in such terrible weather? Their women were at home, keeping the fire going, feeling simple relief. This was the British Empire, after all. Yankees and halfbreeds may be a threat but only for a while. Only till just order was animated to prevail. Look at the map of the world. There was something right in the path of history.

Presiding at the McLean hearing were four Justices of the

Peace. Clement Cornwall was there in his coat with the corners buttoned up. He could not wear his sword in the courtroom, he had decided, but it was in the back chambers. He and his Clinton posse had been late for the showdown at Douglas Lake, but he was here for his Queen's business. John Tait was there, a man who had put McLeans in jail often in the past. He did not hate McLeans. He just thought they were bothersome remnants of the race that would disappear in another generation or two. John Edwards was there. He considered himself the captor of the McLeans. For the next ten years he would give interviews to newspaper and magazine men who wanted to hear about the siege at Douglas Lake. And John Andrew Mara was there. He had been told often enough that the McLeans were planning to get him.

Mara was wearing his best black suit and waistcoat. He had summoned his barber this morning. His white shirt collar gleamed under his thick beard. He had eyes that could look through any solid object.

Alex Hare knew as well as anyone else what the outcome of the hearing would be. He and his companions stood in the dock, their hands and feet in irons, two of them shoeless. Charlie McLean had a huge swollen ball of dark flesh around an eye he could not open. He had scars on his forehead. One of his ears hung a little more than it should from his head. Allan must have been hearing a voice close to his head again. He was standing as straight as he could, but he had to think before he moved. Little Archie would not lift his eyes. He was counting something on the floor.

Alex Hare looked at the four Justices of the Peace. He looked at them one by one and then he returned his eyes to Mara. Could be that Mara was a handsome man, with thick wavy hair and a big nose.

Alex saw Mara leaning over Annie. He saw Mara's white skin that never felt the sun, and he saw Annie's light brown legs. He tried to see a hatchet sunk into the middle of Mara's white back.

17

* * *

EVERYWHERE THE EMPIRE went, the poets went along. But in the places where the settler population was thin, there would be no book publishers, no verse magazines. People would publish poems in the newspapers. These poems always resembled editorials. Or sermons. Editorials and sermons.

The *Inland Sentinel* carried advertisements for the Hudson's Bay Company, the Pacific Railway, and J. Kurtz, Havana cigar manufacturer. Support Home Industry! it urged. The *Inland Sentinel* reported events in Europe, of course. The Empire had its work cut out for it late in the nineteenth century, and people living far from the Old Country needed to know how it was doing. But there was also the romantic British Columbia story to be told as well, incrementally. In the tight columns of the *Inland Sentinel,* readers from Yale to Kamloops and beyond could keep track of the story, from the Chilcotin Uprising to the latest arguments in the McLean case.

But the *Inland Sentinel,* published one poem at least in each of its issues. Sometimes they would have a name attached, as in "Alphabetical Quotations From William Cowper." Usually they were unsigned, like an editorial. Usually they were placed in the upper left-hand corner of the page. You were supposed to take poems as advice in those days. A lot of the rest of the paper was meant as a kind of gentle admonishment, too. Early in 1880, right after the coldest winter on record, there appeared a poem called "Equal Justice to Rich Rogues and Poor":

Clothes that are worn at the people's expense
    Sometimes are fine and sometimes are coarse;
Men are shut up for a few paltry pence.
    Others go free, by favour or force.
He who grows rich by defrauding the State,
    Bidding the public to dance as he pipes,
Dressing in broadcloth and dining from plate,
    Ought to wear stripes.

Cobblers who labour with lapstone and awl,
    Pegging and stitching the work on their knees,
Earn what they get, tho' their gains be small,
    Not so with others, who rob at their ease.
Men who bore holes in the public purse,
    Thousands to gain, and nothing to lose,
Making our freedom a fraud and a curse,
    Ought to peg shoes.

Criminals languish in prisons today,
    Men who were trained from their youth to steal;
Others, more guilty, are brilliant and gay,
    Rich with the wreck of the public weal.
They who have thieved from one man or the State,
    Brothers in crime, like brothers sho'd dwell;

Justice should hold the small rogues and the great,
Shut in the cell.

Hard are the stones that the convict breaks,
Slowly the rocky mass crumbles away;
Easy the ruin that bribery makes,
Quickly corruption begets decay.
Truth will move onward, although it be lame,
Justice for tardiness sometimes atones;
Men who make freedom a cheat and a shame
Ought to break stones.

Every day people would say that they had reached the bottom of the winter, and from now on it would have to warm up. Every morning it was colder than the morning before. They wrapped the hoofs of their horses with bear skin. The sky above Kamloops was filled with woodsmoke. Old Indians, it was reported, were dying. The ice was more than halfway down to the bed of the Thompson River. You had to bring a frozen beef quarter in from the shed three days before you wanted to start making a roast. The traplines were bounteous, animals standing stiff.

George Caughill helped Constable Livingstone take the outlaws to Cache Creek. Caughill was thinking about his boots. Caughill was bundled up in his bearskin coat and bearskin hat. Charlie McLean had no boots and no coat and no hat. Charlie was riding in the back of a wagon with his wrists inside iron circles.

Caughill walked his horse up beside the wagon. He had his right hand on the butt of his handgun.

"I guess the shoe's on the other foot now," he said.

Charlie did not even look at him. Neither did the other outlaws on the wagon. George Caughill was not thinking of the fact that he had not made any money out of this whole capture, except for his daily special constable wages. Enough to buy tobacco and beer, not enough for Scotch whisky.

"Reckon you boys were going to shoot it out to the death, but you got cold feet," he said.

Charlie looked from time to time at Constable Livingstone. The Provincial was riding straight ahead, a scarf over the bottom half of his face. Caughill could say anything he wanted to the outlaws.

"I was going to criticize the way you boys handled this whole thing," he said. "And then I remembered. Dont say anything about a man till you've walked a mile in his shoes."

Caughill's horse was about six or seven feet from him, but Charlie looked back toward Kamloops, toward Savona, toward Dead Man's Creek.

Allan McLean was looking in that direction, too. His hands were manacled in front of him and attached by chains to his ankles. Allan's thick black beard had crusted blood in it. When the wagon's wheels banged over rocks hidden under the snow, he winced, but he never cried out. Hector McLean was sitting in the front of the wagon, beside the drover, but he was attached in such a way that if he tried to jump off the wagon he would choke to death with a chain around his neck. Alex Hare was lying down, pretending to sleep. But it was too cold to sleep. If anyone went to sleep in this air he would probably never wake up, even if he were wearing thick winter clothes. Archie McLean was sitting beside Charlie, in the middle of the wagon. Now Archie turned to the persistent Caughill.

"You better shut up, mister," he said.

He was shivering. He was fifteen years old, he figured. Fourteen, at least. But in the middle of all his shivering he could not get his voice to sound anything over ten.

"Oh no," said Caughill. He shifted in the saddle, exaggerating his comfort. "That's where you got things turned around backward, breed."

Archie hadnt lived long enough to begin to understand his brother Allan's quietness. He grew up working in someone else's mud. He had an Indian mother who was still taller than he was, and no father except in history. His father was a story no one liked. He had trouble with this bulky white man on the horse.

"I'm going to put a bullet in you, man," he said.

"Oh, your bullet days are over, breed. Where you're going they dont let you have bullets. You should just be glad you're still wearing boots. Look at your brother. Got bare toes sticking out of them sorry-looking socks. Goddam breeds dont know how to dress for the weather."

"I'll see you in hell, you bastard," said Archie.

Caughill put a big fake smile on his messy face.

"Least I got a white woman for a mother."

"I'll kill you and your fucking mother," yelled Archie.

But Allan McLean grabbed his little brother by his skinny neck and gave his head a shake. That meant shut up.

When they arrived in Cache Creek, Charlie's ears and toes were frozen. He was shaking in his irons. The five outlaws were utterly silent, and George Caughill had a satisfied smile on his whiskery face.

But Charles Semlin was the big cheese in Cache Creek. After

Donald McLean had invented ranching at Hat Creek just up the Bonaparte River, Semlin had grabbed the second-best bottom land in the valley. He had got in good with the Colonial government and then with the Province. He got them to start a school in Cache Creek, on his property. Three of these captives had gone to his school on days that werent nice enough for other activity. Charles Semlin had a feeling for Sophie McLean, but he was not John Mara. He knew what Mara had done to Annie McLean.

When Semlin saw the half-frozen children of Sophie McLean, he jumped all over Livingstone and Caughill. He told them that the Government was watching this case with special interest. Frozen prisoners would be bad news for outriders.

So now the miscreants had blankets. Charlie had boots on his swollen feet. They wore coats and shaggy hats pulled over their ears.

But they were still the ice of fear in white people's hearts. In Toronto a newspaper featured a drawing of cruel Indians dressed in breechclouts and feathers, waving axes in the air. Blood was represented by ink.

In Cache Creek the curious came to look at the uprising. Children would remember the Wild McLeans. Poets were ransacking their pockets for pencil stubs. Archie McLean looked in the direction he thought Hat Creek might be. Fifteen years ago he had been born in a log house up there. His mother had used English to tell him about his gone heroic father. The ranch hands told him a different story in Shuswap.

Now he was on his way to country he had never imagined that he would see. The McLeans and Alex Hare were dressed in coats and blankets, but they were lying face down on a layer of straw in another wagon. This time they were secured with heavy irons to rings of iron built into the wagon bed. Iron was going to define the rest of their lives.

The two old old Indians could not believe that they had survived this winter so far. They were really old. They were so old that none of the Elders along the whole Thompson Valley could remember when these geezers werent old. They spoke about a hundred languages but they spoke them all with an accent. People did not ask them where they came from. Only white people were rude enough to ask people where they came from.

They wanted to ask them a few things, of course. Such as why did they live in a mat teepee in the middle of winter, instead of in a pit house?

"Did you ever wonder," asked one of the old old Indians, "why we never tried living in one of them hole houses?"

"Call 'em pit house," said the other old old Indian.

They had forgotten which one of them was older, so they made a deal. They both thought of the other one as the young fellow. Both of them claimed to have been the other man's teacher back in the misty days of old.

"I think I remember when the Indians around here started living in hole houses. 'Bout the same time they started them steam houses."

"Or the other way 'round," said his old friend, putting a little tobacco into the tea can.

"Eeyup, reckon you could be right for a change."

"Heard a story once said that steam house idea came with some people from down south a ways."

"Wouldnt be surprised," said the other old old person.

"Whatever it is, it always comes from somewhere else."

"Not like us, eh, old timer?"

"Haw haw."

"What's the name of that Indian devil you were talking about last year?" asked one of the pipe smokers.

"Wasnt last year. I was talking about Sh-teen must a been 'bout two weeks ago."

"Weeks. Years. What's the difference?"

"Aw, you are getting old, my friend. First thing starts going is you cant remember names. Next thing you get all the years mixed up."

"Cant remember my own name some mornings."

"Dont know if I ever knew it," said his chum.

They smoked their cherry-wood pipes. There wasnt a cherry tree anywhere in the area.

"Well, anyway, I figure this Shu-mix fellow must have been sneaking around these parts lately."

"Sh-teen. Why you figure that? You been having impure thoughts again? You dirty old old man!"

"I only wish," said the first old old man. "I wish I could remember what a woman looks like so I could imagine interesting things to do with one."

"That's silly. You catch a glimpse of a woman from time to time. You even hear them talking. How else do you know what's going on around this place?"

"Indian magic. It's in the air. The wind speaks to me. The animals pass me messages."

"I have a message for you, from Coyote."

"I think I know what it is."

"Eeyup."

"More Indian magic."

"Not likely."

The second old old man went through a long elaborate series of gestures that had no particular meaning but that helped him to rise to his feet. He took very short steps during which his feet did not rise far from the matted ground, and eventually got to the large pile of sage roots and pine twigs. He picked up as many as he could carry and brought them back to the centre of the teepee, where he dropped them an arm's length from the little fire. Then he went through a series of gestures that resulted in his sitting again, his ancient legs tucked under him and his back straight. He was so old that he had had many years of practice in not looking old. He picked a piece of root and placed it on the fire. The two old old guys did not speak while they moved, and they did not move while they spoke. Now they were both still again. The fire made the only sound they could hear. The fire and the light breath of the animal that was smelling at a little hole where two sections of mat did not meet quite right.

"That Sh-teen fellow must have been goat-footing it around Douglas Lake all last week," said the first old old Indian. "Or whenever it was."

"You're talking about the McLean boys getting captured. I dont figure Sh-teen had much to do with that. People like that got their own devils."

"You talking about the McLeans?"

"Maybe some. Mainly I'm talking about all the white people was shooting at their door."

"What you figure they going to do with them boys?"

"Most of 'em is boys. That Allan McLean thinks he's a

warrior. Tries to forget he's young Donald McLean's first son
in his second what do you call it marriage."

"You figure they will hang 'em?"

"They like hanging Indians. I think they will figure out a
way to hang the Indian half of them. They just have to find
out a way to let the white half of them go."

"White magic," said the first old old Indian.

In the summertime the stages ran from Cache Creek to Yale,
where steamboats picked up passengers and Cariboo gold and
wafted them to New Westminster. But this was wintertime.
It was worse than anyone could imagine a winter to be. Constable Livingstone was tired of the McLeans. He would have
liked to go back to Kamloops with Caughill. But here he was
riding beside another wagon along a trail they had to dig
through the snow from time to time. He sat on his horse and
watched the others with their shovels. They were all new to
him except young Constable Burr. Burr looked like the kind
of young man who would rescue people from cliffsides. He
hardly ever said anything. Someday he would have a beautiful
grave in some small town in this cattle country.

Livingstone did not speak to the McLeans. Now that they
had blankets and coats and boots the McLeans were talking to
one another, face down in the hay. Livingstone thought about
punishment for outlaws. Maybe they should just manacle them
face down in a wagon and ride them forever over rough stage
roads. Maybe shoot them in the side first. He had seen blood
on Allan McLean's waistcoat.

All winter the telegraph lines had been coming down. They
worked yesterday but they did not work today. Last week they

worked for an hour one morning. Semlin had sent two men on horseback along the trail south. Policemen along the way would know the McLeans were coming. So would everyone else.

When they were finished with rolling hill country, and the gorge of the Fraser River was before their eyes, it was goodbye to wagons.

Now constables and prisoners were on horses, the prisoners in shackles, with their stirrups connected by chains. If a horse were to slip on the thin trail midway up the cliffside, there would be no chance to jump free. Horse and rider would bounce down the rock face and disappear in the fast river. Hell's Canyon was a maelstrom no ice could capture. Allan McLean looked down and saw something like himself. A few times he kneed his Government horse and felt the animal press back, away from the edge.

The brothers were all in a line, all cold, all weary, all hungry, covered with their bodies' dirt. Hector rode last, even behind Alex Hare. Allan had not spoken to Hector since Kamloops. In Kamloops he had spoken to him only once, only two sentences.

"Where were you? Where was your gun?"

Wherever the rock was not vertical there was snow on it. Little slopes of dirty ice made the horses walk slowly, with heads down. The McLeans gave themselves up to the horses and the policemen. They did not lift their heads to look back at any of the citizens who gawked at them whenever they stopped for food or mounts.

"Look at that young one," said the people who came out of their shacks and caught a glimpse of the news.

"Doesnt look any more than about twelve years old."

"Going to hang the little savage just the same."

"Clear the country of them animals, maybe we can make some progress."

"Just a child, though."

"You like 'em so much, why dont you just pack up and go live on a reserve?"

"That's exactly how all this trouble started. Started with all them squaws let loose in white people's business."

Men who found some kind of work along the trail to the Interior were hard. They thought that being hard was the right thing in this country. They thought the country itself was hard. They thought the country would give up its treasure only to something harder than rock.

They were not easy with anything that moved around the country without leaving marks.

In Victoria Premier Walkem was thinking about lunch. All the windows in his office were covered with frost. The frost patterns could capture a man's attention for long moments, as if a premier were a boy. The frost was on the inside of the windows, and the patterns were made by the unseen paths of the warmed air in the important room. Some people of an aesthetic bent would say that the patterns of frost looked like art, like paintings of the coldest winter ever known by white men in this country. Premier Walkem imagined tall frozen fir trees. He imagined a frozen sun dropping bright splinters on mountains he had never seen but was responsible for. He would have the table closest to the big stone fireplace. Slowly the leg of lamb would disappear from his plate, leaving patterns of gravy. He wondered what gravy was. Perhaps today he would take three spoons of mint sauce. That afternoon he had to go outside. He had decided to talk to the newspaper men outside, in front of the Legislature. He wanted to illustrate the fortitude of the Province's employees. He wanted the newspaper men to think about the inevitable but hard-won victory of the Empire over the most dangerous threats that nature and nature's dark brother can set in its way.

When the chained and silent halfbreed hunters arrived in Yale, they saw Christmas trees in windows. There were cedar boughs over the doorways. Yale was an important town, with lawyers and dentists and real estate offices. The biggest store in town was the Hudson's Bay Company, on Front Street. There you were promised the lowest prices on the biggest stock of dry goods, groceries, wines, liquors, and cigars.

The prisoners were taken past the Hudson's Bay Company because it was next to the water, the wide lower reach of the Fraser River. They each turned their heads and gave the big store an expressionless face. Allan, riding first, behind Constable Burr, said something in Shuswap. Charlie managed to find some moisture in his mouth. He spit on the wooden sidewalk in front of the Hudson's Bay Company store.

And they were pushed down the slope to the water's edge, the edge of ice, to the big wooden canoes. Reporters wanted to speak with the captured desperados, but the captured desperados only shouted at them in Shuswap and Kamloops French and Chinook. Then important men from Victoria spoke to the reporters in English, and moved between the reporters and the captured desperados. The reporters would have to make up their own stories. They knew what their stories should look like in Victoria.

The constables helped the iron-hobbled men into the big wooden canoes, and soon they were out in the quick water, finding green rolling space between the expanses of ice. The ice was flat in places, and in other places it was piled up on itself, forming jumbles of garbage ice. Some of the ice was jammed into piles and some of it was floating in chunks, fast down the river. The white men with the paddles were cursing just about all the time.

The McLean brothers and Alex Hare were terrified but they had decided that the closer they got to the white people's coast the more they would be Indians. They were Sophie Grant's boys, and they would sit in their chains in the fast boats, no expression on their faces. If the romantic reporters wanted them to be fearsome rifle boys, they would not tell them anything different. If they wanted them to be eagle eyes, they would not correct them.

They were hungry. They were sleepy. Their bodies were cold and their eyes were red. They were in a strange country. Over and over they heard angry strangers shout at them.

"You're going to hang, you dirty fucking Indian halfbreeds!"

The water pulled them south and west. There was never any blue in the sky now. The air was as cold as it had been on the plateau but now there was water in the air. The wet air lay heavy against their clothing. It went heavy down their throats.

Allan and Charlie were seated in one canoe, with the white paddlers and two constables with shotguns, and an important man from Victoria. Hector and Archie and Alex Hare sat in a row in another canoe, with more shotgun men. The third canoe was filled with constables. Sometimes the constables in

the third canoe practised aiming their shotguns at trees floating in the river, at man-sized ice floes.

The white paddlers had to use their paddles to push floating ice away from the canoes. They had to move their paddles
quickly, and often they made water splash onto the prisoners.
The water was a degree warmer than ice.

After most of a day's canoeing there were only narrow paths
of water between high jumbles of white ice. Still there was no
fear to be seen in the boys' shadowed faces. But their bodies
were not as straight as they had been in Yale. The heavy manacles pulled them down, toward the river.

Now there was no water's path through the ice, only wide
floes banging their edges against one another, and crooked hills
of ice. The water continued to pull, but under the ice. If they
stayed in the canoes those edges of ice would tear everything
apart and the water would pull almost every loose thing under
the ice.

Ice was piled up against the riverbanks, and there was no
use thinking of getting the canoes out of the water. They had
to abandon them and get over the ice to safety.

They all thought, back deep in the oldest sections of their
brains, that they were going to die in the river. But they were
all men on the frontier. They knew they could make it. Out
of the canoes they got, and onto the tipping ice floes. The
constables were carrying shotguns. The five prisoners were
wearing heavy chains. They had to hobble on the ice. Save your
lives, the white men were saying. Justice needs you.

They jumped from one piece of ice that sank beneath their
feet, to another piece of ice that gave way under their weight.
Allan McLean jumped, and almost collapsed his pain into the

water that suddenly opened up between the moving islands.

"Jump, you murderin' halfbreed son of a bitch!" shouted a constable. The ice made big echoes as it struck.

"Take his chains off!" shouted Charlie.

"Fuck you, Siwash!" rejoined the constable, a blond beefy person, probably three years older than Charlie. "Jump!"

They had not slept more than an hour at a time since the death of Johnny Ussher. Now Ussher was under the frozen earth in Kamloops, and they were on the water, looking for something that was not moving. Charlie looked up and almost lost his balance on his sheet of ice. He saw a white-headed eagle. He knew the eagle was looking at him, too.

The ice was piled high. No one could get over that pile of ice with chains holding his feet close together and pulling down on his hands. Not even if he was rested and well fed and warmly dressed. No McLean could get over that jumble of ice. The crooked slabs were frozen together at all angles. Any kind of range boots were going to slip on that ice. The McLean brothers pulled at the ice pile and slipped down. They fell on slabs that dipped into the moving water and back out. If someone took the chains off them they might be able to get over the ice. There were three eagles in the air over the river.

Nobody was going to take the chains off the McLean brothers. Two constables handed their shotguns to the other two constables, and then they grabbed the chains on Archie McLean. Archie weighed a hundred and nineteen pounds. Some hangman was going to have trouble figuring out the arithmetic on Archie McLean. Now the two constables grabbed Archie's chains and pulled him over the little mountain of crooked ice. Archie tried to help. He tried to get a knee on the sloping ice, but they pulled at him. They were like a river. Once they got pulling there was no stopping them. Archie's face was on the ice, and they were pulling him feet first. Finally they dumped him face down on bare gravel. He turned his head and saw the side of a steamboat frozen in the ice.

"Dont move a muscle, breed, or we'll blow your fucking leg off!"

And they went back to get another McLean.

When they pulled Allan toward the bare gravel, they left a pink line in the snow frozen to the surface of the ice.

It was the only writing Allan could read.

The next morning they were on the road again, and now the road was full of pilgrims. Steamships were frozen in the river, and anyone who wanted to be a passenger was riding in a coach very slowly toward New Westminster. The McLean brothers and Alex Hare did not want to be passengers. They were lying face down on wet straw in the back of a wagon again, feet and legs fastened with iron, iron belts around their waists.

This was the main highway from the gold fields to the coast, but it was made of stones and frozen ruts and covered with hard packed ice and drifted snow. The wagon created a terrible noise as it banged over stones and ruts, and when it did, the faces of the prone were bounced on the thin cold straw.

They were never going to agree to good behaviour. They would never be model prisoners.

There was a caravan along the lower Fraser Valley. The white people were sitting in covered stage coaches. They thought the ride was quite uncomfortable. The crews of the frozen steamships rode with them, hoping that they would be paid for these days of sitting on a bouncing leather bench.

When they stopped for the night the passengers gawked at the dark prisoners. Some of them made loud remarks that were meant to be overheard. A few of them spoke directly to the thin iron-weighted boys. The only answers they received were in a language they had never heard. The constables grinned.

At Chilliwack the constables found a stagecoach. There was a Christmas wreath hanging from the back of the coach. The horses had bells as well as iron and leather attached to them. The outlaws did not care where they were. They were too weary to imagine escape in this foreign country.

Allan McLean's hair had become long. It was shiny, blue and black, like the wing of a raven. There was none of his father's red in his hair or his beard. His eyes were black and there was no light in them. They were somewhere else. He was think-ing about the Indians at Douglas Lake. One of them was his son. His son would grow up in a village where the people were just sitting around waiting for the railroad. If the white men could finish making the railroad, they would be able to round up all the Indian people and send them somewhere else. The railroad would be far worse than the priests.

Late in the morning on Christmas day they arrived at the edge of the wide river, across from the smoke of New West-minster. A crowd of men and boys watched them hobble in their chains for an hour across the ice.

18

★ ★ ★

ARITHMETIC WAS ONE sure way to separate civilized human
beings from the dumb beasts.

The main thing you had to learn about arithmetic was how
to use it for your own benefit.

Now the people with pencils and waistcoats were talking
about arithmetic and Mrs. Annie Ussher. They were trying to
figure out how to get her a pension without paying too much
for it themselves. Johnny Ussher was a hero, and the community owed a lot to him. On the other hand, a lot of the jobs
Johnny Ussher had were Government jobs. No sense throwing a lot of dollars in the pot if it was the responsibility of the
Government. On the other hand, it would look good to
demonstrate a certain gratitude and community consideration.

So the civic leaders of Kamloops were talking about the
arithmetic. They wanted Ussher's Annie to get a pension, and
they wanted the news to get around. J. A. Mara was already
calculating how much he could throw in to start the ball rolling,
and then how much he could work his pencil on the next Government contract. With the railroad coming in J. A. Mara
knew all the places where money could appear and disappear.

He also knew how to talk to people in Victoria. Mrs. Annie

Ussher was going to get her pension, and the people of Kamloops and area were going to feel good about helping her get it. They were really grateful to Johnny Ussher. Some of them had their rifles and horses back, and the ones that never had any rifles and horses felt as if they didnt need them so much any more, what with the Indian uprising over.

The Indian uprising had a lot to do with arithmetic. One of the Government jobs around Kamloops and area was to count Indians. To get that job you had to be able to add and subtract. It got a little complicated when people like the McLeans showed up. The old Hudson's Bay men muddied up the arithmetic when they got offspring from Indian women. But now that there were four McLeans and that Hare boy safe in the Provincial Gaol in New Westminster, the counting was a little tidier.

Every once in a while an Indian person would learn a little arithmetic. Thirty years or more ago there was an Indian came from back east somewhere, name of St. Paul. He was very good at arithmetic, especially adding. Before he was finished he had progressed from arithmetic to mathematics. A lot of civic leaders on the Kamloops side of the river spent hours and hours trying to figure out how this St. Paul had gathered up all that land and all those buildings over there under that mountain. They spent their spare time studying up on long division and real estate.

Sophie McLean understood arithmetic. When her Scotchman had got himself reduced to zero in his iron breastplate, she had seen how fast pencils can move and how slowly dollars can find their way to widows. She had gone inside courtrooms and Company offices over and over again, with little McLeans behind her. After five years the white men had flashed their pencils and granted her a quiet little pension for five years. When the pension was over she was a widow with three boys and two girls.

She managed to get one of them into school. Archie. Learn reading and arithmetic, she told him. Remember who your father was.

Now in Kamloops nobody remembered Sophie McLean. Annie Ussher would have her pension. If J. A. Mara could manage it, she would have a free pass on the railroad.

The Provincial Gaol was made up of two buildings. One was a simple cell block, long and narrow. It had been emptied of USAmerican badmen and unpeaceful Indians, so that the McLean gang could be kept alone. The McLeans were history and news. They were a true story no one could hush. They showed signs of becoming a legend. For the oldest people with newspapers in their hands there was no difference.

It was a long cell block with two rows of eight cells each. These were as high as they were long, and they had little barred windows higher than a man could reach. White men with uniforms that came right up to the tops of their necks put the four killers of Johnny Ussher in alternate cells along one side. They put Hector in a cell on the other side, facing an empty cell between Charlie and Archie McLean. The warden wanted space between the McLeans. He wanted them divided. He knew a little about arithmetic, too.

It was damp in the Provincial Gaol, and these young men were from the interior plateau. They felt as if they could wring the water out of their clothes. They were wearing regulation prison pants, light coloured stuff that had been sewn by other prisoners somewhere, and whatever jackets they had come in with.

For the first day the four McLeans and Alex Hare sat on their bunks. That was all the furniture they had, that and a piss pot. Allan was lying down with new bandages wrapped around his body. They were dog tired, and they were in the semi-dark. They would not speak to anyone. They were murderers, everyone said. They had not had any whisky for two weeks. It was the day after Christmas. People had forgotten about the Wild McLeans for a day.

But the next day they were noisy, and the day after that they were noisier, and for four days they made the noise worse and worse. They shouted up and down the row of cells. When the guards came to throw wood into their stove, they laughed at them and insulted them in Chinook. When the guards brought them their limp food, they threw it back at them. Tin cups clattered against the doors.

Archie's high-pitched voice could be heard in the yard.

"Charlie! Charlie!" he shouted in his high-pitched voice. "You working on it? You got it figured out?"

Because he knew that Charlie had been in jail a lot. Archie had never been in jail, only in the school in Cache Creek. Charlie had got out of the jail in Kamloops over and over. They were McLeans! They were jailbreakers. They had business to attend to back in Kamloops. They were going to get a hold of J. A. Mara and take all his fancy clothes off and drag him down the main street to the river and chuck him in. They were going to piss on his clothes.

"Charlie!" He tried to rattle the door of his cage. It rattled a little. Rust came off in his hands.

"We'll be out of here, brother," shouted Charlie. "*Maudit* jail dont have a chance. We'll be out of here before break-up!"

Allan didnt say anything. He was thinking of his baby and the round belly of Chillitnetza's daughter.

Charlie was seventeen years old. He knew about jails. He was not thinking about Douglas Lake or Kamloops or Cache Creek. He was not thinking about his father the famous Indian fighter. He did not think of his mother or his sisters or the other McLeans. He was thinking of the high window at one end of the cell block and the rotting door at the other end of the cell block. He was thinking of horses and guns and the road he had memorized, even the part he had travelled with his face in the straw.

Hector had shouted at the guards while they were in the cell block, but his half-brothers were not speaking to him. He had not been in the cabin at Douglas Lake. He had been captured without a rifle in his hands. He had not brought the Indians for Allan's army.

Alex Hare was shouting and moving as much as he could and as fast as he could inside his cage. He was shaking the door as much as it would shake. When the food came he threw everything, food and metal dishes. He cursed the young guards. He shouted at the McLeans. He screamed at his father and every other white man he had ever known. He filled the dank air around him with noise because there was too much going on inside his head. He was trying not to imagine Annie McLean.

Allan told them many times that Annie was the reason this had all started. This war. Some war, thought Alex Hare. For me it is bad luck. I could be in Kamloops with a gun in my hand, and I could be just outside John Mara's window. If I get out of here. If I get away from the McLeans, I am going to get Mara. I dont care what happens then.

Alex Hare wondered whether he had been hanging around with the McLeans all this while just so he could see Annie from time to time. Waiting for her to be a woman. But Mara didnt wait. Maybe he could dump Mara's body in Mara Lake.

Nobody was ever going to name anything after Alex Hare.

Warden Moresby came to have a look. The McLeans were wild boys from the dry hills. They yelled in languages he could not understand. He heard them clicking in their throats.

Warden Moresby said, chain them. One by one the five prisoners were chained to the stone wall.

They could all remember doing something like that to bad horses.

In Victoria they wanted to be seen doing things right. The Province was a young man out on his own. He had to do things right or a lot of people would make jokes about frontier stupidity as compared to the estimable traditions of fair play and justice for which London was correctly envied around the globe.

The McLeans and Alex Hare had never been to London. They had never seen a judge with a tightly curled wig. They didnt vote for Confederation. They would never get used to the damp air down at the bottom end of the Fraser River.

Sometimes they would sink into a damp depression, and the cell block would become quiet and dim. Warden Moresby would order the wall shackles removed. But the next time a guard got too close, or a priest came to administer to their souls, or a Provincial official would enter the cell block, the McLeans would spit at them, and curse them in four languages.

Other times they would set to whistling, all five of them, whistling as they had done on horseback on the Plateau. No one could stay in that cell block when the McLeans started their whistling.

Then the McLeans would dance. Sometimes they danced the dances of their mother's people. They would dance for an hour at a time.

When they danced the dance of their mother's people, they remained silent except for the sound of the awkward boots that had been made in another part of the Provincial Gaol. But when they danced the awkward steps and stumbles of a Saturday night in the Dominion Hotel, they shouted and cursed in four languages. They fell against the bars and crashed into their bunks.

The whisky that had thinned their blood for several days before Johnny Ussher rode into their camp was long gone from their bodies. Now they danced the memory of whisky. Alex Hare danced with his left hand held high. He was holding an imaginary pewter goblet.

Sometimes they got out into the late winter. They could see ice on the Fraser River. It was two months later now. A man would have to test the strength of the ice, and quickly. He could live forever on the far side of the river in the Alaska tea and bulrushes. He could walk beside the river, and it would appear that he was going very fast because the river was hurtling past him, in the opposite direction. He could live forever in the sagebrush and kinnickinnick, still walking. It would all be the outermost edge of the world.

Sometimes they were let out into the persistent drizzle, and they could see the catalpa tree without a bud on its thousand branches. They were taken to a building to be fitted with boots. They were allowed to stand for an hour in front of a small frame house and then they were led away in foot shackles without finding out what was inside the small frame house.

Sometimes they were allowed outside to shuffle around under the eyes of four shotguns, while Warden Moresby and his men searched their cells. Warden Moresby often found home-made knives in the bunks. He found the remains of tin cups that would never again be used for drinking coffee made from barley.

"When will you ever learn, Charlie?" asked Warden Moresby.

"This aint a school," said Charlie.

Outside in the drizzle the boys talked to one another in Chinook and Shuswap. They talked about their escape plans. There was no wall around the Provincial Gaol, only a fence that any mountain boy could fly over.

"What about your Indians, Allan?" asked Alex Hare in one of his dark times. "Why dont you send for your Indians to come down and get us?"

Sometimes Allan would not say anything when you asked him a question. It didnt matter whether it was an ordinary question or Alex Hare's kind of question. Sometimes Allan would stand with his thumbs stuck into the pockets of his crude prison trousers and look right through your eyes into the back of your skull, the black shadow of his brow making his eyes disappear.

But sometimes he would answer any kind of question.

"No more Indians," he said.

The rain fell lightly and there was no sound of the rain landing on anything. On the plateau you could hear the rain. It sounded like a lot of animals coming through the aspens. It sounded like people on the roof.

"No more white men," said Allan.

What else is there, wondered Alex Hare.

Warden Moresby had just found a knife in Allan McLean's bunk. Now the guards held their shotguns on an angle, pointing at the sky over the river. It was time for murderers to be shackled to the wall again. Four of the prisoners hobbled into their cells. Allan McLean stopped in front of the open door of his cell and turned to face Warden Moresby and the guards.

"Get inside, please, Mr. McLean," said Warden Moresby.

Allan McLean just looked through Moresby's eyes into the back of his skull.

"Allan, return to your cell," said the warden.

Allan McLean put his thumbs into his pockets.

Moresby unsnapped his hard leather holster and pulled the long Government revolver out.

"*Túm'kst,*" said Allan.

Moresby pointed the revolver at Allan McLean. The other prisoners were quiet.

"Allan," said Moresby.

He cocked the revolver without moving the barrel a bit.

Allan McLean did not have an iron breastplate. He was not hidden in the bushes. Warden Moresby used his left hand to gesture to the guards with their shotguns.

"Return to your cell, Allan," he said, with a dangerous patience in his voice.

"I go where I want to go," said Allan, moving nothing, not even his lips.

There was nothing now for anyone to say. It was dead silent inside the cell block. The rotting door was wide open, and late winter light showed dust particles in the cold air. A piece of pitchy wood snapped in the stove and the barrel of Moresby's revolver did not move.

"Shoot!" said Allan, without moving his lips.

Everyone was perfectly still, as if posing for a photographer.

At Douglas Lake Allan McLean's wife lay with two blankets in the night, wrapped with her baby, weighted with the new baby inside her. It was the month of the spring wind, but this year the snow was piled high against the north side of the lodge-pole pines. Inside the pit house all the odours of a long winter had accumulated. Her father was in the council lodge, with the men and the smoke. Her husband was gone. He might be dead. He was always gone. He might be in the white men's prison. Her son was larger inside her. He would be the greatest warrior of all the McLeans, and he would be the greatest warrior of all the Douglas Lake people.

In Kamloops and Cache Creek and other little places along-side rivers on the plateau there were a lot of people named McLean. There were white people named McLean and darker people named McLean. The darker McLeans were not taking any chances these days. Their name and their colour were being spoken all over the Province.

At Douglas Lake it was still winter. The ice had no soft circles in it yet. Far out in the middle of the lake William Palmer's best horse lay frozen. One hoof was in the air above the ice. From time to time a finch would light on this hoof, having flown out to see whether the dark spot in the middle of the lake meant something about food. It was a long winter for finches.

Annie McLean knew what to do with a baby. She just didnt know how to get a father for him. She never took her son to see John Andrew Mara. John Andrew Mara was a great success with no time for little McLeans. Sometimes he did not look at Annie's dark red hair. He was doing enough to give her a job cleaning the worst parts of the hotel. Ever since his family had joined the British Empire he had tried to live up to its standards. He read the New Testament and thought that he could recognize himself there from time to time.

In Kamloops George Caughill kept his eye out for Donald McLean's sons. There were four in jail but there were still a few around. Caughill had been working on McLeans for more than a year, and he hadnt made much money off them. He was a special constable. He knew there were posters with other faces on them, and sums mentioned. The valleys were still full of USAmericans. But George Caughill was a McLean specialist. And he was still wearing boots that someone else had scuffed up.

Ana Richards would teach at the school for two more months. But she would never completely leave the snow country. Her boot heels left thousands of marks every day. Finches followed her, looking for seeds in her boot marks.

In his warm drawing room, standing on a thick carpet from Hyderabad, Justice Matthew Begbie practised his tennis stroke. He kept his shoulder and elbow limber all winter. He imagined the thick grass of Victoria in May, and imagined the figure he would cut in his white trousers. He swung the racquet briskly. He knew how far away each Indic urn was. He had never broken one.

19

✷ ✷ ✷

T HESE COURTROOMS WERE always small, a lot smaller than
the courtrooms in the large city in England. In New Westminster the air outside was still cold. Inside the courtroom
the packed crowd felt the genius of the carpenters who had
contrived to keep the outside air from entering and the inside
air from escaping. The people in the crowd were wearing
overcoats and mufflers. They were sweating. Those with
copies of the *Colonist* or the *Sentinel* were waving them in front
of their faces.

On the high *banc*, wearing a long white wig for this Special
Assize, was Judge Henry Pering Pellew Crease. A few years
later he would have a Sir in front of all those names. His long
white wig fell to his shoulders, longer than the crinkly beard
of black and white that fell as far as it could in front. He had
thick cascading mustaches. Under his beard he was wearing
the crisscross starched collar and valuable pin these men loved.

Judge Henry Pering Pellew Crease was from England, they
said, but anyone looking at him could see that he had some
blood that came from somewhere in the Empire. He looked
as if he might be a quadroon, as they used to say. He had a

deep voice that filled the spaces left in the room and entered the bodies covered with heavy cloth in the public gallery.

Henry Pering Pellew Crease's tale is still there, in books, in old newspapers, in magazines and journals. This is how the people from England passed their true stories and legends down from generation to generation. The descendants of those unemployed miners and curious shop clerks stuffed into the public gallery of the New Westminster courthouse are not telling Henry Pering Pellew Crease's tale to their children and nephews. Their children and nephews can read for themselves.

"The occasion which has called us together is of grave import," said Judge Crease. He said that the crimes were high ones and the law was sombre. He said that the case was famous, and that all across the country there were people who wanted to know what would happen in British Columbia today. The newspapers had settled on the phrase "the Kamloops murderers." Judge Crease wanted to put the trial of these Kamloops murderers into the context of history.

"We are brought face to face with the condition of our numerous and growing halfbreed population throughout the country," he said in his deep voice.

Some of the faces in the crowd settled themselves into the shape that comes with generous sympathy. Others were glazed over with impatience.

"What is their future?" asked Judge Crease.

A lot of people in the crowd were ready to resist generalization. They were interested in the future events of the McLean story.

"Sons of the hardy pioneers, who pierced the Rocky

Mountains and freely flung themselves into the heart of the wilds and forests of the Interior and up to the Arctic Ocean in search of furs, often to save their lives, allied themselves to the native tribes who surrounded them."

The crowd was quiet and attentive now. This was *good*.

"So long as civilization kept away from them, or they from civilization, all was well. They fell into many of the habits of the natives among whom they lived, and many a trapper and trader owes his life to the fidelity and sagacity and courage of his Indian wife. The offspring of these marriages, a tall, strong, handsome race combined in one the hardihood and quick perceptions of the men in the woods, with the intelligence and some of the training and endurance of the white man, which raised them into a grade above their mother's but not yet up to the father's grade."

Allan McLean thought that sounded a little too much like arithmetic.

"Quick shots, unrivalled horsemen, hardy boatmen and hunters, they knew no other life than that of the forest. They never went to school or had the semblance of an education, and when the wave of civilization, without hurry, without delay, but without rest, approached, it met a restless, roving halfbreed population, who, far from imitating, did not understand the resistless agency which was approaching them."

Archie did not whisper. He spoke quietly to Charlie.

"I went to school," he said in Chinook.

"But you are not civilization," said Charlie. "You are population."

Judge Henry Pering Pellew Crease stopped and waited.

Despite what the judge had said, the two guards towered over the boy in the prison-made trousers.

"So long as the white father lived, the children were held in some sort of subjection, but the moment he was gone they gravitated towards their mother's friends and fell back into nature's ways."

It was Alex Hare's turn. He let out a whoop that cut like lightning through the dense hot air of the little courtroom. The visitors in the gallery felt nature in their nerves.

Judge Crease argued that there is no effect without cause. He raised the possibility that civilization could have done better with schools and constables.

The jury listened. They liked a good story. Who didnt? But they had pretty well made up their minds about these halfbreeds.

On Tuesday the four prisoners were again behind the railing in the courtroom. Today the McLeans and Alex Hare would be indicted for murder and a jury would be gathered for their fate.

Archie was looking at the floor in front of his crude boots most of the time. Once he looked over at his brother Allan because Allan was eight years older.

Allan had shorter hair now, but tucked into his hair behind his right ear there was a little feather, painted red and black.

The jury knew it was just a jury. The jury waited for the lawyers. The lawyers could talk all they liked about responsibility and widows. The jury would get to the hanging.

The newspapers loved it.

The great Indian uprising of 1879 had not panned out, but the dastardly murders near Kamloops were high-grade ore.

A forty-five-year-old husband with a neat brown beard was reading the words set in type by the Victoria *Colonist*. His forty-one-year-old wife was perfectly capable of reading the *Colonist* herself, but her husband was holding the opened newspaper in both hands and reading it aloud to her. He did this every time he brought the *Colonist* home with him after his day in the office at his school.

Then they would have a discussion of the news. The husband did not say so in so many words, but he considered this a continuation of his work as an educator. The wife, who could read four languages, two of them used in the Church and among medical people, and the other two used by fur traders, agreed with the husband's views as often as she could bring herself to do so. At other times she attempted to focus his attention on the relationship between words set in type and the feelings of normal human beings in families.

"A systematic opposition to authority," said the husband.

"Are they going to hang those boys?" she asked.

"They murdered two men in cold blood," he said. "The Good Lord knows how many others they might have killed in their rampage."

"Others?"

"That we do not know about," said the husband.

"They are boys," she said. "Just boys."

"Savages," said the husband. The wife was doing something with her hands, repairing something.

"But Robert, how old are those boys? They are children. Some of them," she said.

Now the educator did look up from his newspaper.

"In the paper one day last week," he said, gruffly patient, "the law which obtains in this Province was explained. No person can be found guilty of a crime until the age of seven. Between seven and fourteen he can be found guilty of committing a crime. In such a case the court must determine whether the criminal was cognizant of right and wrong and whether he was aware of the consequences of his wrongdoing."

"How old is that youngest boy?" she asked. "I have heard that he is fifteen. I have even heard that he was fourteen when the terrible things transpired."

"It is probable that he is sixteen. When *I* was sixteen I was working in the shipyard, trying to keep my family in food and clothing."

It was his opinion that he had made a very good point there.

"They are surely going to hang them, Robert?" asked the wife.

"Men are hanged every week, Martha. It is the consequence of their murderous ways. And it is the law of the British Empire."

"Boys."

"I beg your pardon?"

"Boys. You said that men are hanged every week. These are boys. Do you know how old our oldest daughter is, Robert?" asked the wife. She had not stopped her work with her hands.

"She is fourteen," he said. "Fifteen."

"She is seventeen," said the wife, her voice low and even. "Can you imagine a man pulling a hood over her head and tightening a thick rope around her neck and stopping her life?"

It was rare that she should try to prompt his imagination in this manner.

He stood up. He pulled his rumpled jacket down at the sides of his body.

"Good God, woman!" he shouted. "My daughter is a school-girl! She is not some animal, running loose in the trees!"

The lawyers performed and the jury sat silent. The prisoners sat silent, but for the occasional remark addressed to one another in Chinook or to the witness who was at the time vilifying all McLeans.

The defence lawyers decided that it would be for the better if they did not summon their clients to the witness stand. They looked like injured hawks in a cage.

The four halfbreed youths sat silent while white men in white wigs created perfect sentences out of words such as "gallant" and "irrefragable."

The name of Annie McLean was not spoken by anyone.

And now the lawyers were finished. Henry Pering Pellew Crease addressed the jury.

"Malice," he instructed them, "makes all the difference between homicide and murder."

The words described the death of John Ussher. They described the wounds found on the frozen body, and the way in which they were made.

John Ussher died on the frozen ground, and his blood poured out of knife wounds. The bones in his forehead splintered. There were stained boys all over him. He called their names and they killed him.

John Andrew Mara's name was never mentioned.

Alex Hare was trembling. He dropped his face and put his hand over his eyes. His back was shaking the way a horse will shake after you hit her between the eyes with a sledgehammer.

Charlie McLean began to shake as well. He put his hand over his mouth and the thin hairs that would not grow into a mustache, even in the Provincial Gaol. Then he dropped his hand but his head dropped too. His rough haircut was all that anyone could see.

Allan McLean was not there. Those who could catch sight of his face saw no eyes. No one knew where he was. His black beard could have been a lightning burn in the trunk of a red pine.

Little Archie was trying to look like a killer from the high country. He wanted to be wherever Allan was.

"It rests with the jury," Crease was saying, "to re-establish the moral effect of the law in the Interior. There has never been so serious, so open, so flagrant a defiance of the law as this, and should the jury fail in its duty the consequences would be almost irreparable."

That was the equation set before the jury. If they could hang these four people, aged twenty-four to fifteen, the Province would be saved.

"I have great pity," the Judge said, "for the prisoners. I have great pity for their youth. But the force and majesty of the law must be carried out, here as in the home of justice. You must give your verdict without fear, without favour, and without affection."

The jury left the room, which filled with the voices of those lucky enough to have found a place. A few men went outside in the drizzle to smoke tobacco.

Will I die?

The jury came back in twenty-one minutes.

Am I going to die, really?

The foreman said, we find the defendants guilty of the wilful murder of John Ussher. Quickly the judge said, I concur with your verdict.

What are they saying, I am going to die?

I ask your Lordship to pass sentence.

I shall pass sentence ". . . tomorrow." Ample time will be set aside for the accused ". . . to prepare."

For death.

What does that mean, what are they saying? There is still a chance? Tomorrow? Look at Allan. He is not here today.

There was a sheep farmer near Lower Nicola who one day looked up from an animal he was putting his identification upon, and saw a group of horsemen riding at a walk along the crest of a grassy hill. He watched as the horsemen, about a dozen in all, turned toward him and rode at a walk down the gentle slope of grass. As they neared he could see that they were not exactly cowboys, and certainly they were not the kind of roustabouts who worked for the railroad.

He stood and watched as they came closer and closer. Now he could hear the sounds of leather, and steel rubbing on leather. He could hear the horses breathing.

He walked over and stood next to his own horse, which was attached to a small wagon. The wagon was carrying paint cans and shears and other items a man needs at work.

Now the dozen riders were so close that he could see what they were wearing. They were dressed half in Indian materials, buckskin and feathers, and half in the shapeless dark cloth of the western cowpoke. They were all wearing wide-brimmed hats, but the hats had feathers in them.

Under their hat brims they all had light brown faces.

The sheepman could see the stocks of carbines and shotguns sticking out of scabbards on their saddles. He could see pistols lying against their chests and sticking out near their waists. He saw bandoliers of ammunition crisscrossed on their bodies.

Closer still they came, and now he recognized the four riders at the front.

He could not help speaking aloud.

"It's the McLeans. God Almighty. The McLeans have got loose again."

Everyone knew what the sentence would be when Henry Pering Pellew Crease came back to the New Westminster courthouse on March the twentieth. But the room was packed again.

The four outlaws stood in the dock. No one could tell from looking at them that they were going to be told about their frightening end. Did they understand the last few days differently from everyone else? Were they some kind of people who did not understand how justice worked? Were they some kind of people who did not care about life or about death?

"Allan McLean," said Judge Crease. "Do you have anything to say against the judgement that is to be passed upon you for the murder of John Ussher, of which this court has found you guilty?"

Allan stood straight. The wound in his side was not yet healed but it was over. It was part of him.

"John Ussher was not the person," he said. "Your witnesses

from up there in the country all know who the person is. The people."

The judge and jury and the guards and the reporters did not know what Allan was talking about. But his brothers did.

Alex Hare saw Annie McLean on her knees. Her dark red hair was not tied in braids. It was falling over her undressed shoulders. Alex shook his head and opened his eyes as wide as he could. He had to get Annie out of that courtroom.

"Archibald McLean," said Judge Crease, veiling his impatience with Allan's unknowable references, along with his reluctance to do this on this day. "Do you have anything to say against the sentence of death to be passed upon you today?"

"I did not kill Johnny Ussher," said Archie, in his high thin voice. "He killed us."

Even his brothers wondered whether little Archie knew what he was saying.

"Anything else?" asked Judge Crease.

Archie did not say another word. His chin was moving.

"Charles McLean," said Judge Crease. "What have you to say against the passing of judgement upon you for the crime of murder?"

Charlie stared at the Judge for a long time. He was interested in the Judge's English accent. The white men in the Interior had several kinds of accents. But the ones that owned ranches and the ones that were Government men had that English accent. Some of the others might shoot you or stick a knife in you, but the ones with the English accent were going to hang you.

"We just wanted to stay out of jail," said Charlie.

"You killed Constable Ussher because you wanted to stay out of jail for theft?"

"There was something we had to do. Couldnt do it in jail."

"Will you tell us what that was, Charles McLean?"

"That's all," said Charlie.

When they got out they would take care of J. A. Mara.

"Alexander Hare," said Judge Crease. "What have you to say against the passage of the sentence of death upon you for the murder of John Ussher, of which you have been found guilty by this court?"

"I pick my friends poorly," said Alex.

Judge Crease repeated his question. It was a question he had to ask powerless men over and over. It was a part of his duty that he tried to forget when he was performing his role elsewhere.

"I never killed anyone, ever," said Alex, his voice rising. He shouted angrily. "Everybody's been lying! Your goddamned witnesses sent their souls to hell! These boys might have killed somebody. I dont know. Every word I've heard in this goddamned room has been a goddamned lie!"

Dark red hair. Long fingers touching things that.

"The men who were at your camp with Constable Ussher have testified that you were one of his killers," said Judge Crease.

"I have nothing else to say," said Alex Hare. He turned his back toward the Judge.

Henry Pering Pellew Crease stood up to pronounce. His long curled wig fell perfectly on both sides of his head and fell against his chest, longer than his frizzy beard. His African eyes looked out from his disguise. If such a face with such a beard and long curled white hair had appeared suddenly at a camp-fire in the middle of the night, the men around the fire would have run into the trees.

Now he gave his third speech. He told the four soon to be condemned that they had had a long and patient trial, with able counsel and many challenges. Then he said something that perhaps explains why the McLean brothers do not appear in recent histories of the Province.

"You have caused great terror throughout the country, and by a campaign of robbery and assault and murder you have disgraced British Columbia."

Heads were nodded in the visitors' gallery.

"You, Allan McLean, were not content to forfeit your own life by your errant course, but have led your younger broth-ers into a short life of crime. Such a case as yours has seldom occurred in any civilized country."

Heads were nodded.

"You have disgraced the name you bear, instead of honour-ing it."

Disgrace again. They knew that one.

"Your Saviour may be merciful," said Henry Crease. "But you know that you need not expect mercy here. I counsel your atten-tion to the mercy of your Saviour. The sentence of this court is that you be taken to the place whence you came, and from thence to the place of execution, there to be hanged by the necks until you are dead. May God have mercy on your souls."

Then the guards, happy to be in motion again, led the boys in their chains toward the side exit. As luck would have it, William Palmer was standing near the door, hoping to have a last good look at the dirt cleansed from his part of the world.

As he was hobbling by, Allan McLean managed to swing a leg. His boot caught Palmer hard, just next to his crotch. Palmer screamed and fell against a wad of bodies. The force of Allan's actions against his own chains threw him to the oiled floor. He felt blood seeping again.

"Send that to your partner Mara," shouted Allan.

Then the guards were on Allan and his brothers and Alex Hare. Clubs descended on their heads and backs and arms. The guards were joined by other men. Chains protected them and damaged them. The prisoners cursed and tried to hit back, but there were too many men bashing them. It was the same way after they surrendered at Douglas Lake. Then their faces were pushed against the packed snow and stones. Now their faces were pushed against the oiled boards.

20

Archibald Minjus waited for the rain to stop. He waited for almost a week, and then on Tuesday morning the sun came out, bright as a new axe. Brighter. It slashed off the whitened walls and turned dark things white. It was too white for his lenses, and he would have preferred to wait for an overcast day, when the shadows would differ and allow details to be celebrated by silver.

But Warden Moresby was not a subtle man. If the sun was shining the picture-maker could work. He gave Minjus half an hour. He told the McLeans to put on their best clothes and brush their hair.

They were going to get their pictures taken for the first time in their lives.

"Do they have to wear those devices?" asked Minjus.

Allan McLean raised his hands and smoothed his hair. He was almost natty in his first photograph. He was wearing the standard prison pants made of shapeless white duck, and prisoner-made boots. But he still had the dark dress jacket he had always insisted on wearing to mark him off from the riffraff, and the vest that went with it. He had knotted his kerchief around his neck. His hair was longer than the hair of his fellow prisoners, who had scissor jobs, the thick stuff pushed forward. Allan's hair was parted and brushed. It had Scottish waves in it. His black beard was short and even. The bright sun flashed off his forehead and left his eyes in darkness under his brows.

He had a little painted feather in his hair, behind his right ear.

Warden Moresby would not let Minjus pose the four together. He did not want anything to do with threatening groups. These boys were facing individual fates, and they would have individual lives till that moment and afterward. Warden Moresby knew how the people in Victoria and Kamloops felt about groups of certain kinds of people.

So Minjus set his three-legged box in the bright prison yard and took away their images, one by one.

Archibald Minjus, photograph-maker, was at war with himself. In Victoria the beldames and the politicians with expansive bellies identified themselves with the birth of a great city. They wanted a permanent record of their weight. Archibald Minjus ducked under his black hood and transferred them to silver. He posed them in front of thick carpets on the wall. He sat them before a waterfall that would never move. They were interested in solidity and he was selling solidity. He made a tidy living among the high society of an ocean town full of eager prospectors.

But silver is an old argument. Place it in an upturned hand and you can purchase a human soul. Shine a trace of light on it within a profound blackness and you can glimpse the edge of a spectral wing. In his laboratory Archie Minjus ran flecks of darkened silver down his sink drain. In his infernal liquids a succession of faces appeared, death by death. He had killed hundreds of well-coiffed citizens.

Now he wanted to see a wing. Optimistic and powerful men were laying iron rails in the mountains and they required proof of their heroism. Minjus was going to Kamloops. He would climb stone with his big square camera. He would take away buckskin souls.

In New Westminster he had been waiting for days in the rain. Now he was under his black cloth, looking at an upside-down Allan McLean. The world may come through the glass, but he was alone in a hooded darkness that always seemed final.

He whispered to himself to stay alive.

Charlie McLean stood the way Allan did, with his thumbs in the front pockets of his crude prison trousers. He held his dark cap in one hand. He looked like a boy who had never lifted a rifle. His eyebrows were squeezed against the bright sun and the eyes were slits in the darkness under them. He had a thin mustache and a thin beard on the end of his chin. Minjus did not know that these had grown at last in the three months since Douglas Lake.

The McLeans did not know how to be photographed. They had no waterfall to sit before. They just stood with their feet close together because of the iron bars that ran the length of their legs. They took turns standing in front of the whitewashed wall with a dark narrow rifle slot in it.

Later, in his room at the inn, Minjus would lay the prints side by side on a table. He placed his hands over each body, and looked at the faces. They could have been soldiers. They could have been a family. He placed his hand over the bottom half of Archie McLean's face. The child's narrowed eyes looked as if they were filled with pain, from the white sun.

Archie McLean stood with his bandaged right hand tucked

part way inside his shirt. The waist of his rough prison trousers, with the belt of the leg restraint around it, was too high. He looked like a boy in men's clothes.

Alex Hare was wearing a dark shirt several sizes too large for him. The sun whitened his Gallic Indian face. Not a whisker grew on him. His eyes looked as if they belonged to a veteran of terrible wars in nations no one had ever heard of. Alex Hare was not a wild McLean. He was a son left behind. Archibald Minjus was a little afraid of this upside-down *peri*.

Under the hood he could not see Warden Moresby and his shotgun fellows.

He was making shades out of dead silver. These four half-breeds were dark shadows and white ones. They were the zone of translation. They were bad news of the future for the Indians, and bad news of the past for whites. They were trapped in a ghost life, like a high waterfall caught by a slow lens. They could never have participated in either community.

Community? Minjus asked himself. What the hell is community?

When they hanged these boys they were going to weigh shadows. They were going to hang images. The graveyards of British Columbia would be full of stones with the name McLean on them, but there would be no stones for these boys.

All the way up the rivers people were going to be busy adding and adding. From time to time someone had to be called upon to do some subtraction.

Archibald Minjus closed the legs on his tripod and put it over his shoulder. Arithmetic was over for the day. It was the third day of spring. By summer he would be in Kamloops and the McLeans would be out of the sunlight.

But the sun shone all summer, and the McLeans and Alex Hare knew the darkness of their cool cells with the high windows. Their lawyers visited from time to time, not to listen but to inform them about politics and law. Their priests came often, one old Irishman and one young Frenchman. They told the prisoners that suicide was out of the question. Only God, they counselled, had the right to take lives. This opinion did not go down well with three teen-aged boys and a young adult who had been condemned to a gibbet in a New Westminster yard.

As for the four prisoners, they were thinking of getting out of this dark building and killing a few businessmen in the Kamloops region, starting with Palmer and Mara. Father Harris and Father Chireuse advised that vengeance belonged to the Lord.

"This Lord of yours," said Allan McLean. "We've been hearing about him all our lives."

"He is your Lord as well, *mes enfants*," said Father Chireuse. He was two years older than Allan.

"So why are we in here? Why is our Lord going to let us get hung?" asked Charlie. Charlie had never cared much for priests and churches and the like. The first robbery he had ever done took place in a church at night.

"Our Father works in ways we cannot always understand," said the young priest from France. He had been ordained less than a year before. Father LeJeune had asked him to go to New Westminster.

"Our father worked in ways everyone could understand," said Allan. "If you were a Government man, get out of the way. If you were an Indian, say your prayers."

Allan laughed. When Allan laughed his brothers laughed.

But Allan's laughter struck a kind of fear into their stomachs.

"I have heard stories about your father," said the Frenchman.

"Dont believe them," said Charlie. "Some of them are lies and some of them are true stories you'd be better off not to believe."

The young priest from France had a dark shadow of whiskers. He shaved twice every day. He was very masculine in appearance, and he wore a black skirt. He spoke to the prisoners in English and French, but he always let them pick the language. Sometimes when he was there the prisoners spoke to each other in a language he could not begin to understand.

"Will you pray?" he entreated them.

"We'll talk to Coyote," said Allan.

"You will talk to a fox, an animal?"

The Church represented by Father Chireuse did not approve of the presence of animals in religious practice. Not unless they were sacrifices, or metaphors.

"Our father is dead," said Allan. "Coyote is still alive. You will meet him one day. When you do, you might think of praying. But dont pray to an animal, priest."

"I will come back to see you," said the French priest. He was impatient with himself. The French boy Hare had not said a word.

After the McLean trial the warden moved other prisoners into the cell block, so now the place was a lot noisier. The four McLeans and Alex Hare were in adjoining cells, and when the other prisoners were taken out in the morning for their work details, the killers of Johnny Ussher could hear one another without shouting so loud.

They sang loud enough to hear one another. They danced,

each alone in his cell. They made careful weapons and had them confiscated. When they spoke to other convicts they boasted about their death sentences.

But they were beginning to adjust to their fates. Judge Crease had said "not less than two months' time." The words were confusing, heard through the ringing in their ears. But they understood, at last, that they would be alive in these hard rooms until the end of May. The Shuswap people called it Digging Roots month.

Alex Hare was the only one who could scratch his name on his whitewashed wall. He scratched his short name and added a word in his father's language. Mort. In another corner he scratched tiny capital letters. AM.

Allan McLean could not write anything, but he spoke to his lawyer, a message for his wife, the daughter of Chillitnetza. While the lawyer held pencil to paper, Allan looked at the wall. He did not know what to say, a father in a death cell. Another father in the unknown ground far from home. A man who would never know that his son would be the last great warrior of the plateau people.

"How is the boy? What is the new child? I send you my love with this. Write me the answer soon or I will never know. I die before summer. Goodbye from your husband Allan McLean."

Would she dig bitterroot this year, or would she remain beside the lake with her babies?

Two more McLean brothers.

Not two months. Now the Premier and the Supreme Court became embroiled in an argument that had been lying beneath the case since the beginning. This was a new province in a new country. Ottawa was important and Victoria was important. Here was the technicality: had the Assize Court been commissioned properly? There had been no reading of a commission at any time in the trial. Had there been a trial? Famous lawyers and judges and politicians remembered every bad feeling they had ever had about one another.

There had to be an enquiry. Premier Walkem was there. Henry Pering Pellew Crease was there. John Hamilton Gray was there. Matthew Begbie, the hanging Judge was there.

The McLean Brothers and Alex Hare were not there.

The enquiry would reach its decision on June 1. The McLeans were reprieved till June 2.

The enquiry was taking longer than expected.

The McLeans were reprieved until June 17.

Chief Justice Begbie grew angry. He shouted at people to sit down.

Everyone shouted. First they were polite in the lawyer's way. Then they shouted impolitely.

The McLeans were reprieved until June 31.

Allan McLean sat in his poorly lit cell and filed the iron on his ankle. He had a pretty small file with fine teeth. He had been filing for several days. When it was dead quiet in the middle of the night, except for the snoring of the prisoners you could hear Allan's file. Archie listened to Allan's file. He still thought that his oldest brother would save him. The warden had taken away dozens of home-made weapons. But the warden had never seen Allan McLean sitting at the base of a lightning-struck tree.

Judge Gray and Judge Crease and Judge Begbie knew who

killed Johnny Ussher. But they were British. They knew that the majesty of the law recognized no favourites. They decided that there had been no commission, and there had been no trial.

The accused killers were granted a new trial.

Allan McLean waited for a letter from his wife at Douglas Lake.

His brother Charlie had a dream about camels.

Mary Anne Moresby was like a dream. She was always singing. During the long afternoons when the other prisoners were away at their work details, the McLean boys could hear Mrs. Moresby singing in the yard outside her house. She sang songs they had never heard. They had never heard a woman singing in the plateau country. The only songs they had heard were the mountain songs of the Shuswap people and the bawdy or sentimental songs the white cowboys performed badly around a campfire.

Mary Anne Moresby was sitting in front of Allan's cell, probably because she and Allan were the same age. She thought of the other members of the gang as the young ones, or at least that's the way it seemed to them. That was all right with Archie. Archie had not really had time to think of women as anything but mothers, or big sisters, like Annie.

Mrs. Moresby was reading the Victoria newspaper, all about the terrible waste of money the legal system and the politicians had committed, holding a trial that turned out to be illegal. According to the newspaper, the lawyers and police and politicians deserved the fate that the McLeans were sure to face.

"Do you want to hear this?" she would ask Allan.

"Read it all," he said.

"The McLeans are not going to face any fate," said Charlie. "The McLeans are going to be riding their own horses in their own country come winter."

"Damn right," said young Archie. "Sorry," he said.

"Read it all," said Allan. It was just barely light enough to read in the corridor of the Provincial Gaol. It was just enough for Allan to see the pile of light brown curls that fell around Mrs. Moresby's forehead.

Mrs. Moresby had a little boy, Willie, who came to see the prisoners. Allan turned his back as soon as he saw the little boy. He went to the opposite wall of his hard room and would not turn around. Whenever Willie was there, Allan McLean looked at the wall.

She read the whole article to Allan and the others, and then she read some other items. She read the quotations from Tacitus. She read a story about an optician in Yale who had made a pair of glasses for somebody's pet dog. She read about crimes.

"A shooting affray took place at Mudslide on Friday evening, June 25th. The circumstances are as follows: An Italian called upon Captain Thomas and requested him to furnish him with some eggs, to which Mr. Thomas consented. During the time occupied, the Italian had divested himself of coat and boots and taken to himself a bed, to which the other objected, also ordering the visitor to leave immediately, to which the Italian replied by using some profane language; the captain then produced a revolver and shot him in the calf of the leg, after which the Italian proceeded on to Cook's Ferry, and lodged a complaint; the assailant has been arrested, and will shortly have a hearing before Justice Murray."

"He'll get off," said Charlie. "He just shot an Italian."

Charlie was comfortable with the visits of the warden's wife. So was young Archie. Alex Hare gave the impression of being withdrawn from just about everything, even the McLeans, but he was leaning against the bars of his cell, listening.

Allan McLean was not comfortable. He had his jacket and shirt buttoned. He saw the collar that came up to just under her small pink ears. He hated Warden Moresby.

"If you're tired of reading that there noose-paper, ma'am, would you sing us a song now?" asked Archie. He knew that she would. He knew that she would sing a song he did not know. She would sing songs in the courtyard after he was a dead boy.

Mary Anne Moresby had a lovely heart and no irony. She stood up from her kitchen chair and put her hands together behind her striped dress. She swayed from foot to foot as she filled the dark cool building with her unhesitating girl's voice.

> What noble courage must their hearts have fired,
> How great the ardour which their souls inspired,
> Who leaving far behind their native plain
> Have sought a home beyond the Western main;
> And braved the perils of the stormy seas,
> In search of wealth, of freedom and of ease!

Mrs. Moresby's eyes were looking at something far away. Archie could not see her eyes, but he loved her voice. He felt like a child while she sang. When she had done, and after she had taken her chair outside with her, he would be tough and funny again.

Allan did not hear the words of the song. He stood perfectly still, watching her sway lightly, back and forth.

They took Hector away. They wanted to find out whether he could be found guilty of conspiracy in the murders of Johnny Ussher and the sheepman Kelly. Up to Kamloops they took him, and applied the white man's oral culture to him, in a little courtroom with jail cells in the back.

The times were confusing. The law of the white people, especially the real white people, liked to tell stories about individuals, as if people could be made into ones.

Standing in the little dock in Kamloops, surrounded by white people in white wigs, and white people in town clothes, he pretended to be one. He was thinking in Shuswap and trying to listen in English. It was really hard to keep the pronouns straight. The white people were so persnickity about pronouns.

The white people wound up telling this story.

Hector knew that his young half-brothers had committed crimes of a serious nature, but he let them stay at his place. He gave them food to eat. If he could have got food and water to them in the cabin at Douglas Lake, he would have. McLeans are McLeans, no matter who their mother is. Hector McLean was probably going to get a lot of halfbreeds or Indians together eventually, and help Allan mount his uprising.

But Hector McLean was not an accomplice in the murders of Johnny Ussher and the sheepman Kelly.

They had to let him go.

This made people around Kamloops pretty nervous. If they let Hector McLean go, what were the chances that they would have to let Sophie's sons go, one by one, on some technicality?

In the Provincial Gaol in New Westminster the boys were perked up a bit when they heard about the verdict. If Hector could be released by those wigged white men in front of those angry white men, maybe there was hope for the rest of them. Or maybe now Hector would not fail them as he had failed them at Douglas Lake.

The younger ones looked at Allan when they got the chance. They were in the courtyard in the filtered sunshine, in their irons, watched over by the shotgun boys. What was Allan thinking? It looked as if Allan had given up thinking. That meant one of two things. Either they were as good as gone on fresh horses under the pine cones, or they were dangling on rope.

21

THIS TIME THE JURY was out for an hour, an hour and fifteen minutes. People in the visitors' gallery were getting nervous. Everyone knew that the McLean boys had killed Ussher and Kelly. Hadnt they been found guilty once before, and in a few minutes that time? Their lawyers had rejected seventy jury candidates. They had raised every legal argument they could lay their hands on. The murderers had smiled and whispered together and gazed with contempt upon the witnesses. Were they going to get off with some technicality? The jury was out for almost an hour and a half.

The jury came back and pronounced the Queen's people guilty again.

Once more Henry Pering Pellew Crease asked the condemned whether they had anything to say before he pronounced the sentence everyone knew was coming. The young man and the three boys in the dock glared at him and said nothing.

Judge Crease then told them what was going to happen to them, and offered his prayer that the god of the white part of them would have mercy on their souls.

He said that the gibbeting would take place in January.

Unless the Governor-General of Canada had it in mind to commute the death sentence.

The Governor-General was John Douglas Sutherland Campbell, the Marquess of Lorne, later to become the Ninth Duke of Argyll. All those Scottish names did not bode well for the dark children of Donald McLean.

They had been in irons and inside their small cells for over a year. They had been there forever, it nearly seemed. Yet their lives were going to be short. There was not going to be any mercy from the white men they had seen or the white men back east they had never seen. Their lawyers were working late into the night, hauling out old books and looking for a lever in them. But the white fur traders and gold jumpers and land grabbers wanted to hang the halfbreeds. Their sister was condemned to carrying a land grabber's spawn in her belly. Their mother was pushed off her ranch. They had been forced to find their own food and boots before they were ten years old. The fur traders and gold jumpers and land grabbers were not going to give them ten acres of cliffside each. They were going to give them a hole in the ground and never tell anyone where it was.

The only hope they had was escape. They rubbed every piece of metal they could get and made knives that were found a few days later by a guard or asked for by a priest. They worked diligently in the night while other prisoners snored. But they knew they were not going to ride into Kamloops again.

Charlie would not speak to the others prisoners, and then he would not speak to the Warden's son Willie, and then he would not speak to his brothers except in the Shuswap words he could remember. Charlie was trying to remember something his mother had told him, about a grandfather who had the gift of death. He wanted to die as an act of will and cheat their hangman.

The priests talked to them in French and English. The priests said that suicide would lose them their souls. They offered the glory of God's presence. They would be in God's bright house. No more sleeping on the ground. No more running away in the snow.

Allan looked at the young man in the black skirt for half a minute without speaking, though it was obvious that he would speak. He was wondering whether the priest would know exactly what he was saying.

"Father, when I am up there in the glorious presence of this Lord, will I be able to watch what he does to Mara and the others?"

While the McLeans and Alex Hare spent 1880 in their hard rooms the dynamiters blasted their way through the Province. While they danced in their daytime gloom small Chinese men were falling down the faces of granite cliffs. It would have to be left to the ghosts of the McLeans to ride against the railroad.

The railroad did a lot of business with Member of the Provincial Parliament J. A. Mara and his partner W. B. Wilson. The Member of the Provincial Parliament thought it would be a sensible thing to get the city renamed. What kind of name was Kamloops? People back east were going to know the most important stop on the Main Line. They would laugh at a name like Kamloops. What the hell did Kamloops mean, anyway?

He never thought of asking the thin woman who starched his shirts.

"Dont read us any more about the railroad," said Allan.

Mary Anne Moresby was sitting on her kitchen chair, reading from the *Mainland Guardian*. Little Willie leaned against Archie's cell bars, staring at the older boy inside. Willie's father had told him over and over to stay two steps away from any cell, but Willie was a boy. What boy is going to do what his father tells him to do when his father isnt there and his mother is? Sometimes Archie would be in one of his good moods, and then he would teach Willie to count to twenty in Chinook. Sometimes he would teach him the language you can do with your hands. Little Willie already knew how to move his hands to say let's get on our horses and ride into the hills.

"How about we go for a walk?" suggested Charlie, coming up out of his darkness and speaking for the first time that afternoon.

Little Willie did not yet understand gallows humour. He did not understand, either, what grown-ups meant when they talked about halfbreeds. He knew about the Chinaman who fetched their firewood. He had seen Indians and heard what his father and his friends said about them. He looked at Archie's light hair and the dark red in Charlie's hair and thought about half. He looked at Allan's black beard and the thin hair over Charlie's lip. He knew that the word "breed" had something to do with hair. When people said it they sounded as if they did not like some kinds of hair.

His father's friend said that when they got the Chinamen to work on the railroad they made them cut off their hair.

"Here is a story about the new Indian schools," said his mother.

"The Indians are going to have their own school?" asked Allan. He knew better.

"It appears that the Government will supply the means and build the necessary buildings, but the churches will supply the teachers and the lessons," said Mrs. Moresby. "Shall I read it?"

So she read the story about the new plan to take children away from the treacherous environment of their parents' villages and collect them in residential schools, where they could be instructed in the English language and other civilizing courses. Soon all Indian and halfbreed youngsters, said the story, will be integrated into Canadian and Christian life.

"Oh, they already done that to us," said Alex Hare.

Allan McLean did not make any movement of his body. He did not even have to raise a hand. It was understood that it was time to listen to what he had to say.

"Dont read about these schools," he said. "They are just the railroad again."

Just a little south and west of Monte Creek the three wooded mountains had a dusting of New Year's snow on them. These were Thlee-sa and his younger brothers, standing where the dancing woman had left them. Ike Willard told us this story, and it is a legend, s-chip-TACK-wi-la. But it is a true story. When we get old enough they are the same thing.

People dont honestly know whether Thlee-sa and his brothers still talk to one another, there with the little valleys between them. Animals walk all over them, they dont care. Some recently arrived person wants to cut trees down, so what?

But they do talk to one another. They are always talking about the old days. Or making comments about the young people these days. You just cant get down in writing what these old mountains are saying to one another. Who cares?

A guy like Ike Willard could take a little ride off the truck road, just a little south and west of Monte Creek. He was old enough to remember when the word was *Montée*. Ike could sit still under a little mountain and smoke tobacco and listen. He didnt understand what Thlee-sa and his brothers were saying, but he listened. He knew who was there. They knew who he was, too. They liked Ike Willard. He made them happy that they had fixed up this country for people.

Ike lived in a world where white people put their names on lakes and mountains and just about every other old thing they could find. On rocks, maybe. On puddles. Didnt bother Ike. Just gave him an extra set of names to remember.

Ike smoked his tobacco and listened.

Thlee-sa and his brothers were talking about Ike.

Now, there's one good fellow.

Yes, too bad he has to die one day soon.

He doesnt really die.

Yes, but too bad, anyway.

Least those new people didnt kill him, not this one.

Oh, who knows how people die?

Sometimes we know. Sometimes the new people kill the regular people.

Do they really die?

They get lost. No one knows where their bones are.

Bones are roots. Spring is always coming around.

Find those bones, jump over them three times three times, see what happens.

You remember that woman dancing and us in front of the chokecherry bush?

Eye-yeah! She was something to see.

Ike heard himself thinking these thoughts while he smoked his tobacco. He was outdoors. He could smell the tobacco and he could smell snow on the fir needles. Douglas Fir, they called it at the saw mill.

She lit the lamp on the wall and they were home. It had been a forlorn party as January parties always are. Not really a party. Dinner for eight. A little piano music, nothing strenuous. Quite a lot of talk about politics, about Victoria and Ottawa. The men drank some fortified wine from a British concern in Portugal, but not much. So the party broke up, or rather crumbled away quite early. A light angular rain streaked the carriage windows on the way home.

He did not make a fire. He stood beside his dark wooden dresser and slowly removed bits of shiny metal from his clothing. These he placed quietly on the dresser top. Usually he dropped them, enjoying the last punctuation of his day. She noticed this, and half-consciously slowed her own complex removals. She wondered whether this was going to be a talking night.

Sometimes she perceived that she should start. But tonight he had not said a word on the way home. He had not said thank you or good night to the driver. She cleared her throat in the cold room. Their shadows loomed up the walls.

It was not until they were under the tartan blanket of their dark wooden bed that he began the story. The wall lamp was out, and the window was shuttered. As much as their eyes could tell so far, they were in complete darkness. Their bodies were not touching, but they could feel one another's weight. Mary Anne knew that when he came to a gate in a story, she should open it with a word.

"I dont want Willie going into the cell block from now on."

It was his voice, but it seemed to come from somewhere else in the room.

"As you like."

She lay on her back, with the palms of her small hands on her belly. She knew that he was lying as always with his hands outside the tartan. A little triangle of cold air always crept into the gap thus made between them.

"How old is he?"

"Willie? You know how old he is, dear. He will be four at his next birthday."

"God willing, he will have one," he said, his voice across the room.

"Of course he will have one. And we will have a notice in the newspaper." Now she was seeing whether she could make a light and bring his voice over to them.

Then he came to a gate.

"Why were you thinking about our son's age?" she asked quietly from her side of the dark bed.

It took him a while, but she knew that it would. She felt no movement from his side of the bed. When he spoke his voice had returned to the place beside her head.

"That youngest McLean," he said, sounding less like a father than like a boy himself, "is hardly a decade older than Willie."

"Yes." She wanted him to say it all.

"Today he found out that he is to hang on Monday week."

"Oh, God."

She could not hear him breathing. Usually she could hear him breathing before he slept, and the change in his breathing when he fell away, wherever it was a warden goes when he is no longer awake. Now he moved and the bed moved under her. She could not see but she knew that he was turning the pillow over, for the cool side of it.

"Sheriff Morrison came to my office. He had them brought in one at a time in alphabetical order!"

Mary Anne pulled her left arm out from under the tartan and reached for his hand. He let her hold it, that was all.

"So Allan was the first to enter the room, in his shackles. They have grown used to them. They take those little steps."

"Yes."

"Morrison told him about the thirty-first. Allan was perfectly collected. Not a blink. He said all the knives we have taken from him were not for suicide. He could have torn his shirt into strips and hanged himself, he said. No one has done that in my jail. Morrison asked him whether he had anything to say. He said something in one of his languages. He said he would speak from now on only to his French priest. After a while he said that I should write a letter for him. Tell his brother Hector not to do anything to Palmer. Tell him the McLeans knew how to die."

"I saw William Palmer," she said. "I did not like that man."

She wondered how she could be saying such a thing. To her husband the law. In the middle of such a story. But he was through another gate now.

"While Allan was saying this, little Archie McLean came in. He asked when it was going to be, right away. Allan looked away somewhere. I couldnt help watching him, a condemned man with eleven days left. Mary Anne, he was somewhere else. I felt a shiver go through me. Am I sounding daft?"

"No," she whispered. "No," louder.

"Morrison told Willie. Ah. I have never heard a sheriff tell a child he has to die. The boy tried to appear staunch. But I heard the air go into his mouth, over and over. I saw his chest heaving."

She held his large hand.

"Archie," she said.

"Archie."

"You called him Willie."

She thought that this time he would not start again. She held the gate open without saying anything.

"Then Charlie. He did not say anything. I think he has been crazy for the past year. His eyes are there but they are filled with something. Then the Hare boy. When Morrison asked him whether he had anything to say, he only replied that he would write some letters before the great event. He can write. Hardly any of my prisoners can read or write."

Now there was the faintest hint of light in the room, but she could not see the warden. She squeezed his hand.

"He called it the great event, Mary Anne."

Chillitnetza's daughter emerged from the women's door of the pit house, into the cold air of Stay at Home month. This was not the terrible freeze of last year's winter. The snow was sprinkled here and there with soil from hoofs and wheels. High grey cloud was fixed over the lake country. It was only the cold of the new year. She brought the babies out for the beautiful light and the air without smoke.

The boy could walk alone now, even in the snow. This was a warrior. Chillitnetza's daughter knew this already. An old woman had told her that this child would one day capture many enemies. She did not tell where this war would take place.

The baby was tied to the board on her back. She wanted the baby to breathe the cold air without smoke, and to see the flat snow on the lake. Slowly she walked across the little bridge and up the road toward the cabin with the bullets in its walls. She would not make the boy walk the whole way. Just as far as he could.

When she bent to pick the boy up she saw a sparrow hawk's feather on the snow. She picked it up too.

The morning of January thirtieth was filled with winter light on the Coast. It was Sunday, so the families dressing for Service felt the energy of internal faith when they saw bright sun on their curtains. The remnants of last week's snow quickly vanished. Someone saw a robin hopping on the moist earth behind his house. The ocean lay like shining metal, brighter than the sky.

But the McLean brothers and Alex Hare had never in their lives seen the ocean. They often felt its moisture in the air. They saw salt in the detail of hat badges. On still nights they heard a foghorn but they had no way of knowing how far away it was. Now on the morning of January thirtieth three of them were out in the bright sunlight. Not the crisp sun of plateau January. But they had lived most of their days with direct sun on their skin, and this peculiar coastal light was a bend of memory.

Sunday was the day before. Ten days had disappeared. The

English priest and the French priest were often in the cell block. *Courage, mes enfants,* and he was two years older than Allan. But no brothers, no sisters, no wife, no parents, made the downhill trip to visit the boys. It was Stay at Home Month.

Charlie would not come out. He turned his head away from the others and sat entirely still, facing the other wall of his hard room. The other three almost staggered in the brightness of the yard.

"I didnt hear no hammering and sawing," said Allan.

"You think we'd make a special one for you breeds?" asked one of the shotgun boys. Warden Moresby gave him a terrible look, and the shotgun boy nearly stumbled.

Moresby met them and walked out into the yard with them. He was perfectly accustomed to walking slowly to keep pace with manacled men. He would not embarrass them.

"I must go to church shortly before eleven," he said.

He saw the feather in Allan's hair. It was red. He knew what Allan had used for paint.

They were taking tomorrow's walk. Today they would see the thing and walk away. Why, Alex Hare was thinking, didnt Johnny Ussher go away from the boys with the whisky? Here it was so warm in the middle of winter. Alex Hare could feel his heart pounding in his whole chest. As if it was himself at last, known for the first time, and too late.

Allan McLean could feel his heart beating him. He thought about counting the number of beats it had left before it would stop, but he had no arithmetic. He had no letter from Chillitnetza's daughter. He had decided that the second baby was a boy. He saw himself walking up the little hill toward the wooden structure with the little roof over it in case of rain.

He prayed that it would not rain tomorrow. He saw himself and the yard he was walking through, and it seemed as if it was all happening but he was not quite in the middle of it. He yanked at his manacles and grabbed his thigh as hard as he could, to make himself be there. But he did not know the names of the trees he saw beyond the fence. The Indian names or their names.

"Will we have these goddamned things on our ankles tomorrow?" he asked Moresby.

"I'm sorry, yes," said the warden in his church suit.

"Oh, dont you be sorry, Bill," said Alex Hare. "It's us that are supposed to be the sorry ones."

"I am sorry, nevertheless," said the warden.

Archie did not say anything while they hobbled up the hill. His heart was nearly knocking him over as he moved the boots that were too big for him. He wanted to stop and breathe, but he remembered what Sophie had said. He did not remember what his father looked like except his face in the hard picture. Archie kept his eyes on Allan instead. He almost expected to be Allan's age.

Allan had told Moresby that they wanted to see the contraption. Now here it was. The platform was as high as a second-floor balcony on Mara's hotel. Allan counted the steps as he climbed, straining the limits of the metal attached to his ankles. There were nineteen steps. He had always been told that there were thirteen steps. But no man decorated with Government iron could climb to the second story in thirteen steps.

Moresby stood beside the boys and answered their questions. In the clear sunlight there was a good view of the river with its islands from that balcony. "The Fraser empties into the

Pacific just a couple miles in that direction. The smoke you see is one of the new sawmills, even works on the Sabbath. That's the new Provincial Government building going up on Hudson Street. Those mountains keep going till you get to the Arctic circle, just about." William Moresby was their guide, but they were not hunters now, not soldiers.

Archie and Alex needed help getting down the stairs. The gallows was not built for prisoners who did such a thing. Moresby stayed on top with Allan, careful to keep off the long door near their feet. Allan was gone to his place or he was trying to get there. Moresby did not attempt any words now. He had seen just about every kind of prisoner but he had never seen one who stood so still. It was Sunday morning. A tugboat on the river hooted. There was no ice anywhere to be seen. The only snow was the bright snow on the mountains.

A quick flock of small grey birds fell from the air and covered the moist ground in front of the wooden structure. Somewhere nearby there was a dog barking, and then another dog answering from farther away. The birds hopped about, looking for anything. Allan was away now, or he wanted to look as if he had managed. He was just about twenty-four. Getting old.

Archie and Alex shuffled their way underneath the platform. They could see a long iron bar on their ceiling. Alex was wondering how they would line up. He expected to be at one end because he was not a McLean. He was just a French boy, and not even an orphan.

Archie and Alex stood side by side. Two shotgun boys were standing out in the sunlight. One of them had a smile on his face. Archie's heart was thumping so hard and so fast that he thought Alex and the guards must hear it.

"It's a pretty fair piece of work," said Alex.

"What?"

Archie could hear but it seemed to be a new way of hearing. He could understand Alex but it was as if he had never done this, only seen other people do it. A story, but not really, just something you knew how to do but you were not really there doing it.

"Whoever put this thing together was good carpenters," said Alex.

Archie put his connected hands out and rubbed a piece of upright lumber. Alex Hare's hands were there in front of him. The boys had been in a dim cell block for thirteen months but they were still not pale. They held up their four arms and shook hands in the shade.

Alex heard a heart thumping. He spoke to his young friend.

"Archie, you and I will meet down here again tomorrow morning. I'll stay with you when we go."

They will put bags over our heads.

"I'll keep you in sight, Arch."

Archie's eyes looked at nothing, at the chopped hair in front of him, at the hoofprints of horses in the snow, looked out of the photograph in the tray. I see them in the dark. You see them. The squinting eyes of little Archie McLean.